# PSYCOP
## BRIEFS

# PSYCOP
## BRIEFS

*Jordan Castillo Price*

jcpbooks.com

**PsyCop Briefs: Volume 1**
Print edition published in the
United States in 2016 by JCP Books
www.jcpbooks.com

This book is a work of fiction. The characters, incidents, and dialogue are drawn from the author's imagination or are used fictitiously.



ISBN-13: 978-1-935540-84-7
Cover art by Jordan Castillo Price
Audio edition available

# Contents


When Did THAT Happen? ...................1

Coffee O'Clock. ........................ 3

Thaw ................................. 15

Mind Reader ......................... 19

Stroke of Midnight..................... 25

No Sale ............................. 33

Most Likely To... ..................... 36

Jock Straps On Sale..................... 40

Piece of Cake ........................ 43

In the Dark........................... 47

Let the Chips Fall ..................... 72

Memento ............................ 74

Impact............................... 90

Everyone's Afraid of Clowns ............. 96

Waiting Game ........................141

On the Road.......................... 146

Wood................................ 149

Off the Cuff ......................... 159

Locked and Loaded ................... 165

Inside Out............................ 169

Witness ............................. 183

About the Author ..................... 227

# when Did THAT Happen?

## A ROUGH TIMELINE

The PsyCop shorts differ from the main series in various ways: tone, pacing, even subject matter. Some of them don't fit neatly into a specific slot in the series. Some of them may even contradict small facts from the main books. They're tangents, really, bits of story that would warp the pacing of a longer book, but things that seemed to be worth exploring.

*Coffee O'Clock* takes place soon after *Among the Living*, when Vic's relationship with Jacob was still tenuous and new. A few months elapsed before *Thaw*, so it would be set between *Body & Soul* and *Secrets*. So would *Stroke of Midnight*, their first New Year's together.

*No Sale* is the first story that takes place after they move in to the cannery, so it's after *Secrets* and *Camp Hell*. *Most Likely To...*, *Let the Chips Fall*, *Off the Cuff* and *Memento* all happen after the move-in. Vic's baking effort marks their first anniversary together, so *Piece of Cake* occurred just after *GhosTV*.

*In the Dark*, which expands on Jacob's relationship with Keith, would be their second Halloween together, which puts it between *GhosTV* and *Spook Squad*. That would make *Everyone's Afraid of Clowns* a future Halloween.

The stories where Vic tangles with Crash happened closer to the beginning of their friendship. *Mind Reader* would be pretty early, in the Fall just after *Criss Cross*, but in *Jock Straps* they're more comfortable together, so it's the next Spring, after *Body & Soul*.

Since Lisa is in town with *Waiting Game*, it happened during the gap between *GhosTV* and *Spook Squad*, which was the longest continuous stretch she was in Chicago.

In *Impact*, Jacob is beginning to explore his own abilities, so that's after *Camp Hell*. *Wood* and *On the Road* are set around the holidays of their second winter, and Vic is at ease with Jacob's family by then, so they occur after *Spook Squad*, as do *Locked and Loaded* and *Witness*.

*Inside Out* is a prequel set before *Among the Living*, but it wouldn't be as interesting to read it chronologically. I think of it as a flashback episode of a sitcom where none of the characters know each other yet; the fun comes from viewing it through the lens of knowing that those ships passing in the night will eventually collide.

These snatches of stories—vignettes and flashbacks, and a few longer meaningful moments that happened when the novels weren't looking—form a mosaic of Vic and Jacob's relationship that's still recognizable as them, but shows the two of them in some new and unexpected colors.

# coffee o'clock

I was awake. I'd been awake forever. Contorted in a weird jumble of limbs with only the corner of one flat pillow to cradle my head, I'd watched the cheap plastic mini blinds go from dark-striped to light as I tried to tell myself everything was hunky dory, but the crick in my neck wasn't buying it. All the while, mashed against my back, Detective Jacob Marks, big shot PsyCop investigator of the Twelfth Precinct, snored and snuffled his way through the wee hours of the night, blissfully unaware.

I'd been pleasantly surprised the first time he spent the night. Puzzled the second. Now I was downright suspicious. Nobody other than me ever tolerated my sagging mattress more than a single night in a row, but he'd stayed the better part of a week.

He was after something. But what? Try as I might, I couldn't come up with anything he stood to gain from spending so much time at my crappy apartment.

If I craned my neck just so, I could make out the glowing green numbers on the clock radio, but I didn't bother. I'd stopped checking somewhere around 4am when I determined that while time was not actually standing still, it was only moving forward in excruciating five-minute increments.

The room brightened further. A shadow up in the corner of the ceiling resolved itself into a cobweb. My place isn't haunted, yet I was spooked by the thought of something lurking there all night just beyond my threshold of vision. I used to leave the lights on in the adjoining room when I slept. Jacob presumed I'd just forgotten, and "helpfully" turned them off. I didn't say anything. I didn't go turn them back on, either. And now look where I'd ended up.

Jacob sighed and squashed me even tighter against the wall. I should be counting my blessings. Sex. Right? I'd be an idiot to take sex for granted. Especially with someone who looked like him. Such enthusiastic sex, too.

Okay, sex was definitely in the plus-column. It was the fact he didn't leave afterward that made me leery.

The alarm bleated and I flinched, and felt a twinge of pity for Jacob. Being roused from such a sound sleep was never fun. He didn't budge, though. Already awake? The alarm kept on bleating. He burrowed his head deeper into the pillow...then snored.

Oh, for crying out loud. I levered myself up and over him, smacked the alarm and perched on the edge of the mattress. He made a wordish sound and hunkered down even more obstinately in the comforter cocoon.

"You working today?" I asked.

"Nuh."

"Oh. Okay. Well, they expect me back at the Fifth today—I've got eight million forms to fill out." I considered adding, *So I'll be leaving, and I suppose it's time for you to mosey along too,* but that was implicit. Wasn't it?

Jacob took a long deep breath. Then resumed his snoring.

Maybe not.

Clearly, it was time for coffee. Very strong coffee. I was pondering how full I could fill the basket without causing a countertop flood when I tripped over something and nearly cracked my head open on the radiator. I whirled around and glared at the offending object: Jacob's shoe. And then I spotted his other shoe. Then his discarded socks, wadded in the bedroom doorway. Underwear too. Not that I'd brain myself stumbling over socks and underwear, but they bugged me nevertheless.

My joints creaked as I trudged into the kitchen. The coffee pot needed a good going over. Not only is my water incredibly hard, but the last dribs never exit the carafe and end up caramelizing to the bottom. I gave it a quick rinse, dumped in water with lots of grounds, and let it do its thing while I washed a cup for me and another for the big, sleepy guy in my bed.

The coffee dripped. Slowly. Very slowly. The holes where the water forced its way through to the grounds were probably caked with lime.

I sighed.

It was stupid to be discombobulated because Jacob was sticking around. What else would I do with myself if it wasn't for him? Other than the excruciating bureaucracy, there wasn't much to keep me busy back at the Fifth until they dug up a new partner for my PsyCop unit. No overtime, not when the only thing on my agenda was two-fingered typing. Which meant I'd be home before sundown with the whole empty evening stretching out in front of me. Getting to spend it with Jacob? I should be ecstatic.

Maybe I was. I just had no idea what ecstatic felt like.

Best not think about it too hard. I looked to the powdered creamer to kill a few seconds while I waited for the world's slowest drip, only the spot at the corner of the counter where it normally sat was empty.

Sometime over the course of the past few nights, Jacob had appeared with groceries, so maybe he'd put it away. Why he would take it upon himself to put away something with an established footprint when he couldn't pick up his own socks, I couldn't begin to guess. But creamer doesn't just disappear.

Cupboards? Empty. Drawers? Empty. That weird mesh basket thing hanging behind the door? Empty too.

On the off chance that maybe I'd done something dumb with the canister myself yesterday morning while Jacob was distracting me with his tongue, I checked inside the fridge. No powdered creamer in sight...but there was a fresh new carton of real dairy half & half. I hardly ever treat myself since I wouldn't want to get used to the good stuff. Too many instances of chunky curds in my cup—or worse, in my mouth—alerting me to the fact that it had expired a month ago. Safer to use the armageddon-proof stuff in the plastic cylinder, even if it was barely reminiscent of milk.

Oh, who was I kidding? I just wasn't used to someone else going through my stuff. But Jacob wasn't snooping. Or judging. Or criticizing. He was buying me better creamer, for God's sake. So what if he left a trail of dirty laundry wherever he went? I should be grateful, not annoyed.

I checked the coffee's progress. Still thick enough to eat with a fork. Since I only half-jokingly thought the pot had gained sentience and was going even slower just to spite me, I wiped down the countertop where a few faint coffee rings showed. It was a mundane action I'd taken innumerable times before. Spray, wipe, toss. Except this time, when I went to toss the paper towel, I noticed something different.

Namely, my old powdered creamer. Just lying there. In the trash.

If that didn't count as a criticism, I don't know what did.

Before I could think through the ramifications of sticking my hand in there, I was brandishing the damn thing, angry and defiant. Luckily, the coffee was still not done. Otherwise, I might have actually used creamer from the trash. Creamer covered in the slimy, crusty remains of last night's chicken parm—which were now all over my hand.

I flung the gooey canister back in the trash. No way could I use the half & half in the fridge now. On *principle.* I rinsed off my hand, tugged on my jacket, stomped into my sneakers and marched straight out the door.

Three blocks down Montrose was a hole-in-the-wall bodega where I'd bought my fair share of sudoku books and frozen burritos. Even though walking there was a lot faster than driving, parking and shopping at a real store, usually I found myself wishing it was closer. Now I was hoping the walk would cool me off before I blurted out anything I'd sorely regret. Time and distance and brisk fall air. That's all I'd need to screw my head on straight. That, and a blessed few moments to gather my thoughts in solitude.

"Hey, white boy. Where you going?"

Really? *Really?* The dead hooker picks this particular moment to get on my very last nerve?

"Slow down now, I only wanna say hello. Just being friendly."

"Right. You're the picture of congeniality."

"Whoever told you that be talking out their ass. Free clinic say the test come back fine."

Kill me now. Wait, no—don't. I might end up stuck with no one to talk to for all eternity but Jackie.

"Need a date? Twenty dollar get you some *fine* company."

It would be satisfying to turn around and face her when I told her off, but I've never had a visual. Just a voice. A very annoying voice. "Go away."

"Maybe you'd be nicer if you treat yourself to a li'l TLC. I'll do you good, baby. Twenty dollar."

I kept walking. I don't know the exact boundaries of her territory, but I was pretty sure that in another block or so I wouldn't hear her. I was almost to the bodega. Just a few more feet.

"Nineteen?"

"What, you're gonna make change?"

She clucked her tongue. "I'm just saying. They can break a twenty for you in the store. Or if Tanya there, she sell you a rock. I do you real good for a rock."

The mood I was in, this "Tanya" would be lucky if I didn't call down to the precinct and have someone from Narcotics pay a visit and see if she was holding. Luckily, the pimply teenage boy at the counter didn't look much like a Tanya, so I was spared the moral dilemma of letting a crack dealer slide so I didn't have to divulge that my informant was the disembodied voice of a phenomenally irksome dead prostitute.

The dinky corner store was cramped, and it smelled overwhelmingly of corn tortillas. Ravenswood is a healthy mix of nationalities and ethnicities, and the bodega sold all kinds of foreign packaged goods, Latin American, Korean, Greek, Indian, Middle Eastern and more. Faded little boxes with obscure labels, things with uses I couldn't begin to guess. But they sold plenty of off-brand, marked up, run-of-the-mill stuff too. Not just powdered creamer. Three kinds of powdered creamer: plain, hazelnut and diet vanilla.

Normally, I go for the plain. Call me a purist. But today I chose stinky-sweet hazelnut to ensure Jacob fully understood whatever point I was attempting to make.

The kid at the register was in the midst of a phone conversation, and he wasn't about to interrupt it on my account. He counted my change with glacial inattentiveness, then spent several long, baffling moments attempting to bag the purchase. The plastic bag was stuck to itself so firmly he couldn't find the opening. He plucked at it again and again, all the while mumbling some inarticulate stream of nothing at whoever was on the other end. I crossed my arms. Tapped my foot. And wondered what else I could possibly do to signal my displeasure without resorting to saying something.

Finally, I couldn't hold it in any longer. I sighed.

The kid looked up at me as if I'd just now appeared there, like an intersection car crash repeater at sundown. He looked down at the plastic bag just as stupidly, then licked his thumb to try and tease open the handles. Like getting slimed by last night's entree wasn't bad enough. "Give me that." I snatched my creamer out of his hand and strode out the door.

Fully aware how ridiculous I looked charging down the street with my canister of powdered nondairy creamer, I could at least appreciate that Jackie had found someone else to bother. Or so I thought. When I stopped for a traffic signal, she blurted out, "You got my rock? Huh? White boy, you got my rock?"

I re-routed myself to the opposite side of the street in hopes that it was out of range, and charged toward my apartment, power-walking with my creamer.

"So now you can't even answer me back? Why you be all moody and shit? Prolly need to get laid. When's the last time you been with somebody who show you a *real* good time?"

Well, actually....

My expression must have shifted, because suddenly Jackie changed her tune. "Hold up, hold up, now I feel you. The reason you don't wanna party with me is cos you got a lady upstairs. Know how I know? That fancy cream. Only reason anyone would bother this early in the morning. You trying to make an impression."

That was one way of looking at it.

"You and her," she asked, "is it a one-night-stand, or something serious?"

We were drawing abreast of my car now. Jacob's black Crown Victoria was squeezed into the spot behind it, bumper to bumper, dwarfing my subcompact. Taking up my mattress, my floor and my fridge weren't enough. Now he was edging into my parking space, too. "It's pretty serious. Apparently."

"Whatever you do, don't let her catch you looking at no naked pictures on the computer. And make sure you always say her hair look nice."

As if Jacob ever had a hair out of place...and as if my computer ever ran anything but an antivirus program crying wolf. I paused beside Jacob's car and a thought almost fleeted past before I saw it for what it was: an opportunity to bail. I could "helpfully" bring whatever stuff he'd strewn around my apartment down to his car. Then he'd take the hint to back off and give me a little...space.

Except his car was full of stuff. Not just stuff he'd tossed aside in his eagerness to get where he was going, either. The backseat held several gym bags, a milk crate full of notebooks and a couple pieces of luggage. A garment bag stretched along his passenger seat, and a slim case on the floor looked suspiciously like a laptop carrier.

"You be living out your car now, white boy?"

"It's not my car."

"Cos if you don't move it every day or two, the police come 'round and start bugging you."

"Yeah, thanks," I said absently, and slipped back across the street through a break in the early morning traffic. Jackie, hot on my heels, rattled off some more sage advice about how to sweet talk a lady, but I was no longer hearing her. By that I mean, I still *heard* her, but my brain had been hijacked by the stunned realization that Jacob wasn't in my bed because he was feeling clingy.

He simply couldn't deal with going home.

And that changed everything.

What if I hadn't stormed out the door for predawn powdered creamer? What if I'd succumbed to my own demons, shaken that big lug awake and told him to back off?

What if I'd killed this thing between us before it even

managed to take its first gurgling breaths? Somehow I'd managed to squeak by without cramming my foot so deep in my mouth it came out my ass. It was close—too damn close. I'd almost blown it. Almost. But thankfully, not quite. Not yet, anyway.

Jackie's admonitions to make sure I take my lady out for a real sit-down dinner somewhere other than McDonald's began to fade as I crossed my courtyard, and by the time I started up my stairwell, I was alone again—at least for the amount of time it would take me to tiptoe up three flights. When I slipped back into my kitchen, the coffee was just about done brewing. I probably didn't need to be so stealthy, since Jacob was capable of sleeping through an air raid siren. But I'd managed to well and truly spook myself and I wasn't about to take any chances.

I filled my favorite mug, a cheesy workplace birthday gift that announced *It's Coffee O'Clock!* in wobbly lettering. I consider it my favorite not because it dredges up any sentimental feelings—we're always being hit up to toss in a couple bucks for some occasion or another, and no less than five other guys down at the precinct owned that same mug. I just liked the way it held an extra few mouthfuls. I tried a sip that nearly melted my nose hairs, dumped those extra few mouthfuls back into the carafe, then cracked open the fresh new half & half and attempted to dilute the napalm.

About the last scenario I envisioned for myself was pampering a guy by bringing him breakfast in bed, complete with a cutesy tray and a bud vase holding a single flower. Or a mimosa in a fancy glass, heavy on the champagne, as Jackie suggested. But waking someone gently with a big cup of coffee? I could handle that.

Jacob was sprawled belly-down in a perfect diagonal, with one foot wedged between the mattress and the wall, and the opposite arm shielding his head with the elbow grazing the headboard. The top sheet and comforter were wound around him like he'd purposely reeled them around his naked body in a strangling spiral, and both pillows were bunched under his face.

He was adorable.

I set the coffee on the corner of the nightstand and perched on the unoccupied corner of the mattress. Detective Jacob Marks, a pervy perp's worst nightmare. I hadn't really considered he might be having nightmares of his own. And leaving the lights on wouldn't do much to dispel his bad dreams; his place had been lit just fine when he took a soul-devouring incubus to bed.

I cleared my throat a few times, realized the subtlety was lost on Jacob, then gave him a gentle shake and said, "Hey."

He mumbled, groaned, and rolled onto his back. One pillow slid to the floor and the sheets wrapped around him even tighter. His eyes were puffy and pillow-marks creased his face where the goatee left off.

Still adorable.

He squinted at me. "Hey."

I considered telling him his hair looked nice. But that would be weird.

He zeroed in one hundred percent on me and whatever had been haunting his dreams fell away. His shrewd, dark eyes went big and liquid as he beheld me in all my unassuming glory. We coexisted in that moment without too much awkwardness, just looking at each other. He was a puzzle to me, and he had plenty to learn about the way I operate too—such as, don't paw through my shit and throw it out, at least not without saying something first.

Given all he'd been through recently, I supposed I could let it slide. This time. "Brought you some coffee."

"Thanks." He got an elbow under him, tore his focus away from me and considered the mug. "Maybe you should take this one. I drink it black."

"Try some before you make any rash decisions."

He took a sip. Winced. And nodded.

"Sleep okay?" I asked. Because maybe mornings had always been an ordeal for him, even before…everything.

He gave me a fleeting leer and said, "Can't complain about the nightcap," then forced down another few sips of my coffee. The man was clearly made of stronger stuff than most.

I searched for a way to tell him that he didn't need to live out of his car. My crappy apartment was small, but we'd make do. Since my workload had recently conspired to make space in my life, the least I could do was figure out how to make room in my closet.

I'd never asked anyone to move in with me before. Hell, I'd never even nudged anyone toward spending the night. As far as I was concerned, once we'd both had our jollies, a guy was more than free to leave.

No doubt this arrangement between Jacob and me was just temporary. He had a condo on the lake. If he didn't want to live there, he could sell it in a heartbeat and find some other picture-perfect showcase to call home. But would it really be so bad to play house with him, just for a little while?

He began extricating himself from the tangle of covers, and paused to trail his fingertip across the back of my wrist. I tamped down a shiver, not quite successfully. He conveyed all the dirty, dirty things he wanted to do to me with a single naughty grin, then took another tentative stab at the coffee.

No, seeing more of him wouldn't be bad. It would be the opposite of bad. That's probably what I was so afraid of. Once I got used to having him around, how could I feel reasonably content alone?

Both of us were scared. Him of an exploding incubus, me of venturing out of my comfort zone. I supposed I could cut him some slack. Maybe I'd seen so many ugly spectral surprises I hadn't been terribly scarred by the thing that went splat in his bedroom, but any normal person would've been totally unnerved.

"So," I said, "what's the verdict?"

He forced down another sip. "I need to treat you to some better beans."

I half-laughed and went to pour myself a cup. In the kitchen, it was tempting to fling open the trash lid and be reminded that he'd thrown away something that belonged to me, but all the steam had gone out of my indignation. He'd seen it as a way of "treating" me. Was it his fault I had no idea what it was like to be pampered any more than I knew how to pamper someone else?

Most people have a still, small voice that tells them when something is worth pursuing. Not me. Mine was murmuring, *Better not get used to it.*

Undoubtedly that voice had saved me from plenty of disappointment over the years, yet I could also see the value in striking while the iron was hot. Not only was Jacob inexplicably taken with my creepy psychic talent, he was also currently unwilling to sleep in his own bed.

I'd be an idiot to let that opportunity slip through my grasp.

I sifted through my junk drawer. Twist ties and rubber bands, gummy old masking tape and half-dead batteries. I went through everything twice, was on the verge of giving up, when I located a little something that was sure to make a big impression: my spare keys. But before I could present them in a totally casual way, emphasizing it was absolutely no big deal, I tucked my new hazelnut creamer onto the highest shelf I could reach, well out of Jacob's line of sight.

Maybe I was reckless in ignoring that still, small voice that insisted I should probably run the other way, but I knew better than to tempt fate.

Thaw

I'm the last guy in the world who cares about sports, whether we're talking about the Cubs, Sox, Bulls or Bears, or for that matter anything even remotely athletic. So I was a little surprised when Jacob suggested that we take a trip downtown to go ice skating. But nowhere near as surprised as *he* was when I told him I thought it was a great idea.

What Jacob didn't know was that I'd played pee-wee hockey the winter I was eleven. (I didn't give a rat's ass about hockey. I had a crush on the goalie.) And what *I* didn't know was that the ice rink would look so cool after sunset. All the bare trees along Michigan Avenue had been wrapped in white Christmas lights, and the whole Chicago skyline blazed behind them. Millennium Park was insanely cold, but it was gorgeous.

Jacob must have figured out that I could skate before we even got out on the ice. Not only is he smart that way, but I'm about as easy to read as a billboard. Even so, he still spent more time checking me out than he did enjoying the scenery. It's weird, the way he stares. He doesn't stop when I catch him at it. He just smiles a little.

And what a smile it is. Jacob is drop-dead handsome, dark haired, dark-eyed, with an immaculately trimmed goatee that's just this side of supervillain chic.

He watched me lace my skates as if I were doing a strip tease for his benefit, and then gave me a hand up. He didn't let go of my hand once I was on my feet. It almost felt like he'd pull me against him and kiss me—right there beside the bench, with people milling all around us. Straight people, I was willing to bet, at least for the most part. Families. Kids.

I gave his hand a squeeze and he let go. "You ready to see some action?" I asked him.

"Oh yeah."

I launched out onto the ice and glided into the stream of skaters. Y'know that expression they always use, "It's like riding a bike!" It never made much sense to me, since I was a crap bike rider at any age. But skating? It came right back.

My black wool peacoat wasn't particularly aerodynamic, but it didn't matter. My legs were longer now than they had been when I was eleven, and the blades bit into the ice with a satisfying crunch when I pushed. I veered easily around the tottering couple in matching yellow parkas trying to support each other. Another skater, a fit looking woman crouched low to the ground, caught my eye and smiled, glad to see someone else on the ice who was willing to turn up the speed. She looked serious, lycra leggings and all. I bet I could beat her.

But then someone caught my elbow. I turned. Jacob was there, sexy as sin in his leather jacket and Indian patterned scarf. "Vic—want to know what I'm thinking?" he said. His scarf covered his mouth, but I could tell by his eyes that he was smiling.

"Is there a G-rated version?"

"No."

There was a long gap in the crowd in front of me, so I spun around to skate backwards and watch Jacob watching me. The white lights sparkled behind him. The night was magic. Even though car crash victims that only I could see wandered around on Michigan Avenue like Night of the Living Dead, if I tilted my head at just the right angle, I could block them out and pretend my whole world was just Jacob, Christmas lights, and the dark night sky.

I turned back around to avoid bodychecking an innocent middle-schooler and let Jacob glide up beside me. He slipped his arm through mine and slowed me to a pace less likely to put someone's eye out. Other couples were arm in arm, but none of them were two men. Unless you counted the kid dragging along the runny-nosed brat who looked to be his younger brother.

I tugged my arm to see if Jacob would disengage. Nope.

Oh well, why not? If anyone wanted to be a prick about the two of us skating together, I was sure Jacob would be happy to subdue them with a withering look. And if things turned physical, I could always skate away really fast while Jacob taught them some manners. But other than the transparent cabbie with a crushed face who stood half-in, half-out of a light pole, no one even made eye contact with me. Jacob and I skated together under the Christmas lights for a good hour until I started to shiver, and Jacob steered me off the ice. He seemed to enjoy watching me remove my skates just as much as he had staring at me as I laced up.

It's nowhere near as much fun to slide across the ice without skates on, especially if you aren't doing it on purpose. On our way back to the El I hit a slippery patch, shot forward a few feet, arms flailing, then caught myself and staggered upright.

"We can go back if you're not done," said Jacob.

I ignored the remark, even though he was grinning at me, trying to goad me on. "I was way faster than you," I said.

"Uh huh."

"With better moves."

I waited for a zinger, but there was none. We both

stopped and looked at each other. He was still staring, still grinning.

"Wha—?"

Jacob grabbed me before I even finished the word and dragged me into the recessed doorway of a deli that was closed for the night. He spun me around, backed me into the door handle, and covered my body with his.

His lips tasted like winter. His face was cold, even his mouth, but his tongue was hot as he pressed it against mine. My hands in their thick gloves fumbled around his neck, pulling him against me. Jacob blotted out the rest of the world—other than the door handle, which could be ignored, at least in the short term. The whole night with him felt like something stolen out of a much simpler, much happier life. Only it was actually mine. I sighed into his kiss while he drew back reluctantly, lingering over my mouth until the unmistakable sound of people crunching through frozen slush drew near.

"Do you know how happy you make me?" he said.

Good thing it was too dark in that alcove to get a good look at his eyes. That would've been way too much. I swallowed hard, the metallic taste at the back of my throat from skating and exertion mixing with the cool flavor of Jacob's kiss. "Same here," I said.

I pushed Jacob back onto the street and fell into step beside him as I did my best not to go all head-case on him, though the realization that I was actually happy had hit me pretty hard. I moved a little closer to Jacob, and slipped my awkward gloved hand into his. He gave my hand a squeeze.

# Mind Reader

I leaned over the display case and stared down through the glass.

"Pretty messed up," Crash said.

I thought for a second that he was reading my mind, but then I realized he was talking about the display. I shrugged. The mummified babies were just some brown, withered husks. I'd seen worse, lots worse.

"What does it say about a culture, that they're so obsessed with their dead that they go through all this preparation and ritual to preserve the body?"

I glanced up at a small sign on the wall I'd noticed that said something about it. "They, uh, thought they'd need this stuff in the afterlife. Just being thorough, I guess."

A female security guard watched us with the same expression she probably wore while she was waiting for a load of laundry to dry. Crash petted the pocket of his leather jacket as if he was jonesing to have a smoke right then and there. "I take it you can't find any Egyptian ghosts to talk to."

"Nope. They're probably in Egypt, not in a museum in Hyde Park. And they probably didn't stick around more than a few dozen years after they died. I hardly ever see ghosts that are more than a century or two old." Then again, there weren't many white people in the Midwest before that, and maybe all the Native Americans were smart enough not to stick around once they'd died.

"If you can't see mummy ghosts, then there aren't any to be seen."

"I didn't say that."

"But it's true. I can't wait to blow a hole in ScienceFiend's theory that the whole mummification process ties the spirits to the physical realm."

"ScienceFiend."

"It's an online nickname."

I knew that. It just sounded stupid when Crash said it out loud, especially because he said it like he cared about what someone thought of him even though they'd never actually met in person. "You never know," I told him. "Mummification might keep a spirit around a lot longer than normal. Say a ghost was going to stick around for ten years, and instead it stayed here for fifty." I shrugged. "You'd need some newer mummies to test that out."

"They mummified a guy in Baltimore in 1994."

They? Who were They? I thought it was better not to know. "Too recent. Plenty of ghosts have bodies that died in '94. You'd need some mummies from the sixteen, seventeen hundreds."

We turned a corner and found ourselves in the gift shop. Mummy keychains. Gummy mummies. No ghosts.

"And this concludes our tour," said Crash. "Unless you see any spirit activity in here...."

I thought I felt a cold spot, but when I looked up I saw an air conditioning vent set into the ceiling. "Nope. What if I just make something up? Will you be happy then? There's a Sherpa in the corner chewing on some ectoplasmic yak fat."

"No use lying to an empath, even a lowly level-one like me." He took another look around the gift shop. "What about that doorway? We haven't been in there."

"That doorway" led to one of those museum displays that looked like they'd been conceived by the cheapest guy on the board of directors, then executed by the apprentice display makers on a day they were all hungover. It consisted of a narrow passage with some signs in it that were covered in tiny little type, and a few faded photos.

"I don't see anything," I said.

Crash narrowed his eyes. I looked again. Maybe I really had missed something. He was the empath, right? Maybe he had a feeling about that room.

I stepped into the cramped space. It felt close and overly quiet, a windowless corridor in the center of a building.

"No. I don't hear anything eith—"

Crash shoved my back against the display wall and planted his hands on either side of my head.

He'd say something nasty, I was sure. It was always push and pull with him. He'd begged me to drive him to the Oriental Institute and look at mummies, and yet he'd followed that up with some remark at me about being too narrow-minded to do it. He'd cranked my passenger seat all the way back and sprawled in it with his leather jacket hanging open and his hips tilted up in such a way that it looked like he'd shoved a pair of socks down the front of his jeans to get my attention, and yet he'd scowled at me every time I looked in his general direction. And now, here we were in the most awkward position I'd been in since I could remember, and it was only a matter of time before....

He kissed me.

I stood there. I don't think I kissed him back. I was too floored to move.

His mouth didn't feel like Jacob's. His face was clean shaven. His lips were warm and slightly wet, as if he'd just licked them. And he hadn't come at me as hard as I thought he might, as if he'd changed his mind at the last second, decided that maybe this kiss wasn't such a hot idea after all, but the momentum had built up behind it so long that there was no way he could put the brakes on even if he'd wanted to. Or maybe he was just more gentle than I figured he'd be.

Neither of us had closed our eyes. His were open wide, and they looked as surprised as I felt. Maybe he had herded me into that room with the intention of putting the moves on me, but if so, I don't think he'd planned it out all that carefully. I searched for something to say, but the look he was giving me had me pinned to the wall, helpless to do anything but stare right back.

"Sir—take your hands off the wall."

I'll admit it. I jumped.

Crash eased back, cool as can be, turned to the security guard who was standing in the doorway, and smiled. He held his hands out, palms forward, the universal I-give-up sign.

"Sorry," he said. He didn't sound sorry at all. "My mistake."

How long had she been standing there? Jesus. I wanted a hole to open up in the floor and swallow me, despite the fact that there was probably a basement full of mummies underneath. Sure, they were creepy dead bodies. But at least they wouldn't have seen me liplocked with Crash.

I turned and headed back toward the gift shop, walking with giant strides to get out of there as quickly as possible without actually running. I didn't stop until I was fumbling in the parking lot with my keychain, its half-dead battery and my automatic locks. Crash went around to the passenger side, put his forearms on the roof, and rested his chin on his folded hands. Even though I was doing my best not to, I looked. He was still smiling.

"So," he said. "Where do you want to go for lunch?"

I shook my head. "I've got things to do."

The lock finally popped open. I could go to the car

dealership and get the battery changed. There. I wasn't lying. I did have things to do. For real.

We climbed into the car and snapped on our seatbelts. I could tell he was watching me, but I kept my eyes on the parking lot. There was a ghost on the lawn with a parasol and gigantic hair that looked like she could've been pretty old, 1800's even, but I didn't mention it. She was old, but not thousands of years old. I didn't trust my voice to sound normal, anyway.

I merged onto the highway. Crash played with the radio. I didn't say anything, and neither did he. It wasn't that "companionable silence" that you hear about all the time. I just suspected I'd get roped into a conversation I didn't want to have if I asked him what the fuck it was he'd thought he'd been doing back there, but I couldn't think of a single damn thing I could bring up to change the subject, either.

Traffic was light enough that I got back to Crash's store before I exploded and sprayed gobs of skin, blood and brain on the windshield, so I supposed I should be thankful for that, at least. I double-parked in front of his building. Crash turned the radio down and stared through the windshield, looking thoughtful. "All that history," he said, "I'm surprised there weren't any spirits at the museum."

"I didn't say that. I said there weren't any mummy ghosts."

He looked at me and raised an eyebrow. "You held out on me," he said. Like he was surprised.

I shrugged.

"It really is that fucking easy for you." He sort of looked like Billy Idol when he was mad and his lip curled like that, even though he hadn't been born yet back when MTV-punk was in its heyday. He got out of the car and slammed the door. He lit a cigarette before he'd even made it to the sidewalk.

A car pulled up behind me and laid on the horn. Had I

really been thinking about going after Crash and explaining myself? There wasn't really much to say. If I piped up every time I saw a ghost, I'd never shut up. There was one at the corner, and another few wandering around in the grocery store parking lot across the street.

He didn't realize how stupid it was to be jealous of my so-called talent. In terms of psychic ability, more is definitely not better, even for empaths. Who could stand to feel the weight of everyone else's baggage as acutely as if it was his own? How would you ever know what you actually felt?

The car horn blared again. I did a quick check in my rearview, flipped on my blinker and pulled into traffic. The thought that Crash might actually know how I felt was something I didn't want to dwell on. I did my best to channel all my mental energy into the phrase "really bad idea" whenever he got anywhere near me. So what was that kiss all about?

He probably had no idea how I really felt, not without a bunch of meditating and centering and whatever other maneuvers he had to go through to beef up his talent. He was just a level one, after all.

# Stroke of Midnight

It had seemed like a good idea at the time. Famous last words, I know. But originally we would've had four hands to carry the six-pack of microbrew and the sub platter. Then we got a call (okay, Vic got a call). There was a body, and he had to go…which left me by myself trying to figure out how to ring the doorbell. I could've knocked on it with my foot, but I really wasn't in the mood to hear SWAT team jokes for the rest of the night. I really wasn't in the mood to be there at all anymore, but it seemed better than sitting alone in that minuscule apartment with a platter full of subs.

I managed to connect my elbow with the doorbell, and pretty soon a silhouette filled the frosted glass window. I hoped it was Manny. That surprised me. Keith might've been the one I'd known forever, but Manny had an easy-going way about him that Keith had never managed. Sure, Keith tried, or maybe he just tried to fake it, but all those bitchy remarks he made and then later claimed to be "just kidding" about, all the backhanded compliments and derisive eye-rolls—they added up. The front door opened. Keith. "Oh, here, let me get that." He wrangled the platter through the door, then did a sudden stop as I mounted the single stair so he could peer over my shoulder. "Where's this Victor person we've been hearing so little about? Parking the car?"

"He got called in. You'll have to make do with me."

He shooed me in out of the cold and bumped the door shut with his hip. "And what have we here? Alcohol and nitrates? Very decadent. And just in time—there's been some grumbling about the gazpacho." Civil enough. Maybe he was turning over a new leaf. A pleasant new leaf. He leaned over the platter and kissed me on the cheek, then headed for the dining room.

Whatever snow had landed on my leather jacket beaded up into water droplets in the heat of the foyer, and I shook them off before I tucked my coat into the closet. If Vic were there, I would have mentioned how nice it would be to actually have a coat closet. If he were there.

Either the dining room was packed, or the helium balloons crowding the ceiling with their curlicue ribbons dangling down made it feel that way. Or both. There were guys from the gym, guys from the bar. Keith's sister Marie and a few of her friends. No guys from the force, other than me. There weren't enough of us to make up a demographic.

"Look, it's Jacob," Manny called out from across the dining room table. He's the kind of guy who really knows how to make you feel welcome. Keith did good, landing someone like him. Manny rounded the table, hugged me, and kissed me on the corner of the mouth with champagne on his breath. "And where's your secret boyfriend?"

"He had to work."

Manny clucked his tongue and quirked his eyebrows. He'd never been a cop. "What're we gonna do with you, Jakie-pie? We're starting to think you're ashamed of us. All we've got on your mystery man so far is a quick peek across the grocery store parking lot."

"And you call yourself a P.I."

He leaned into me and pressed his mouth to my ear.

He was a grabby drunk. Charming, but grabby. "He's deliciously tall. And cute."

"I thought you said you only got a quick peek."

"So color me observant."

Marie looped some strings of Mardi Gras-type beads around my neck, black, silver and gold, and Keith pressed a glass of champagne into my hand. "Any chance loverboy will make it by Midnight?"

"Doubtful. 10-71."

Keith furrowed his brow. "Stray animal?" Maybe Manny's sense of humor had finally started to rub off on him. He finished his champagne and took another glass from the pyramid of flutes on the table. "Let's see. What kind of PsyCop would they send to investigate a shooting? Precog? Telepath?"

"Keith, stop it."

"Oh. It's classified." His voice went cold enough to chill the champagne in his hand. Maybe it hadn't been humor at all. Maybe he'd just been trying to lull me into a false sense of camaraderie so I'd be wide open when he took his shot. You'd think I would expect it by now. "I'm sure a civilian like me couldn't possibly handle knowing what your secret boyfriend's talent is—card tricks or spoon-bending."

"If I didn't know better, I'd say you were jealous." Jealous of me for staying on the force, or jealous of Vic for settling down with me? Hard to say. But right after I said it, I regretted it. Keith was working through big-time anger, the resentment of being squeezed out of the Twelfth. Officially, he could have dug in his heels and stayed. With that temper of his, though, I couldn't say I was surprised when he hadn't.

A deafening noise ripped through the house. Saved by the bell. Keith gave me a faux laugh, tossed his head, and went to see why an alarm was going off in his kitchen. I lost myself in the press of the crowd that was razzing Manny for not knowing how to use his own broiler, and joined in the cheer when Marie climbed on the countertop and knocked the batteries out of the smoke detector with the Swiffer handle.

We all dispersed to open the windows. It was below zero out, but the small bungalow had been so packed with bodies that the cold air was a relief. I went into the back hall and undid the chain and deadbolt on the outer door to see if it was too cold for me to prop it open and channel some of the smoke out into the yard.

Your typical inner-city Chicago backyard won't make the cover of Better Homes & Gardens. There's the utility poles, the rat-control garbage cans, and the inescapably seedy alley that connects them all. But Keith's yard had this untouched blanket of snow that sparkled under the streetlight, the way snow does when it's cold enough to sting—and it was pretty. Pretty enough to keep me there despite the ice forming in my beard.

The door to the kitchen opened and someone slipped into the hall. Keith, I thought at first, back to revisit my jealousy comment. But the body language was all wrong. Manny, then. They're built alike, and both dark-haired and dark-eyed, but aside from the generalities, they're very different. Manny's a quarter Guatemalan, so his features are more exotic. Also, I don't feel like strangling Manny. "Whoo, it's nasty out here. Good thing I'm fortified with champagne against the cold." He pulled a pack of smokes down from a shelf that held peat pots and gardening gloves and offered me a cigarette.

I shook my head. "I can't believe you still smoke."

"They say it's harder to kick than heroin." He lit up, took a drag, and blew a stream of smoke over my shoulder. "The ball's gonna drop in Times Square in a couple of minutes. I'm sure Marie and her girlfriends will be happy to kiss you. It'll be ninety percent platonic, too. Well, maybe eighty-five.

Cherise might slip you some tongue."

I sighed. My breath left a trail of vapor almost as sharp as Manny's cigarette smoke. "Speaking of slipping things in…lately your boyfriend's been sneaking so many digs into our conversations, they're more hostile than not."

"He's just jealous because your new man still has hair."

"Keith looks decent with a shaved head. He has a good skull for it."

"Sometimes that's all it's good for." Manny dropped his cigarette into a terra cotta strawberry pot where it snuffed itself in the snow with a long hiss. "Just ignore him, baby. You know how he is."

I did. I suppose I hadn't really expected him to act differently. Not with champagne involved.

Manny said, "Private practice ain't nothing like being a detective. People are a lot less likely to call on Keith to do their dirty work now that they gotta pay him out of their own pockets."

"If he misses it, maybe he should—"

"Uh-uh. No way. My name is on the mortgage and that's how it's gonna stay. I'm not going back to sneaking around 'cos my boyfriend's a cop." He slipped an arm around me and gave my ass a quick grope. "I already bragged about us to too many people to take it back. The way things went down…I gotta think they happened for a reason. Keith and that Sergeant Owens falling out, maybe it made him get his booty in gear and start his business. And the two of you, maybe you never caught on, but now he's got *me* in all my fabulousness."

Manny always knew how to make me smile. "That he does."

"So what's he got to bitch about?"

I followed him back inside and we congregated with everyone else in the slightly smoky living room. The ball dropping in Times Square looked as big as life on their massive TV. Marie and all her friends did kiss me, lipstick and champagne, and not too much tongue. It wasn't really New Year's Day yet, not in Chicago, however it seemed like once the ball dropped and everyone on the East Coast kissed and partied and set off fireworks, celebrations in the Midwest were more of a formality. Technically, it would be New Year's Day in an hour—but it just wasn't the same. Kind of like going through the motions of ringing in the New Year without Vic.

I was home by eleven thirty and in bed by quarter to twelve. I planned to read some of the paperback I was currently crawling through two pages at a time in an attempt to take my mind off of Keith. He might be pissed at me, though he'd never admit it, for staying at the Twelfth despite the grumblings of a few homophobes. But it was stupid of him to feel jealous. Now he set his own hours. No 10-71s on New Year's Eve for him.

And like Manny said, maybe things did happen the way they did for a reason. I'd like to think we're not just sacks of biological goo careening through a random universe.

My eyes burned; it'd been a long day. I rested the paperback on my chest and rubbed my eyes—closed them for a moment, only a moment, to rest. The quirky hangtime of pre-sleep stole over me where time stretched. My limbs felt weighted down, like maybe I could move them, but only with more effort than I was willing to expend.

So when Vic's face filled my field of vision, I figured I was dreaming, that hyper-real sort of dream you have when you first fall asleep, the kind you only remember if something jerks you awake.

Like cold lips pressing against yours.

I snapped back into waking awareness with a big heave and a gasp. And I blinked. The room was its usual time-yellowed white, and Vic stood in the center, a pillar of dark in his black peacoat. His hair stuck out, glistening with melted snow, and he had a day's worth of stubble that emphasized the cleft in his chin. He smiled down at me with a boyish grin that seemed like it shouldn't even be able to exist in the same face as his usual scowl. "You fell asleep with the lights on. Didn't you go to that party?"

"I put in an appearance. What about you—are you home for good?" Unlikely, since he would have hung his coat on the back of the kitchen door before he came into the bedroom if he was. But you never know. Maybe I'd been snoring and he wanted to call me on it, so he rushed in without ditching his coat.

No such luck. "It'll be a couple more hours. The spirit took off fast, but we've gotta walk the grid and make sure we didn't miss anything." He glanced at the alarm clock, and I did too. Three minutes past twelve. "When I saw your car outside, I told Zigler I had to run up and take a pill."

"That excuse'll wear thin someday."

"Someday," he agreed. He bent over me and parted my lips with his tongue, then sucked my lower lip into his mouth and hummed as if I tasted good. It made me tingle all over. I thought about pulling him into bed with me— damp peacoat and all—and starting off the year on a high note; unfortunately there's only so long I'd expect his Stiff to wait down there in the car.

When he pulled back, he cupped my face in his palm. His fingers were like ice, but so what? I covered his hand with mine and stared up into his eyes. So blue. I've always been a total goner for blue eyes. "This wasn't exactly the way I pictured tonight turning out," he said, "but for some reason I feel pretty okay about it."

"You got out of going to a party."

He smirked. "That's not what I mean." He pressed his mouth to mine again, firmly—just lips this time, but with his hand still cupping my face and his fingers growing warm. Our breath mingled. His stubble scraped my upper lip. When he finally pulled away, the ghost of his touch lingered on my cheek. "I think it'll be a good year."

"Pretty okay" and a cautious optimism was as wholehearted an endorsement as I was likely to expect from Vic. He gave me a parting glance over his shoulder—a naughty one, like he was thinking about waking me up again once he got home for good—and flipped off the overhead light. I lay there in his bed, his mattress that was too small for the both of us sagging toward my side of the bed, and stared at the ceiling. Though the light from the living room wasn't shining in directly, I could see well enough. Awful room. Small and cramped, with a dozen coats of economy white paint laid on so thick the detail in the crown molding was gone.

Awful apartment, when it came right down to it. The hallway smelled like boiled cabbage, the bathroom was so narrow I could hardly turn around in it, and the furniture was all slightly out of plumb because the pressboard was starting to work loose from the screws that held it together.

I had no idea how long we'd be stuck there. The only property we could both agree on was bound up so thick with red tape we might never unravel it all. For the foreseeable future, this four-room flat was home.

Home.

Our bed now, our room, our apartment. So despite the fact that my living situation hadn't turned out exactly like I'd always pictured it, I was "pretty okay" with it too.

# No Sale

Shopping malls don't tend to be haunted. They're too new. Too frequented. Too high-profile for your average murder, with security cameras everywhere. And don't forget the mall cops.

These little boutiquey joints in Boystown where Jacob wears out the magnetic strips on his credit cards, on the other hand....

"This eight-inch chef's knife is finished with a long taper rather than a short bevel so the edge stays sharp longer..."

A hundred bucks, on sale. Not a set of knives, mind you. Just the big, stabby one. Jacob wanted it. If there was one Jacob-expression I was confident I had a handle on, it's the "I want that" look. The clerk was flirting up a storm, too, which really didn't hurt his chances of scoring a sale.

Combining two households worth of crap should have left us with extras, and yet lately, we constantly came up missing various items we couldn't live without. Maybe if *someone* wasn't so eager to toss things out, we wouldn't be stuck shopping in our precious spare time, but I'm not one for unnecessary conflict, so I'd chosen to pick my battles and tag along.

Besides, a spiffy new chef's knife that cost more than

our outrageous cable bill would probably net me some fine eating as Jacob put it through its paces. Visions of home-made guacamole and stir fry and sushi danced in my head. So tasty I was tempted to ignore the oily, cold slither of deadness creeping down my spine. Even to pretend the whuff-whuff rasp was a quirk of the radiator. But a passing headlight shone through the storefront's plate glass, lighting a figure in the aisle for a fraction of a second. Long enough for me to see the bloated face with its poached salmon eyes trained right on me.

Telling Jacob why. That would be the hard part.

"...though we do recommend you bring it back for sharpening every six months..."

Right. How many gay guys bought one just for an excuse to come back and have another try at picking up Mr. Totally Fake Highlights? I cleared my throat, and Jacob woke from the salesman's spell and shifted his attention to me.

"If you had your heart set on a spatula, maybe a colander, I would tell you to knock yourself out." My eyes went to the spot where I now saw half-formed movement, a flickering outline streaked black with old blood. "But a knife?" I shook my head, dropped my voice, and muttered, "Not from this place."

Jacob shifted smoothly into high alert—one minute calm, affable, relaxed, and the next tensed like a predator. His gaze went right to the spot, but it was a faraway look on his face. Not like he'd actually seen anything, not like me. Only that he'd gleaned that I had.

That was enough for him. Jacob put down the knife and allowed me to steer us away from the bad juju he couldn't actually see. It was encouraging to think that he trusted my lead, even if it was only in the matter of picking the next store. I refrained from giving the salesman a smug look as we filed out the door. His fancy cutlery was no match for my secret weapon. Jacob liked expensive things, but all the pricy kitchen gadgets in the world didn't trump my second sight.

# Most Likely To...

It should come as no surprise that in the eighties, Jacob had a mullet.

If you're forty-something now, back then your hair could've only gone a few different ways. A nerdy side-part. Long and feathered for the stoners and short and feathered for the preps. If your parents were particularly cruel, a bowl cut. But for the non-preppy jocks, it was business in the front and party in the back. Jacob has always liked to present a conservative exterior, so his mulleted hair wasn't too extreme. But it was bad enough that I could tease him about it whenever his mother dragged out the yearbooks.

"I notice you've never coughed up any photographic evidence of your awkward years," he said.

After that I went quiet, which he must have noticed too, because he never brought it up again. My pensiveness wasn't due to the fact that I've never grown out of my awkward years—hell, eventually a guy gets used to being all elbows and ribs. No, it was because pictures from my high school days didn't exist.

Believe me, I was nothing to look at back then. Six-four and a buck thirty. My skin didn't have many good days, either. So I wore my jeans torn, my hair in my eyes, and my expression in a perpetual fuck-you.

I suppose it didn't really matter that I had no documentation of teenage me, but I was surprised to feel nostalgic over it. I wouldn't mind a point of reference, something where I could acknowledge that my skin's okay these days and my hairline hasn't shifted too dramatically. It might be reassuring to concede that I made it through all the bullshit and came out in one piece.

I'm still here. That would need to be enough.

The yearbook incident was long past, or so I'd thought, when I looked up from a magazine I'd been half-reading to find Jacob with a hardback clutched against his stomach, a green and yellow hardback with a telltale arrowhead emblazoned on the front. The "go, Lane, go," school song came flooding back like it was yesterday, and me giving Adam Sherhauer a hand job under the pep rally bleachers—not to completion, of course, but far enough that afterwards he would pointedly french his current girlfriend whenever I was in visual range.

"eBay," Jacob said. "Junior year. I found your senior year too, but...."

"I wasn't in that one." Did I need to spell out that I'd finished out high school in the psych ward, back when "psych" was short for psychiatric? Nah, why ruin the moment...I had my GED, anyway. "I don't remember this one either. I take it by the look on your face that I am actually in it."

He nodded carefully.

"C'mon." I patted the couch cushion. "Let's get it over with."

We spread the yearbook open with one side on my lap and the other on his. He started thumbing through to the juniors, but I stopped him as I recognized a few faces. A sophomore kid I sat with at lunch who could repeat lines from a TV show after seeing it just once. A Filipino girl who refused to wear her glasses even though she was half blind without them. Her sister, who was a sudden knockout after she had her braces off sophomore year. Where were they now? Married? Settled?

Jacob's knee pressed mine. Yeah, hopefully they were all settled by now.

Weirdly enough, I spotted Patty Barnes first. Her locker was next to mine and she sat beside me in homeroom. She told me about how far she went with her dates, in excruciating detail. At the time I figured she was trying to get me to admit that I'd hit all those bases too, and more. With boys. Now, she looked painfully young to my jaded eyes. Even innocent. And it occurred to me—nearly a quarter century later—that she'd probably been flirting.

And there, next to her, was me. Scowling. My hair was gelled into a sort of drooping Sid Vicious. I looked just as painfully young as Patty. Just as innocent too.

"I would've been too intimidated to approach you," Jacob said.

Like he knows the meaning of the word. "Especially given that you were looking at grad schools at the time...."

"You know what I mean."

I flipped forward to Adam Sherhauer. His short feathered hair looked unnaturally stiff, but at least his skin was clear. Decent smile. Not a bad looking kid, but nothing special. Hopefully he'd given up frenching girls in an attempt to force himself to be straight, or at least seem that way. Or maybe he'd just been curious back then, under the bleachers. Who was I to judge?

Jacob leafed forward and pointed to a lunchroom candid of three popular cheerleaders mugging for the camera. He tapped the background and said, "That's you too, right?"

I looked harder.

There I was, regaling the lunch gang with a very dramatic-looking story. My arms were spread wide like I'd just come to the punch line of a big joke, and everyone was watching me in rapt fascination. Who the heck knows what I'd been recounting—I recall that our most pressing topics were sitcoms, music, and the stupidity of jocks.

"I had you figured for a loner," Jacob said.

Funny, I thought I'd been a loner too.

Who knows what I feared I might find in my old yearbook. That maybe my name wasn't really my name, and it had been changed at some point and implanted by Camp Hell scientists? Or maybe that it wasn't actually possible to capture me on film. Instead, I found a kid. Not your most motivated or well-adjusted kid, but not a total mess either. Strong enough to stand up against the ugliness of the next several years. I had to give it to that seventeen year-old Victor Bayne—he was pretty damn sturdy.

# Jock Straps On Sale

"Going through my mail, are you?"

I tore my eyes away from a dog-eared envelope on Crash's countertop I hadn't exactly been staring at, though it probably looked that way to the untrained eye. Or any eye. Mostly I'd just had a wretched, long day at a non-haunted crime scene and my feet really hurt. "Uh. No."

Smooth.

"You're the detective, Detective Bayne. What is it you detect?"

That no matter what I said, I'd be sorry. "I wasn't really thinking about...never mind."

Crash batted his eyelashes, clicked his tongue stud against his front teeth, draped himself over the counter and began to rifle dramatically through the massive pile of letters and papers. Jacob and I combined don't get that much mail. Probably comes with the territory of owning a business. Either that or it had been accumulating for a week. "Bill. Ad. Bill. Junk. Junk. Bill. Ooh, and here's the latest circular for SaverPlus."

Great. Now I'd have to endure some wisecrack about my wardrobe. "Look, I just need to know if you have any Florida Water, and if you don't—"

"Yeah, yeah, I heard you before. Nothing on the shelf. Some tattooed witchy chick cleaned me out a couple days ago—hot damn…would you look at these prices?"

A remark about the polyester blazer was coming for sure. "Is there a good substitute, then? Something similar with a different name?"

"So low. How *do* they do it?" He licked his thumb pointedly, smiled to himself and turned the page with his spit. "Their margins must be paper-thin."

"Maybe another ritual herb with the same properties?"

His eyebrows shot up toward his hairline as he bolted upright and snatched up the circular in disbelief. "Jock straps?" He flipped the paper around and stretched it across his crotch, and the tiny picture of a plastic mannequin torso in a cup landed right over the fly of his jeans in glorious, bulging 3-D. "And they're on sale!"

"Never mind. I can hit the botanica in Uptown on the way to work tomorrow…."

"Let you leave empty handed? I wouldn't hear of it. I'll give you my own personal bottle, gratis…if you'll just do me a solid."

When people ask for a favor, my usual reaction is to pretend I didn't hear them and hope they go ask someone else. But Crash? I owe him nine ways 'til Sunday, so I couldn't just blow him off. He dropped the paper and whisked through the beaded curtain to his inner sanctum before I could agree or disagree, and came back with a slightly used bottle of Florida water, which dangled from his hand where he held it by the narrow neck between his first two fingers like a cigarette. He was also now wearing his vintage wool double-breasted officer's coat.

Great. The favor involved going somewhere.

"I have this friend at SaverPlus," he said.

I was liking it even less. "Uh huh."

"Howsabout we pay him a little visit. Me. You. A bunch of

loss-leader jock straps. Him and his massive love muscle."

"No."

"But you haven't even met—"

"No."

Crash came around the counter, and with a long, put-up-on sigh, pressed his temple into my shoulder. "What would entice you to join in our reindeer games?"

"I'm not a joiner. Just ask the Homeowner's Association and the Fantasy Football League." He did some more eyelash batting and I shoved him off my shoulder. "You know I'd never take you up on the offer. What's really going on?"

"I saw on Facebook that he just got stood up—spent last night sitting there alone at Blue Man Group—and so I figured he could use a little cheer."

"Who?"

"My friend at SaverPlus."

And here I'd presumed Mr. Big was just a figment of Crash's overactive imagination. "I can drop you off on my way home, but I'm not going in."

"Coolness." Crash pressed the Florida water into my hands then twirled away, coattails flaring, and hit the lights. Sticks and Stones went dim. "Let's motor."

When he strapped in to my passenger seat, it occurred to me to refrain from pointing out that it wasn't much of a favor. SaverPlus was on my way home, after all. "If you needed a ride, all you had to do was ask."

"Yeah, I know." He clicked his tongue stud against his teeth a few times. "But it's so much fun to see you squirm."

# Piece of Cake

*Grease and flour a 13 by 9 inch pan.*

**Ash Man:** what r u doing?

I stared at the chat popup with a mixture of dread and relief. Would he believe me if I told him? I was trying to bake a cake...and the instructions on the box were worthless.

**Lets69:** is that mexican bakery across from you still open

**Ash Man:** nope, they lock their doors at 3 - lucky saps

**Lets69:** what happens if you grease & flour a pan wrong cuz im trying to watch a video on it & i think my flash player is out of date & how do you update that

**Ash Man:** this can't be good

**Lets69:** forget it

**Ash Man:** calm down, clearly you're eager to channel your inner betty crocker

**Ash Man:** u don't need a video - wipe down the pan with some shortening, then put in a tbsp of flour and tap it all around so it sticks. easy peasy.

**Lets69:** we dont have shortening…can I use olive oil

**Ash Man:** only if ur making cornbread

Cornbread did sound tasty, but it didn't have the same sort of panache as a cake. Plus, I'd already opened the box.

**Ash Man:** what about butter?

**Lets69:** will margarine work

**Ash Man:** that processed stuff will kill you

**Ash Man:** but yeah it will do

I'm fairly sure butter is way worse for your health than margarine, but I know better than to argue with Crash.

Getting the grease on the pan was easy enough. It actually took longer to smooth the finger-marks out of the margarine afterward. I double-checked the box to see if it specified white or brown flour, and then I saw that not only did the cake take 45 minutes to bake, it was supposed to cool for another two hours before I could frost it. This whole cake thing was a bust—no way would Jacob be Skyping with Clayton for three more hours, no matter how exciting the first few weeks of school had been. I was considering if I could get away with hauling both the opened cake mix and the greasy floured pan out to the alley without getting caught when the chat window bleeped.

**Ash Man:** i just realized what the momentous occasion is

If we were face to face, I'd be able to judge which end of the sarcasm scale his comment was hitting: the chummy ribbing, or the scathing venom. I figured I should give him the benefit of the doubt. And be as vague and neutral as possible in reply.

**Lets69:** yep one year

Damn it, I was covered in flour. I'd have to ditch my clothes, too. And I really liked that T-shirt.

**Ash Man:** one year from the first date, or one year since you moved in together?

**Ash Man:** same difference, I guess

The last thing I needed was him mouthing off to me when I was in the middle of a cake crisis.

**Lets69:** jealous much?

The moment I hit the enter key, I regretted it. If I'd been thinking—which obviously I hadn't—I would've realized that my knee-jerk comeback opened up a whole can of worms that really shouldn't be allowed to slither out. What if I'd just led him to believe that I thought I'd won Jacob away from him?

**Lets69:** not jealous of me

Or worse, that I was conceited enough to think he was hot for me.

**Lets69:** or Jacob

Cripes, the whole remark was so ill-considered I wished I could unremark it, because he wasn't firing back with anything—and he's a really fast typist.

**Lets69:** its just an expression…i didn't mean anything by it

**Lets69:** really

On his end, only silence. Or the chat-equivalent of silence, anyway. He was determined to make me squirm. I probably deserved it. What did I care if he made comments about how quickly I'd fallen into a serious committed relationship? It's not as if I could deny it. We'd stood the test of time, though, Jacob and me. The anniversary proved it. That's what mattered.

**Lets69:** come on…call me an asshole and get it over with

Surely that would get a rise out of him. I watched the chat box, and I waited.

Nothing.

He might be with a customer, at least that's what I wanted to believe. But he might also be seriously ticked off. I pulled out my phone, which left me with a trio of white finger-marks on my jeans. My phone seemed to magnetically attract the flour, too. The black plastic was holding onto it more tightly than the greased pan. I stood there for a moment, wavering between cleaning up all my evidence, and following through with a phone call in which I'd get reamed out. Since both prospects were equally daunting, the decision wouldn't form. Given that it was a Saturday and Crash had chosen to chat rather than call, I figured

Sticks and Stones was seeing some business. That meant the phone call would be short and sweet, and the sooner I got it over with, the better I'd come off. My thumb was hovering over the call button when Jacob shouted from the office, "My connection died. Can you get on?"

I glanced at the laptop perched on the counter and called back, "I'll check."

**Lets69:** are you there?

Nothing. And then I noticed the cursor up in the corner of the screen was shaped like a little clock...and when I backed over the last thing I'd typed, it disappeared. I pulled up a browser and tried to connect to the weather page. Nothing.

Talk about dodging a bullet.

"Nope," I yelled, "no internet." I closed down the chat program. Hopefully it would whisk the awkward jealousy remark into the realm of lost data, the magical place where so many of my projects end up when the computer freezes and shuts itself off for no good reason.

Jacob said, "I'm going to restart the modem."

The last time the internet went out, Jacob wrestled with it for nearly half a day before giving in and calling the cable company. He's the poster child for the word *persistence*, which would definitely work to my advantage. If I got cooking right away, the cake might even be able to cool before I frosted it. Eager to get that sucker in the oven, I grabbed the box and read the next line in the instructions.

*Combine cake mix, two large eggs, 1/4 cup of water, and 1/2 cup of oil.*

No problem. I reached for the olive oil....

# In the Dark

1

I don't hate all of Jacob's friends. Just the ones he's slept with.

No, wait, that's not true. As much as I fight off the urge to knock Crash over the nearest piece of low-lying furniture, I must enjoy spending time with him, because a couple times a week I look up and realize I'm at Sticks and Stones, and the two of us are eating some vegetarian take-out and maybe laughing about something together, or at least performing a synchronized eye-roll.

Maybe I just hate the ones Jacob's slept with, but conveniently omitted mentioning that he's slept with until I've met them for like the ninth or tenth time. And then later on he'll throw in a thing like, "When we were dating." Because Jacob's not a liar—at least, not about things like that. He wouldn't say, "No, I've never been with him," if he actually had. But having a lie detector for a partner all those years has made him an old pro at skirting around any facts he doesn't want to deal with at the moment.

I'm a realistic guy. It was pretty clear that neither of us

were blushing virgins when we hooked up. Not him. Not me. At our age, it would be suspicious if we were. But I'd been in the dark this whole time, and what was nagging at me now was the way I'd accepted "Keith and Manny" as some unit who'd been a couple forever. That I'd invented this whole history between the two of them that spanned back a good twenty years when, in fact, they were together for two. And that it used to be "Keith and Jacob."

Funny, I even used to have trouble telling Keith and Manny apart.

Not anymore.

Manny's the nice one. Keith is the one who gives me "that look." Now that I understand the reason behind that look, I can't see how I ever mixed them up. Sure, they're both shaved-headed and bulging with muscles. But given that one's part Hispanic and one's white—and the white one's always giving me the hairy eyeball—the difference is suddenly crystal clear.

At first I'd been disappointed that this Halloween party of Keith and Manny's (the one I promised I would attend) was a suit-and-tie thing rather than a costume thing. It's easier to scare up a cheap costume than it is to arrange for one of the jackets that actually fits me to be clean. But since it was a non-costume event, I'd get to demonstrate my newfound grasp on the muscular bald guys' identities by calling each of them by name when I greeted them.

No doubt that would earn me a "look" too.

Wearing a jacket reminds me of dressing for work, and dressing for work makes me feel like a sellout, so I dug out a nicer shirt than I was willing to waste on the Fifth Precinct in hopes of looking like more of a guy going somewhere fancy and less like a plainclothes cop. I think it worked. Maybe because it didn't have that telltale permanent press finish. Maybe because I was unarmed, and my holster wasn't making its usual bulge over my right hip. Plus my hair had some serious product going on. My cop-face was in place, though. A vague scowl. At least it was, until Jacob grabbed me on our way out the door, tipped my face toward the hall light and said, "You missed a few whiskers shaving...let's see." But there were no strays—it was just an excuse to maul my mouth with his for a few minutes. Once we came up for air, I imagine I wasn't scowling very convincingly at all.

Not until I realized he had no intention of ditching the dumb party.

We headed down toward Logan Square, a trendier neighborhood where a couple of guys sporting liberal amounts of hair product wouldn't look out of place, and scored a parking space a few blocks from a bar/restaurant with a "Closed - Private Party" sign in the window. When I got out of the car and buttoned my jacket, my hip felt naked without my sidearm. I reminded myself that it was unlikely I would need to shoot anyone in a room full of fancy gay guys. However much I might want to.

The days of stepping through the door into a haze of second-hand smoke are long gone. Bars feel cleaner now, although many, like this one, simply cranked the lights down a bit lower to compensate for the lack of ambience. From what I could see by the occasional tea light, it looked like a hip place. Classy. Disappointing, too. What's the point of throwing a shindig on Halloween if you're not going to have crappy plastic skeletons hanging everywhere and a cake shaped like a tombstone? Then I picked out a few guests and realized that the age demographic was skewed a good eight to ten years older than me. Which was probably why they were sipping wine instead of doing jello shots.

Once my eyes adjusted to the non-light, I could see the catering was definitely beyond my age demographic, too. Not to mention my socioeconomic bracket. Small, fussy food. Shrimp? Caviar? Of course, over by the seafood area.

Not to be confused with the sushi area. That was parked by the wall of predictably low-key local art. Cheeses? Convenient to the wine. Fruit? Yes...but in shapes and colors you could only find in froufrou specialty stores. Pastries, almost too pretty to eat, near the coffee. I was starving, of course, having presumed we'd get some kind of sit-down dinner, and Jacob vague on the details. Mr. Perfectly Vague himself had begun his circuit of affable and completely confident hellos. I'd lagged behind to gaze off into the hors d'oeuvres and try to calculate how rapidly I could consume them without being too obvious and making some mortifying lapse of social etiquette.

"And look who's here!" Someone exclaimed in my ear, because despite all the fanciness, a disco standard was blasting for all it was worth. Thankfully, I don't visibly flinch anymore when a ginormous musclebound guy sneaks up on me. Desensitization in action.

Recognition kicked in quickly—this would be the nice one. Or at least the one Jacob had never dated. As far as I knew. "Manny." I moved to shake hands, smooth as you please. But instead of a handshake, a glass of bubbly was thrust into my grasp.

Manny gave the rims a tiny clink. His movements were delicate for such a big guy, and he had a secret little smile he carried mostly in his eyes that held a certain appeal. I supposed he didn't actually remind me of the orderlies at Camp Hell—I'd just been worried that he should. When he raised his glass, eyes locked with mine, I mirrored him in some autonomic attempt to fit in. Though I steeled myself to camouflage a shudder, the "ew, booze" reaction didn't kick in when the champagne hit. Yeah, it tasted like alcohol. But mostly fizzy. Kind of like a really dry soda.

"Good, right?" Manny slipped an arm around me and turned me to face the far end of the bar, and pointed over my shoulder where a bunch of bottles protruded from a bed of ice. "There's plenty where that came from. One of our clients paid us in champagne...not that I'm complaining."

I tried to dredge up a nugget of small talk, but what I really wondered was what it would be like to get paid in champagne. Could they afford that? They seemed to be doing well enough for themselves, although when I scanned the crowd for Jacob and found him talking to a bunch of stuffed shirts, I realized that maybe they would rather have their invoice honored in a more conventional way. Maybe they didn't have a cake shaped like a tombstone because the type of people who'd be into kitschy Halloween parties weren't the type of people who'd hire a pair of private investigators. And hopefully pay them in real currency.

It was too loud in there to broach such a nuanced subject though, and anyway, it was none of my business. I didn't know Manny well enough get so personal.

More guests arrived and Manny flitted off, which left me some space to work my way through the small, small food. I snagged a couple pieces here, a couple there, avoiding only the sushi. It wasn't the raw fish I was worried about. It was the fear of biting into a surprise hunk of horseradish and having my sinuses drain all over the nearest well-dressed stranger.

Off to the side I spotted a table full of meat-and-pastry somethings, and I slotted myself in where I wasn't too obvious and got to work on rearranging the platter, which was clearly overcrowded. If I ate approximately every third hors d'oeuvres, the pieces that were left fit the plate much better.

Flaky. Warm. And oh so meaty. They went down fast, which was good, because my champagne was gone, and it had left behind a pleasant buzz that made the idea of small talk seem entirely doable. No doubt the warm, meaty, flaky things would be awesome at soaking up the stray alcohol in my stomach before I actually needed to talk to—

"Say, you look like you'd have an interesting request."

*How about you go find someone else to bother? How's that for an interesting request?*

My peripheral vision is stunningly well-developed from years and years of not looking at people, so without even turning I could tell the DJ who'd inserted himself between me and the rest of the meat rolls was all decked out in too-big jewelry in an attempt to seem "urban." Grudgingly, I looked in his direction. He was probably Caucasian, or maybe a mix, mid-twenties, with a shaved head and a pierced eyebrow. Gay, but butch. Like all the other men, he was wearing a suit, so thankfully he'd left his baseball cap at home. I had no doubt if he had been wearing one, it would have been tilted sideways.

He cocked his head toward the sound system and said, "Whatcha wanna hear? Thirty thousand tunes on my iPod—I'll bet I got it."

I stifled a sigh. "I don't know."

"Something classic? Something new?"

"I really don't have a preference."

He crossed his arms and got big—like every other guy there, apparently he had a long-standing subscription to Biceps Monthly—but then he topped off the pose with an exasperated smile that wasn't exactly threatening. "Aw... come on. What's your favorite song?"

*Cripes, none of your business.*

"'Cos I'll bet you anything I got it."

"Um, I dunno." Just think of a song, I told myself, any freakin' song, and he'll go play it...and then you can ditch him and get more of that champagne that tastes like boozy soda. A nasty three-chord punk ditty called *I Hate People* sprang to mind (and it was long-forgotten enough that I bet he didn't have it) but as it hovered there on the tip of my tongue, I glanced up and spied Jacob across the bar. Yes, his suits were all immaculate, and yes, he had great hair and even better bone structure. But even if he hadn't been gifted with a great wardrobe and stunning genetics, out of that whole sea of beefy middle-aged gay guys and their sparkly women-friends, he would be the one I'd stop and take another look at. Jacob didn't just *have* a conversation. He owned it. Not by talking over everyone else, either. Even if he wasn't the one who was speaking, Jacob could exude charisma simply by observing whoever was talking.

Posture. Facial expression. I wasn't really sure exactly how he managed it. Some method way too subtle to imitate. Not that I'd ever have the balls to attempt it.

He did speak, then, and I watched the people around him watching him...and I realized why Jacob and I had been invited to a party among a bunch of potential clients. Not because Keith and Manny thought they needed to woo us into giving them a job—they were already the only ones we trusted when we needed to work around the police force—but because Jacob would put all of those would-be clients in a relaxed and trusting frame of mind.

And if I goaded the DJ into playing something stupid, I'd be totally undermining The Jacob Effect.

2

While the party wasn't exactly my idea of a festive Halloween, the last thing I wanted to do was spoil the mood. I requested some Bronski Beat (hey, it was better than disco) and slipped away as smoothly as I could manage for a guy who's way too tall to be invisible. The crowd wasn't exactly thick—we all had our own elbow room—but it felt like everywhere I went, something was brushing against one of my thighs or rubbing up against my back. I scored another champagne, took a few sips, then ended up knocking it back in one smooth swallow. Fizzy and good—but I'd have to pace myself.

As soon as I thought that, the belligerent part of me that had just been thwarted from requesting something obnoxious from the pushy DJ thought, "Really?"

I gave the room a casual glance. People talking. People laughing. One or two people even singing along to Bronski Beat. No one was getting cut down by bullets or choking on a piece of ham. No one was standing half inside a wall or flickering in and out of existence. No one had a scary, rotted face or a transparent head.

In short, no one was dead.

I eased over to the champagne and helped myself to another glass. It went down as fizzy and cold as the first two.

As I lowered the glass, my arm jostled someone—yet another bald guy in a suit, though this one, I didn't know. He had a soul patch facial hair thing going on, and a small earring. He got all apologetic and started brushing at my sleeve, even though I'd drained my glass dry enough that there was nothing left in it to actually slosh out. Once I disentangled myself from him, I snagged another champagne, then sought out a suitably dark corner of the room where I'd be able to keep from blundering into every Tom, Dick and Harry by standing perfectly still. Yeah, I had a buzz on, but nothing that should send me careening around like a pinball.

Someone had freshened up the meat rolls, so I quickly plotted a course that would take me past the overly earnest DJ while he was talking to someone else, allow me to scoop up a good handful of tasty meat-filled pastry, and then tuck me into a deliciously dark corner without any bald, suited, middle-aged gay man being any the wiser. Zipping my way through the crowd was so effortless it felt like ice skating, and before I knew it I had a napkin full of hot hors d'oeuvres in one hand and a full glass of champagne in the other, and was heading away from all the inexplicably close bodies, when a door emerged from the darkness in front of me.

Even better.

I flicked the handle with my elbow and let myself in, eager to stuff my face with meat rolls in peace...and maybe wash them down with a Valium, because clearly Valium and champagne were meant to go together. One pill, or two? That was the big question. I must have been fairly distracted by the decision of exactly how relaxed I wanted to feel, or else I had a pretty good momentum going, because the chill in the air only hit me once I'd taken several steps out into the alley and the door slammed shut behind me. I turned around. Yep. There was the back of the bar. Flat gray graffiti-cover paint and dumpsters, and a ring of cigarette butts on the blacktop.

Oh well. It was cold outside, but nothing I couldn't handle. No sense in letting the meat rolls go to waste. I savored them one by one, flaky pastry and juicy spiced meat, until they were gone. And then, since I was all alone with nobody to impress, I licked my fingers. I had the impulse to chase the meat rolls with a swig of champagne, but since I was outside in my pleasant bubble of aloneness, I didn't need to drown my awkwardness in carbonation. I could simply enjoy the savoriness melting away on my tongue at my leisure, tasting the spices I couldn't name given infinite chances, and thinking that maybe the Halloween party I'd only attended because I thought it would make Jacob happy really wasn't too bad after all.

Even when something moved out there at the edge of my well-developed peripheral vision, I was still hanging on to that thought. The idea that I wasn't having too bad of a time. Because initially I took that movement for a plastic bag blowing in the wind, or maybe a bare tree branch bobbing in front of a lit window. But no. The thing that swooped past me looked nothing like a plastic bag or a branch-covered window. It looked like a woman. A semi-transparent blood spattered woman. A semi-transparent blood spattered woman running down the alley with her mouth gaping in a silent scream.

I steeled myself and swallowed my champagne.

Revenant or repeater? I can't say I was particularly eager to see either species of deceased humanity. Repeaters are just plain old scary, stuck in a continual loop that replays the moment of their death. I'm not sure which part is worse—dying over and over for eternity, or having a piece of you carry on outside your conscious control. Or maybe it wasn't important which aspect was worse than the other. It all sucked.

The ghosts who still had their personalities intact weren't any treat to be around, either. They tended to glom on to me and drive me nuts with their badgering and whining. And while they were actually capable of carrying on a conversation, they were also pretty tenacious about veering back toward whatever unfinished business was keeping them stuck in this plane.

So which type of ghost was I dealing with? A spectral film loop, or a sentient dead chick? I supposed I'd need to check it out, even though it was the last thing in the world

I wanted to do (and, in fact, going back in and trying to think of more songs for the eager DJ was even starting to look pretty appealing.) Some people can't go to bed without brushing their teeth. And some people can't deal with letting their calls go to voicemail. Me, I can't leave a spirit wandering around until I've determined if it's suffering or not. I set my empty glass on the dumpster and reached for my sidearm, which of course wasn't there. Not that I'd be able to shoot the ghost, anyway. I just felt more secure with my favorite hunk of matte black plastic in my hand.

To get the lay of the land, I tried the door I'd just exited. Locked. I'd figured as much from the sound of the click, but some details are best not left to chance. That settled it, then. My only way back to the party was through the alley. And the alley was where I'd seen the ghost. The champagne buzz didn't feel nearly as welcome as it had mere moments before…but maybe having some booze in me was actually a good thing. Alcohol makes the spirit world shine even brighter to my inner eye, and alleys are creepy enough even without the knowledge that you're not alone…and whatever else is in your proximity is dead.

This alley had several bright lights shining down on it, but even so, large portions of it were in shadow. I'd need to watch out for more than just ghosts. If I ended up getting rolled for my wallet while I was busy staring off into Deadland, I'd never hear the end of it. A few steps forward. A few more. Look. Listen.

Nothing.

The tension in my shoulders was just starting to ebb when I caught a flash of motion. Fast. Crazy fast. My head snapped around, and even though she was soaring at me way too quick to be natural, that brief impression coalesced in a single moment. Wild hair. Wide eyes. Torn clothes. And blood, blue-black in the street lights, running down her legs.

And then she was gone.

I stood perfectly still, suddenly aware of the noise of Halloween revelers out on the street, car doors slamming, traffic, people talking, people laughing. Living people. Eventually it seemed like maybe the show was over and I'd seen all there was to see...and then I saw the flash of movement again. The bleeding woman, running too fast. She disappeared in the same spot as before, a few yards before alley met side street. I allowed myself to exhale: repeater. Creepy. Tragic. But as far as I knew, nothing I needed to do much about, other than flick some salt its way and urge it out of its perpetual death loop.

A flicker, and the bloody woman ran by again and disappeared. How often did it happen, once every minute or so? Multiplied by however many minutes it had been since she screamed her last scream...well, doing the math wouldn't help either of us. I'd end up depressed, and she'd still be perpetually screaming down the alley. I didn't happen to have any salt on me. However, I could easily go around the block, hope I didn't earn too many weird looks by arriving at the same party twice, pony up to the bar and order a frozen margarita with a nice salty rim.

Except....

The likelihood of her death having been an accident or a suicide were pretty damn slim. I don't think back alley coat hanger abortions actually take place in back alleys, so shady medical procedures were an unlikely cause. It didn't look like a case of pedestrian vs. vehicle, either, like I see at so many intersections. Judging by the bloody thighs, my new repeater had been sexually assaulted. But had the crime been solved, or was it rotting in a cold case file? Hard to say. Not my precinct. Not to mention that I couldn't really tell how fresh the repeater was. Could've been two years. Could've been twenty.

If the case was still open, chances of me getting called in to help with it were minuscule. And chances of another medium picking up the level of detail that I could were nearly nil. Even so, if I salted her now and it turned out they needed more evidence later, I didn't want to be the one who'd scrubbed the traces clean.

"So both of my choices here suck," I told her as she flashed by me. "I'm sorry."

The repeater darted to the end of the alley and disappeared.

I straightened my tie, picked up my empty champagne glass and followed. As I neared the side street, someone cleared their throat. I cataloged all the ways I might use my empty glass as a weapon. But muggers don't usually clear their throats to let you know they're in your path—and the guy leaning on the building had the silhouette of a bald guy in a suit. Maybe one of the guests, but more likely one of the hosts. He tipped his chin up and the alleyway lights caught his brow, nose and cheekbones.

Not the nice one. The one Jacob used to "date." Keith.

He didn't move to take his hands out of his pockets, which excused me from a handshake. But we could hardly pretend we didn't see each other. "Cigarette break?" he said.

"Just getting some air."

He grunted, eyes on the pavement beyond me as if the asphalt was more interesting than I was, and he'd only asked because it seemed it was expected of him.

Awkward pause, and then, since he didn't seem to be smoking either, I said, "You?"

"Same."

It's *your* party, I thought. You picked out your guest list and your hors d'oeuvres bar and your incredibly persistent DJ. Why should *you* need to escape? I stuffed my free hand in my pocket and rocked on my feet for a moment since I didn't want anyone reporting back to Jacob that I hadn't been willing to chat. But when it didn't seem as if Keith wanted me there any more than I wanted to be there, I shifted my weight to take a step toward the bar. Once I'd made my decision to walk, of course, he began to speak.

"Manny picked this place."

A chill raced down the back of my neck. Was this guy a telepath? 'Cos it sounded like a response to the very thing I'd just thought. Given Jacob and his hard-on for psychs, I shouldn't be surprised. "Oh. It's, uh...nice. Upscale. Logan Square cleaned up pretty good in the past ten, fifteen years." The gentrified parts, anyway.

"Twenty-third precinct," he supplied.

It was a cop thing to say. Keith is a private investigator now, but he used to be a cop. He hadn't quite shed the cop part yet. If I looked at him as a cop, his lack of niceness felt a hell of a lot less personal. The things we see every day don't exactly leave us cracking jokes. Not unless the punch lines are dark.

The silence between us grew less oppressively weird. Then he said, "I was a rookie. Canvassed the neighborhood after an ugly rape left a girl dead, a twenty-year-old Loyola student. Survived the assault, laid here and screamed for an hour while all the residents turned a deaf ear, bled out... where you're standing."

A flash of ghostly non-color to my right told me that Keith's memory of the logistics might be a foot or two off, but I shifted away from the spot anyway.

"Did you bag the guy?"

He nodded without any enthusiasm, still staring hard at the patch of asphalt I'd just been standing on. "He'd been in and out of prison since he was sixteen, in tight with whatever prison gang tattooed his neck. Fuckhead hardly blinked when he was sentenced."

I leave the court duties to my partner, Zigler. It's in my contract. Probably the only favorable thing I'd ever managed to agree to.

"You work Homicide," he said. "How many years?"

"Twelve." More like thirteen now, probably. It starts to blend after a while. A sick slideshow of things no one should ever have to see.

"Well," he turned to head back toward the bar, "someone's gotta do it."

The chill prickling along the back of my neck intensified, because every time I decided I'd had enough of being a PsyCop, that particular reason was the excuse I gave myself. Someone did have to do it. And the tasks I could accomplish, seeing the repeaters, chatting with the lingering dead, were jobs that would go undone if I didn't step up to the plate and do them. Keith's victim flashed past me and disappeared. "I'm sorry," I repeated. Though it didn't make either one of us feel better.

3

Luckily the guy at the door remembered me from the first time around, so I didn't need to come off like a party crasher by explaining I'd already been crossed off the guest list as Jacob's "+1." The party vibe had intensified while I was outside and the alcohol had been doing its work. People were standing closer, laughing louder. Their gregariousness didn't rub off on me at all. No matter how hard I tried to get back in the swing of the party, I found I had no appetite for spicy meat rolls anymore. The champagne wasn't calling to me either. I couldn't even think of a smartass song to request from the DJ.

The business of death leaves a sour taste in your mouth. There's no expiration date on it, either. A crime doesn't need to be fresh to leave you wishing you'd never known about it, and then wondering what kind of world you live in that things like that can happen.

When I sought out Jacob, it wasn't exactly for comfort. Him and me, we're not the type to kiss each other's boo-boos, cradle each other's heads, or murmur "there, there" in each other's ears. Despite that, he did manage to exude reassurance in a subtle but very concrete way. His posture. His direct gaze. His utter certainty, which usually made me want to scream. At times, though, that certainty washed over me as persistent and soothing as a Seconal on a Friday night.

He spotted me feeling my way through the crowd and disengaged from his conversation by the time I caught up with him, and zeroed in close to me in a way we couldn't usually do out in public, given our jobs. Our thighs brushed. He rested his hand on my hip. "There you are. I thought one of your admirers made off with you."

"Uh huh," I said blandly. Because either I'd heard him

wrong, or I'd heard him perfectly fine...and simply had no idea what he was talking about. Most likely he was just yanking my chain.

"Do you need a drink?"

I shook my head, then angled my mouth to his ear to ask him a question over the club beats du jour. "When did Keith retire?"

Jacob gave me a once-over and narrowed his eyes. It was a simple enough question, but that look must've meant the answer was nowhere near as easy. He thought about it, chose his words to be concise enough to penetrate the music, then leaned into me and said, "He didn't. He quit."

"Really?" Yeah, I'd pegged him for a guy who'd seen a lot of things that rubbed him wrong. But also as someone who'd managed to build up a callus against them. "He doesn't...strike me that way. As a quitter."

The music chose that particular moment to end, and my last word seemed to reverberate in the brief silence. *...itter, itter, itter, itter.* But before I could figure out who'd heard me and how embarrassed I needed to be, a big blat of disco nearly knocked me on my ass, and the crowd of fifty-something queers and their glittery underfed female friends all whooped and started to bump or hustle or whatever John Travolta move they were attempting. Me? I cringed.

The feathered hair, satin jackets and polyester shirts had been bad enough in the seventies. Did it make me less gay to continue to viscerally despise the music?

Jacob, who never misses a trick, steered me toward the door. Though he and I didn't see eye to eye on music overall, he'd never been a Dancing Queen either. He'd aced all his college classes to the artsier, more cerebral indie bands of the early eighties, his cassette tapes spooling out thin from wear as he crammed for his criminal justice exams. College rock wasn't exactly my thing, but it wasn't awful. In fact, when R.E.M. finally broke up, I was the epitome of tact. I didn't point out that Jacob's eyes looked a little swollen and he was sniffling after he'd absorbed the news.

We angled our way through the middle-aged disco flailing and slipped out the front door. Some parties spill out into the street, but this one was contained. It was cold on the sidewalk, while inside the bar the music was loud, the champagne was fizzy, and the meat rolls were periodically topped off. Despite the cold and the damp, I found I could breathe easier without worrying about someone boogieing into me. Jacob gazed up past the streetlights into the night sky, leaned against the building, and said, "Technically, he quit."

"Okay."

"And technically, if he'd been reprimanded because of his orientation, he could've fought back with a major discrimination suit."

I sighed, getting a good idea where the story was going already. I might not fit in with most gay guys in my general demographic, but I understood how police business worked.

"The thing is, *technically* the Twelfth Precinct hadn't officially reprimanded him in any way. But after a year of getting the shittiest assignments with the most asinine partners during the most ungodly shifts, after being passed up for two promotions in favor of guys with half the seniority and a quarter the brains...he'd had enough."

"Wait a minute. The Twelfth Precinct? Your precinct? He told me he worked in the Twenty-Third."

"He used to."

"So when he got outed at work, were the two of you...?"
Jacob nodded.

"I thought Sergeant Owens was okay with it."

"Eventually, more or less, he came around. But at first—with two guys on the same squad dating—that was a different story."

"And you *stayed*, while Keith threw away his pension and his benefits and...." I stopped when I realized I was kind of yelling at him. Because what did I care about Keith? I couldn't stand the guy. Always glaring at me like...hell, I didn't know. I used to think it was because I'd ended up with Jacob, but maybe he was pissed off that I was still on the force. And I wasn't stuck on hooker duty at the crack of dawn.

"I tried to get him to go with the flow, let things calm down before he made any big decisions. But he said I didn't know what it was like, being unofficially demoted." He straightened his cuffs, though his jacket was already sitting on him just fine. "I think I might have gotten the same treatment, if they'd been able to find anyone else who could deal with Carolyn."

And now she'd been left behind too while Jacob networked with the Feds. He didn't look guilty, exactly. Maybe regretful.

Way back when, he'd had the choice between making a stand with Keith or staying on the force. He chose the force. I turned that around in my mind a couple of times, and realized that I might not have done the same. Most likely I would have done whatever served me the most. I'd left Stefan rotting in Camp Hell without so much as a backward glance, after all. The easier choice would have been for Jacob to resign too, but he stayed. Maybe his job was a discouraging cycle of ferreting out lowlife predators and putting them away, only to have fresh monsters pop up like weeds the minute the ground was cleared. But someone had to do it. And if keeping that job cost him his relationship, so be it.

Maybe I wasn't angry he hadn't stood by Keith. Maybe I was mad at myself.

Once I'd been standing there marveling at the parallels for a good long while, he asked, "Do you want to go home?"

Home—where the food comes in big, solid portions and I don't need to be wary of dropping anything on my best suit. I expected relief to flood me. Instead, though, I felt a gnawing sense of non-completion. The way you feel when someone hums three lines of a song without humming the fourth. At least when that song isn't disco.

Despite the cannery's reputation for being haunted, home was a ghost-free zone. This place, not so much. "There's a repeater in back I need to deal with first." Because someone had to do it.

"What do you need from me?" Jacob asked. He was so earnest, I couldn't help but feel the benefit of the doubt creeping up on me. Jacob did what Jacob did because he thought it was the right thing to do. If I couldn't say the same for myself, that was my problem, I decided. Not his. And definitely not my problem with him.

"I don't have my Florida Water with me." Although I did have a few good slugs of champagne in my system. "Maybe I can try it with just the salt."

"Salt. Check." He slipped back inside and returned a few minutes later with a salt shaker. "I said our goodbyes, too."

Good old reliable Jacob. Not only had he rescued my eardrums from the disco, he'd saved me from having to figure out what my face should look like while I signed off with Keith.

Rather than just blundering around back and waiting for the bleedout repeater to barrel past me, I took another moment to center myself first. Centering is an overused New Age term, if you ask me. But I'm painfully literal, so the word felt pretty apt. When I quieted my scattered brain long enough to collect myself, when I focused on the salt and started thinking about things like subtle bodies and psychic energies, it really did feel like I'd drawn everything into myself, like I'd packed a fresh magazine into the center of my Glock and my Glock in the center of its holster. All that potential, all that force, concentrated into a small and easily accessible place, ready for action with the squeeze of a trigger.

I opened my eyes. Things weren't exactly glowy, like they might have been if I'd swallowed a prescription psyactive, or fallen into the range of a GhosTV. Some things looked more soft-edged than others, though. The salt. My hand. Jacob's face. Maybe it was all in my head. Then again, that's where psychic ability lives, so probably, it was. I took a deep breath, let the cold night air scour my lungs, and said, "Okay. Let's do this."

He allowed me to take point and followed close, but he didn't crowd me—a solid presence, like a sidearm at my hip. "There's a flashlight in the glove box," he said. "Want me to go get it?"

"The thing I'm looking for...I might actually see it better without. Can't speak for the rats, though." We both gave a short breath of a laugh and headed toward the side street, easy with one another, secure. I circled around to the back of the building with my white light internal faucet cranked all the way up, and when I came to the spot where I'd had my little chat with Keith, I found a hazy mist rising from the ground that I wasn't seeing with my physical eyes. I planted my feet beside it and held out my arm crossing-guard style to stop Jacob from walking onto the hotspot. He stopped and waited.

A woman-shaped flicker, an impression of screaming and blood, then quiet. Gooseflesh prickled my forearms. I exhaled and saw my breath, but that was probably just from the actual temperature. Still, since my psychic faucet was wide open, lingering on the site of the lethal assault felt like cobwebs wafting against my eyelashes and cheeks. I debated whether I needed to give a verbal confirmation or not. Jacob could probably tell what was going on by the way I was standing or which of my scowls I was wearing. But then

I remembered how the repeater kept flickering through the conversation I'd had with Keith, oblivious to the present. "She died here. I see her running, up to about here." I stretched out a hand toward the spot where she continued to vanish. "Irregular repetitions. Some just a few seconds apart, some more like a minute or two." I could have added that there was a wrongness to her motions, which was typical of repeaters. Never quite the same wrongness twice, it seemed. Distorted features, excess fluidity, awkward rigidity, or maybe just standing a few inches above or below the ground. Ghosts are as creepily unique as snowflakes.

"An accident?" Jacob asked.

"An assault."

"Should we call it in?"

"I checked—she's okay to scrub."

"Good. I've got your back." So. He didn't know Keith's story, not that it surprised me. Keith probably could have told a few dozen stories that ended with the victim dying and the perp getting a slap on the wrist. I'd just heard this particular rendition because I'd been in the right place at the right time.

Jacob eased away from me and started scanning the area. His days of lugging around candles and carrying my incense were long past. I didn't need any of those props— all I needed was some Florida Water, a sprinkle of salt, and my own focus. That focus was a lot easier to come by with someone to punt rats out of the way before they scurried across my feet. I breathed deep and pulled in white light, and despite the cold, I felt comfortable. The shift in my focus from physical to non-physical probably had a lot to do with it. My subtle bodies don't care what the thermostat reads. Now, with my concern shifted away from muggers, vermin or the possibility I'd be expected to get down and get funky—and placed instead on my inner self—I was able to spot the repeater sooner, to follow her motions more precisely as she made her silently screaming final run for the billionth time. Once I really got a bead on her, like most ghosts, she struck me as more pathetic than terrifying.

The anger at whoever'd done this to her bubbled up inside me—because if there weren't any bad guys in the world, there'd be no need for Keiths and Jacobs and Victor Baynes to go around seeing all the miserable shit we could never un-see. Finally I had somewhere to channel the moral outrage that had been plaguing me all night and threatening to spill over and ruin a perfectly mediocre evening. But as I shifted into anger, I felt my white light falter, and the repeater grew more scattered and ephemeral. As satisfying and justified as anger might feel, it wasn't helping me channel my talent. I imagined it as a red syrup draining through my body, drawn as if by gravity, down through my spine, my limbs, my muscles and veins, until it seeped out the bottom of my feet into the ground. The planet was big enough to suck it up without losing too much sleep over it. Even so, I sent the earth a small, wordless apology.

Once I'd drained sufficient righteous indignation, I turned my attention to the salt shaker. It was one of those typical restaurant types, glass with a small chrome screw-on top. The grains rasped against the screw thread as I twisted the top off. I dumped out as much salt as my palm would hold, and I visualized my white light pouring into it. Jacob had probably snuck a peek over his shoulder—for all that he can't see these things glowing like I can, he still gets a kick out of it—and on a good night he can feel it, like the vibration of a low sound wave, but without the sound. But I was so certain of Jacob, in particular of his ability to think on his feet and to do what needed doing, that I didn't give his presence a second thought, except as a comforting knowledge that someone I utterly trusted would handle the outside world while my whole focus was pointed inward.

Sometimes psychic things happen gradually, like a

sunrise. Other times they click into place with the suddenness of a light switch flipping on. This exorcism was one of those light switch moments. One second I was cupping some salt in a cold alley that smelled like beer, grease and the onset of winter, and the next I was all lit up. The world crystallized around me, and the fleeing ghost juddered to a normal-paced run. Or maybe she was still moving way too fast, but now my awareness was keeping up with her. Not only was she no longer a glowing, silently screaming blur, I felt like I could count every hair on her head, every freckle on her cheek—and each and every bruised finger-mark on her neck.

Fucking hell.

"Stop running," I said under my breath. "We caught the creep."

I cast the salt at her, though the action didn't have a damn thing to do with salt. The salt was just the physical thing that carried my intention. And my intention had something to do with the white light. Empathy. Compassion. And while it's an insanely loaded word, in the purest sense of the meaning, love.

Some repeaters fade with repeated saltings, some slow and dwindle, but this spirit stopped in its tracks as if it had suddenly gone brittle. It was like the whole world was made from sheets of wafer thin ice, and this stranded ghost was at the center of it, a beautiful, terrible ice sculpture. If I severed the connection now, she'd probably melt away. Eventually. But instead I dug deeper, opened my connection wider, and flooded her with white light—with the compassion I try to pretend I don't feel, because what if the world is so rotten it uses up all I've got and keeps on going 'til it drains me dry?

My internal faucet was cranked so wide that at the moment the victim's repeater tore free from the world, I felt it—a painful twinge, hot and cold and maybe even electrical, like a sharp rap to the funny bone.

And then she was gone.

I pressed my hand into my solar plexus to soothe away the after-effect of whatever energy had just brushed me... but then I realized, I didn't need to. My sense of my surroundings was beginning to come back to me. The smell of beer bottles. The muffled throb of disco. A patter of rain against my cheeks. But I didn't feel singed where I'd brushed up against the energy. I felt fine, actually. Kind of light. Dare I say...I felt good?

While I dampened down my faucet, I took a deep, cleansing breath and let it out. It wasn't with any kind of psychic sense I knew Jacob was absolutely bursting to ask me if the exorcism was done. I just know him pretty well by now. I nodded and said, "Yeah, it's all right. It worked."

"And how are you?"

"Fine." I checked in with myself yet again, just to be sure. "Good."

We headed toward the car, Jacob casting occasional glances behind us even though he wouldn't be able to see any physical evidence of what we'd just done, me trying to sort out the effect of the bubbly from the positive energetic feedback I'd never expected to absorb. We approached the Crown Vic and he beeped open the locks, and I considered whether or not I wanted more champagne. But mostly I wanted to fling off my suit, toss Jacob onto the bed and rub my naked self all over him to see if we could feel that tingly energy crackling between us.

As he pulled away from the curb, I glanced back at the bar. There'd been no coffin-shaped cake, no rubber bats hanging from the ceiling. But as Halloweens go, I'd had worse.

"I don't hate Keith," I decided.

"Good to know." Jacob gave a half-smile, but opted against exploring that sentiment further, keeping his eyes on the road and the steering wheel pointed toward home.

# Let the Chips Fall

In the cannery, there's a certain division of labor. I shovel the snow and Jacob mows the lawn. He cooks the meals and I do the dishes. I pick up the laundry from all the recesses into which he's strewn it, and he takes it down to the basement and washes it. We're a well-oiled machine, at least until a task emerges that's got both of us stumped.

We stood in the home center a healthy distance from the wall of paint chips where every color known to man was arrayed, square by square, to form an undulating, gradiating rainbow.

"The countertop is butcher block," Jacob ventured, "so it should go with anything."

"Stupid backsplash. I wish that tile hadn't broken against the faucet. I could've just glued it back on."

"It probably would've popped back off...look, I'll paint the thing. I just don't want you complaining about the color."

"Complain? Me?" I eased up to the paint chips, crafty and slow, so they didn't swarm me and leave me bleeding out on the concrete floor from ten thousand shallow paper cuts. "You've obviously confused me with someone who gives a damn about backsplashes." I grabbed a strip of beiges and glanced at the colors. "Blanched Almond. Summer Muslin." I snorted back a laugh. "Alpaca."

"No. And I don't even care what it looks like. Just no."

"Aren't you good at this stuff?" I asked. "Your old place looked pretty spiffy."

"I hired a decorator."

"Oh." Nowadays we only let a short list of people into our abode, since you never know when a stranger will come bearing a surveillance device. "Here's something," I said. "The color of the year. Radiant Orchid."

"Shoot me now," Jacob muttered. "You seriously want a big purple backsplash?"

Not really. "I just figured the 'experts' must know something I don't."

We continued rifling through the varicolored strips, but Jacob glazed over quickly. Once he'd considered and rejected some greens and blues and grays, I said, "Weird that neither of us can pick out a paint. Are you positive we're gay?"

He cracked a rueful smile. "We'll have to give it a test run when we get home. Just to make sure." Now, there was an idea I could get behind. I trailed my fingertip down the side of his hand, and he shivered. "Just pick something." His voice sounded a little husky.

"Anything?"

"Anything."

I grabbed a can from the shelf and did my damnedest to squelch a victory dance. It would be unseemly to gloat.

"Don't you need to have it tinted?" Jacob asked.

"Nope." I gave his ass a surreptitious pat with my free hand as I angled him toward checkout, gazing fondly at the can. My favorite color: Antique White.

# Memento

Words blurred and swam. Had I read this book before, or only this page? Hard to tell. As far as authors go, I have a handful of old favorites I follow, and a lot of their stuff reads the same. That's probably what I like about it. The predictability. Vic was shuffling around the bedroom, and although it wasn't a conscious decision, I had half my attention on him. My mind tends to wander while I read fiction anyway. That's a good thing. I enjoy the fact that no one will actually be raped or murdered while I take my time piecing all the clues together. The supernatural villains don't hurt any real people, either.

"Weird," Vic said.

Another great thing about reading is that it's supremely interruptible.

I put down the paperback with its pages spread across my chest to mark my place...though I'd probably end up backtracking a few pages. He hadn't sounded alarmed, merely curious, so I took my time in answering. He was at the foot of the bed now, crouched by the dresser with a drawer open. I watched him frown at something in his lap for a moment before I lifted my head off the pillow and said, "What's weird?"

"This shirt."

I dog-eared the page I was on, closed the book, and let it slide to the floor.

Vic held up the T-shirt. It was a dingy white with yellowed pit-stains, and it had some obnoxious punk rock design on it, a skull with a spiked mohawk, crazed through with cracks where the silkscreen paint had gone brittle. The fabric looked thin. Not thin like it was a clingy knit, but thin like a majority of the fibers had been stripped off by an untold number of washings, then blown out the dryer vent.

"Okay." I could name any number of things I thought were weird about it.

"D'you know how old this is?"

Rhetorical question. I shrugged and waited for him to tell me.

"I got this in like...ninety? No, eighty-nine. No, wait...." He scowled. Attempted to pinpoint a year. "High school, anyway."

Before Camp Hell. Before the mental ward, too. I stayed quiet, hoping for a rare glimpse into his past. I've always had a feeling he was different then, really different. Granted, we all were. Him, though, more than most.

I watched his eyes. They were unfocused. His scowl deepened. To determine if it was a thinking-scowl or something worse, I asked, "Is that a band on it?"

"Oh. Yeah." His focus slowly returned, and his scowl softened. "The Exploited...they played the Metro. I got lucky sometimes, y'know, getting into a club even though I was underage, depending on how secure the bouncer was about his height. I got lucky then." He smiled, almost. "Not *that* lucky...but once I was done getting kidney-punched in the mosh pit, I ended up pressed right up against the stage. And it's a concert, right? So you'd think I would remember the way they sounded. But I don't." He stretched the shirt between two fists and ran his thumbs over the peeling ink.

"I remember how it smelled. The beer and the Aqua Net and the leather and sweat, it all mixed together into this... this...." He opened his hands and dropped the shirt as words failed him. "It doesn't sound very appealing, I guess."

"No. It does." Particularly if I imagined him in the scene. He doesn't wear leather nowadays—says he's too old and he'd look like a dork. The thought of him jammed into the stage in a battered biker jacket, sinewy and scowling, with a beer-leather-sweat fog roiling around in the heat of the stage lights? Plenty appealing. Plenty.

He turned back to the drawer and rifled through it, picking out another T-shirt, this one with the logo of a radio station on the chest. Neither of us listened to that particular station, and neither of us ever wore royal blue, not that it mattered. He'd been dredging the bottom of the drawer, so I'd guess he was planning on tackling the rotting mass of leaves we'd recently discovered by the downspout. I should consider myself lucky—he'll do some pretty horrific chores if they keep him out of the basement—but really, I wanted to hear more about that concert. There probably wasn't much more to tell. I wished there was, though.

He pulled the blue shirt over his head, then scavenged a dirty pair of jeans off the floor. I watched him dress. The way his jeans fit his ass, he could still carry off a leather jacket, no problem. If I ever managed to let him get farther than the front steps wearing it, anyhow. He zipped his fly, closed the drawer, then lobbed something into the trash.

"What was that?"

"Just the T-shirt."

"But..." I scrambled for a reason he shouldn't toss the thing. Technically, it was an ugly scrap of decaying fabric. But wasn't it more than that? Wasn't it a memento from a time in his past he'd actually been happy? "Why?"

"It's not like I'm gonna wear it." He headed out the bedroom door. From the hall, he added, "I'd look like a big stupid middle-aged loser."

A few of the stairs creaked as he jogged lightly down. Noises from the kitchen drifted up. Running water. The clink of a spoon in a mug. I'd fished my book from the pile of socks and underwear on the floor, and just like I'd expected, I had absolutely no idea who was talking on the page I'd dog-eared, or really, what all the characters were so worked up about. No concentration. My eyes kept going to the trash can.

Finally, I dropped the book, rolled across the bed and retrieved the T-shirt from the trash. I didn't really expect it to smell like that night from Vic's imagination, the beer and sweat and hair spray, but I held it to my nose anyway. It smelled like the inside of the drawer. Wood, faintly musty. Disappointing. I smoothed it out. The band's name wasn't even on it, just the scrawled words *Punks not Dead*. Downstairs, the microwave beeped, then the TV came on, murmuring the morning news. I traced the ink ridges of the words, and then a cracked anarchy symbol beside them. The bathroom door downstairs opened and shut. I smoothed the shirt again and the mental image of a younger Vic wearing it made me smile. And not just because he was bent over the edge of the stage.

If the book could wait, the rotting leaves could probably be rescheduled without too much coaxing.

I headed downstairs with the wad of old shirt in my hand. Vic was perched on the arm of the couch now, triple-tasking in front of the TV. He sipped coffee with one hand while he worked a tied sneaker onto his foot with the other, all the while keeping his eyes glued to the set. He watched as the Saturday morning anchor semi-successfully demonstrated how dental floss could be used for a lightweight travel clothesline, typical weekend fluff. Not that Vic traveled or even particularly cared, but it was better than the murders you usually hear about first thing in the morning. "Is the electric bill on autopay, or is that the gas?" he asked, then took another loud sip from his mug, eyes still on the TV.

Thinking about the utilities: task number four. I don't think he knows he does this mega-multitasking, and I've never pointed it out. It's either an enviable skill, or a coping mechanism. I haven't quite decided which. "Both. It's the sewer bill we keep forgetting."

His sneaker popped onto his foot, and a few drops of coffee splashed over the side of the mug and dribbled onto his jeans. He picked up the remote left-handed and punched it a few times, paused at a Gilligan's Island rerun, then proceeded to a weather channel.

I glanced down at the old T-shirt in my hands. Maybe he was right. The Vic who belonged to this shirt would have stopped at the inane sixties sitcom. He wouldn't be gearing up to vanquish a decomposing mass of slimy leaf mold on a perfectly lazy Saturday. In all likelihood, our former selves could have hooked up, but the fling would've gone its course by now. Eventually Young Vic would have ditched me for someone with a bunch of piercings and an edgy record collection, if I didn't take off with a pseudo-intellectual political activist first. And what was I hoping for now, anyway? That this Vic would slip into the T-shirt and spread 'em, so I could pretend I'd managed to vanquish his rebellious side? That would never happen—institutionalization ensured he found subtler ways to rebel, and I doubted I'd ever discover the half of them.

I didn't mind trying, though.

While he gave his coffee another slurp, I eased the T-shirt out of sight beneath a recliner cushion, then joined him on the sofa he wasn't quite committed to sitting on. I dropped my knees open, canted my hips in invitation, and said, "Kind of cold out there for yard work."

"It's October." Slurp. "It'll only get colder."

I smiled to myself. Subtlety is lost on him. Ironic, since his come-hither signals require the training of a federal investigator to be perceived. His idea of making a pass involves leaning in my general direction, and on a bold day, maybe clearing his throat. "Before you brave the elements…" I dropped my voice low, which was cheesy, but at least he'd get the gist, "better make sure you're good and… warmed up."

He paused at the precipice of a slurp, froze, and cut his eyes to me. I leered. He lowered his cup slowly and turned away, but not before I caught that shy smile of his, the one that makes my heart skip a beat. "I dunno," he drawled. "I'd hate to wear myself out before I even got started."

"Statistics show that men with active sex lives have better stamina when it comes to household tasks."

"Uh huh."

"In fact, they report more efficiency and productivity, and greater satisfaction once the chores are complete." He likes it when I make up fake statistics. Especially the part where he humors me. We're probably insufferable around civilians by now. "Fewer injuries, too."

He stood, smirking. The remote slipped between the sofa cushions while he dug out a coaster and placed his mug deliberately in the center of the coffee table. "I suppose I wouldn't want to pull a muscle." He unhitched his waistband with a quick swipe of his thumb, then planted a knee between my spread legs. Climbing me. His kiss struck, fast and hard. The sofa's leather squeaked beneath his hands as he attempted to angle himself over me while shoving my leg farther open with his knee. My cock shifted in my sweatpants. He landed another kiss, teeth grazing teeth, lingering over my mouth longer than he had that first time. I opened to his tongue while we grappled.

Our mouths slid apart. I was already gasping and hard. His gaze found my face, studied it, mapped it. All four of his tasks (five, counting the downspout-attack he was probably planning while he dressed and caffeinated and worried about the bills and checked the weather) had been successfully postponed. For now, he'd zeroed in on me. The weight of his focus sent a chill down my spine.

Cupping my face, he turned me lengthwise. Once I'd slipped into position with the help of the leather couch, once I was good and situated, I grabbed him by the ass two-handed and worked his buns through the denim. I love the way he fills out his jeans. I could get lost in the topography, the way the pockets ride the curve of each globe and the center seam nestles in the cleft. The texture of the denim grew smooth beneath my fingertips as I trailed across to the worn parts, the surfaces that had buffed themselves against umpteen car seats and diner booths. I squeezed again, then slid my fingers back in, this time angling down to the secret space between the legs, where center seams rub ragged and the denim around them softens. The hot space nestled among taint and ball and thigh.

Vic was supporting himself with one arm caught between our bodies and the sofa back, palm sunk into the cushion. With the other hand he caught my wrist and swung my arm around to his front. This area of his jeans intrigued me too, in an entirely different way. Pocket rivets and zipper teeth, and bulging there, down the top of his thigh, a rock hard rise. I ran my fingers down the length of it. The denim was not so worn that I could make out every last vein, but it had thinned enough that I could easily find the flange of his cockhead and stroke it with my thumb.

He huffed out a breath and scumbled his fingers across my chest, stiffening my nipple with a wayward stroke, then really finding it, fixing on it. Squeezing. My cock throbbed like it was trying to synchronize the pulse in my veins with his tugs. He thrust his tongue into my mouth again. I gave his cock ridge another slow stroke, and he gasped against the wetness on my lips, shuddered, and in a decisive move, rolled off me to rid himself of the pesky clothes in our way. He bumped the coffee table. The half-full mug rocked, but held its ground.

I hadn't realized there'd been heat building between us until his body was gone, and the cold downstairs air crept across my abs where my shirt had ridden up. Heat rises in the loft, and this time of year either the first floor is chilly or the upstairs is sweltering. He kicked off the one sneaker and sloughed his old Wranglers so they bunched around his ankles. His cock sprang free and pointed at me, flush-tipped and bobbing, as he hop-stomped out of his underwear and jeans. Gooseflesh prickled up his thighs. Not the type that raises your body hair when a spirit's in the vicinity, just a good, old-fashioned temperature-related response.

He'd stripped, though not fully, to crew socks and shirt. I did him one better—I shoved my sweatpants down to expose only the relevant parts. He made a grab for me as soon as my cock thunked onto my stomach. The touch of those long, sure fingers had my back arching up off the sofa in three seconds flat, then he dropped me again and straddled my chest. Whereas I was sliding around, his bare skin gripped the leather. He planted one knee right beside my shoulder and angled in for some head. I got off on his enthusiasm—and I knew he knew. He could tell by the way I was squirming. He gazed down at me for half a second and took it all in, caressing my mouth with his cock's silky tip.

"Go for it," I murmured, catching him with a teasing lick that glanced partway down his shaft.

"Oh, I will." He stroked himself across my lips. "For the sake of the yard work."

"For the sake of the yard work." I wet my lips and he pushed in. Not far—and not urgent, either. He jacked himself a time or two, but for the most part he was just holding himself there for me to suck. I grabbed him by the hips and tried to drag him toward me, but he didn't budge. Too much traction. I pulled myself up against him instead, coaxing him deeper, sucking hard. He let go of his dick to grab for my head, and then I went nice and deep, until my throat forced open and my mustache rasped against pubes.

He managed to get hold of some hair up near my forehead, but he didn't exactly guide my head with it. More like he needed to hang on to something. His breathing was deep now, threaded with encouragements. Parts of words and murmurs of appreciation. It was tempting to jerk myself off to be sure I kept up with him, but I decided against it. It didn't much matter who finished first. We'd both enjoy a nice finale. Mostly, I focused on the sound of his breath, with the barely voiced "uhn" sounds he made when I upped the suction or danced my tongue along the underside of his shaft. His fingers tightened in my hair and he prodded deeper. I nose-breathed carefully and inhaled a heady hit of muskiness. I clenched his hips and urged him to go harder. His breath caught, stuttered, resumed. His glutes tensed. He gasped again, paused, then said, "Wait." I raised my eyebrows as he forced me off his cock by the scant handful of hair.

He straightened. Slid off. Bumped the table. A slight tremor rocked the coffee cup. I peeled a wayward pubic hair from the side of my tongue and patiently did as I'd been told: I waited. Meanwhile, he gave the couch a critical once-over, hands on hips and stiff cock glistening with saliva. Once he'd sized up the situation, he hooked his arms beneath my knees and dragged me down so I was laid out flat on the couch cushions. "I like where this is going," I told him.

"You don't say." He swung a leg over my head and straddled me facing my groin. The couch squawked, comically loud, as his bare knees skidded against leather. Positioning is everything. He took great care fitting himself into place.

Lining up. Making sure everything was just so. Trapped beneath him, all I could really do was watch his scrotum sway a maddening six inches from my nose while he figured out where he wanted to plant his hands and knees. He cat-arched his back and peered between us. "How's that?"

I grabbed his dick, aimed it at my mouth and took it deep.

"Fuck yeah," he gasped. The exhalation flitted across the crook of my thigh like a teasing caress. It was the sound of his voice, though, that got to me. Rough. Intense. And although I had needed to pluck him from the stream of his eight million distractions, right now, there was nowhere else he'd rather be than on this couch, pressed up against me half naked, dragging his tongue across the skin of my balls.

I slipped my arms around him so I could grab him by the ass again. The skin was cold—poor guy's got zero insulation—but the gooseflesh there eased once I'd given the cheeks a few good kneads. I considered fingering him. He'd get off on it, sure, but I figured he didn't need to start a morning of yard work with me prodding around in his rectum. True, he's a voracious bottom, but he'll get off on most anything once we get going.

He flexed his hips, judging how deep he could thrust without choking me. I nudged him gently—*More. Yeah. A little more.* He moaned and prodded himself deeper, until I squeezed him a signal—*right there*—and he took up a rhythm. Not quite deep enough to whack me in the forehead on every downstroke, but close enough that I felt his balls quiver just above my brow with the force of each thrust's velocity. And Vic? He licked me up and down and all around, then started jacking me again. Still hard, still even and rhythmic, but with the addition of the spit, a much stronger pull toward the big finish.

Though his mouth wasn't working my dick, it was plenty

busy. He'd poised his head between my legs to have access to anything he wanted, then pinned my body down with his chest so I didn't have any say in what he chose to do to me. He zeroed in on my balls. Initially I was ticklish—but not for long. He lavished a trail of licks and sucks that shot wild sparks through my nervous system. Pinpricks of sensation, some good, and some merely indescribable. When one patch of skin accustomed itself to the treatment, he'd work his way over to a virgin spot and get me squirming all over again.

Not only was I busy fighting the urge to fling him off me—since that was just a reflex from the sheer intensity, and what I really wanted was to bust a nut all over us—but I found myself basking in the sound. Our place is an echo chamber, all hard surfaces of brick and wood, and the leather furniture did nothing to buffer noise. The sound of him sucking my balls was obscene. And buried among the noisy slurps, the steady whap-whap-whap of him jacking my wet dick underscored the spitty sucking.

I was closer than I realized. He probably knew it first since his face was right up against my sack when my nuts started to draw up. That was when he pulled out the big guns. Not only did he increase the speed of his hand-job— but he rocked forward and started working over my taint. I made a noise but it was muffled by his dick. He must have felt it. The word "yeah" slid wetly between my legs. Another sound from me, plaintive. He responded with a gentle rake of his teeth. Then he burrowed in deep, got that tender strip of flesh in his mouth, and really started sucking.

When I arched up, he rode along with me. His dick had slipped out of my mouth, but he kept on sucking and jacking, merciless. The point of no return seethed along my nerves, and I relaxed and gave over to the last few moments of hanging in suspension, the agonizing deliciousness of the brink. He brought me off with a final, agile stroke. The orgasm thrummed through my shaft, but the energy encompassed all of me, organs and skin, body and mind, a single moment of pure perfection. His voice joined me from between my legs, sharing my peak by gasping sweet nothings against my balls. I collapsed back down in that disjointed just-came moment—that diffuse and tingly moment that I sometimes think is my favorite part—and he went into slow-mo, his hand urging out one more drop as he soothed my taint with the hot caress of his breath. I gave a final shiver, then decided I should let him know I was back from the stratosphere by murmuring, "Yeah."

He kissed the inside of my thigh, then pushed up and discovered he could sit his bare butt on the armrest with his knees at my shoulders. Maybe he'd planned it that way. He knows that juicy bukake action is the icing on my cake.

I quickly shed my sweatshirt, then settled back in to look up at him from between his legs. When I grabbed for his cock he batted my hand aside, spit in his palm and started beating himself off. Nothing much for me to do but enjoy the show. I wanted to contribute somehow, so I curled my arms awkwardly around his bent knees and caressed his hips with my fingertips to help coax him toward his peak. His breathing went shallow and rapid. He was close.

Then he surprised me by saying, "Tell me something." Odd, since he's not a big talker at times like these. I gave an inquisitive grunt, and he said, "You came down here to talk about the T-shirt. Why?"

So. It hadn't slipped his notice, even while he was doing five other things. And damned if I knew. I probably couldn't have been able to explain even if I was clear-headed, let alone flat on my back, post-coital woozy, with a load of jiz cooling across my hip and an intimate view of his balls juddering while he whacked off. "It's yours," I said.

I glimpsed a tender expression, upside down and half hidden by cock. "Sap."

Was I? I'd certainly never been accused of sentimentality before. I pondered it, but only briefly, as the sight of his scrotum wrinkling up in anticipation of his peak seemed far more compelling than my attachment to an old scrap of fabric.

His breath hitched and his quads went rigid. The leather beneath his ass gave the smallest creak. And then came a spurt, falling like warm, salted syrup, and another. He gave a small huff of satisfaction, paused, and sighed. I let his load settle into my chest hair briefly, then dragged my fingertips through it and sighed too, spent and content. Vic dropped his hand between his thighs and trailed a single caress down my cheek, only the briefest segue, before he launched off the couch and clocked his shin against the coffee table.

He grabbed his mug and drained it in a few gulps. I winced. How he drinks it lukewarm like that, I'll never know.

By the time he had his jeans back on, I was still lying there drawing swirls in his jiz while I watched him key back into all the other tasks from which he'd been interrupted. Double-checking the weather. Stomping into tied sneakers. Somewhere in the vast corridors of his mind, strategizing his assault on a pile of wet leaves. And then he was off to the kitchen, to put his empty mug in its proper place in the dishwasher before it had a chance to become "clutter." While I gathered the motivation to move, I continued watching him as far as the couch would allow. I was wrestling with the urge to nod off, in fact, when a gentle whump startled me into full wakefulness. A kitchen towel had landed on the back of the couch. Impressive aim.

I grabbed it and swabbed off, then slid a glance toward the recliner. Was it possible Vic hadn't realized that I'd actually fished his old shirt out of the trash and brought it downstairs? Probably. Otherwise he'd be goading me to use it for a come-rag. I waited for the creak of the front door opening, the howl of the wind and the sound of him muttering, "Holy cripes," when it hit him, and finally the sudden silence when the door shut behind him and I was alone. Only then did I grab the yellowed T-shirt and head upstairs.

I opened one of my drawers and considered stowing the thing where Vic had no reason to rummage, but then I saw a real stunner of my own: a clumsy fundraiser design that featured a distorted hand-drawn trumpet in yellow ink on bright red jersey. Supposedly it had sent an old colleague's kid to band camp. If there was ever a shirt that would look better in the back of a garbage truck, that was the one.

I pulled out the awful red shirt, closed the drawer, and dragged my box of mementos out of the closet. Teenage Vic's punk tee fit perfectly, right between a wrestling trophy and a yellowed photo album. It took up hardly any room at all. And to think, he'd wanted to toss it.

Once I'd stowed the box, I glanced in the direction of the paperback I'd been reading, and then at the ugly red band T-shirt. It really was no contest. I dressed and joined Vic in the yard.

He stood with his hands on his hips and the rake at his feet. The cold sun picked out russet highlights in his black hair that never show in man-made lighting. I followed his gaze, but there was nothing much to see but the back alley.

Or was there?

Once, we'd gently exorcised the ghost of a child there— or maybe what we'd done was more of an appeasement. He claimed he'd only had an audio on that spirit, though, so I doubted he'd be seeing her now. Had someone new crept into our turf? Or some*thing*?

Only Vic could say, though I knew I shouldn't jump to conclusions. His scowl could really mean anything. So much of him is easy to read, for anyone who bothers to learn the vocabulary. Yet, other sides of him I may never know, not until he chooses to share them.

"Anything interesting?" I asked.

He squinted harder for a moment, then shrugged. "Those douchebags with the black shutters put up their Christmas lights. In October." He gave me a look. In the harsh daylight, his irises were the color of the pale autumn sky. "You didn't want to decorate or anything...did you?"

"Not particularly."

Bullet dodged. His shoulders relaxed. "In October." He dismissed the neighbor's holiday cheer, and only then did he wonder why I'd joined him. "What the hell's that supposed to be?" He pointed at the T-shirt that showed in the half-zipped V of my hooded sweatshirt. "A bugle?"

"Possibly."

"Even I can draw better than that."

I shrugged. "I thought maybe you could use some help out here."

"It's pretty nasty."

"Okay."

He picked up the rake and prodded the large brown mass with it. "Really. I mean, it reeks of decomp. And it's full of slugs. Plus you do all the shopping and the cooking and the laundry and...well, you don't have to. I got this."

"Don't tell me I put on this awful shirt for nothing."

"Well, if you've got your heart set on it...I guess it can't hurt." Vic smiled his shyest smile, dipping his head. "Especially since you've already been slimed."

I wrapped my hand around his, giving the rake a gentle tug that angled him toward me. I hadn't necessarily planned on kissing him. I just couldn't resist.

Our lips pressed, slow and lingering, yet fairly restrained. None of our neighbors had ever raised a fuss over seeing two men kiss, and whatever surveillance was trained on us had probably seen all that and more. Still, this wasn't about everyone else—it was about us. There are "I want to do dirty things to you" kisses, and "I love you" kisses. For my unapologetically sentimental mood, this kiss was the perfect fit.

# Impact

"Male, Caucasian, strong build." I spoke, Jacob listened, and while he didn't have his notepad out, no doubt the mental ticker tape was running. "Five foot ten. One eighty. Brown hair—and a mustache." A mustache any present-day hipster would kill to have. Hell, maybe his suspenders, too. Who can keep track of what the kids are wearing these days? Our historically mustachioed friend gazed up toward the sky, one hand in his pocket, the other shielding his eyes. A brick appeared just as it was striking him on the temple. He flickered, blinked out, and reappeared a second later, head intact, eyes cast upward.

"How old?" Jacob prompted.

"Nineteen twenties." I guessed. "Maybe earlier." Ancient history wasn't my strong suit.

"I meant his birth age." Jacob quelled a smile. He was totally getting off on the whole venture.

"Forty?" Hard to tell behind that squirrel tail on his upper lip. "No...younger, I think. Thirty-five."

Jacob looked hard at the floor, which was obviously much newer than the repeater, though at least the granite tile formed a grid we'd be able to use. Since we were both wearing suits, and since we both projected the air of,

"I'm entitled to be here and I know exactly what I'm doing," none of the lobby's pedestrian traffic interfered with our training exercise. The current building had gone up in the sixties according to the cornerstone facing Clark Street. It housed lawyers and accountants now, and the occasional inscrutable generic LLC. Whatever it had been a few decades prior, I supposed it didn't matter now. We had no reason to dig and nothing to solve. This repeater was an accident, not an "accident." I figured if someone had actually aimed that brick at him, there'd be more of him left behind to complain about it, even if the brick-lobber was long dead. He was safe to practice on. Ethically safe, I mean.

I hoped so, anyway.

I squatted low and tapped a tile with the clicky end of my pen. "This row, two columns in toward the elevators." Jacob's laser focus shot over to the tile I'd specified. Intentionally, I hadn't said which tile the repeater's other foot was on. I also didn't tell him I was looking to see if he could read some other detail about the repeater, now that he had a general description of the guy. I propped my elbow on my knee and waited, twirling my pen where it dangled between my legs. I gathered some white light too, but not with any sense of urgency, only the idea that it would be nice to power up. Instead of the protective white balloon I usually placed around myself in my mind's eye, I created a mist—a cloud, a vapor—and I imagined it encompassing both Jacob and me. Whether or not it actually accomplished anything, I had no clue. Likely it was wishful thinking, this idea that I could expand my coverage to include him if we weren't physically touching and concentrating like all get-out on the power transfer. But this territory was so damn uncharted that I couldn't say for sure it *wouldn't* work, so I might as well try.

Jacob stared at the floor so hard I saw a vein throb in his temple, then turned to me where I waited and watched, and said, "How'd he die?"

I cocked an eyebrow at him. "Don't ask. Guess." Doubt flickered across his brow. "Yeah, I know, it's about as satisfying as yesterday's decaf. But no one's breathing down our necks, plus I'm here to tell you if you're warm or cold, so you might as well take advantage."

He squared his shoulders, closed his eyes, and huffed out a breath. Two seconds ago he'd been raring to go, but now I could tell he was getting frustrated, fast—he hadn't even offered a passing leer at my suggestion he take advantage of me. Poor guy. He was so used to being good at everything, it was murder for him to keep spinning his wheels. What he didn't understand was that he was already good at Psych, scary good. When the ectoplasm flew, he really was the man of steel, at least in the vibrational sense. I watched him now as he battled to pick up on his own perceptions. Maybe if he hadn't always been told his sixth sense was nonexistent and his third eye couldn't see squat, he'd have an easier time getting a handle on his abilities. That didn't matter, though. I'd seen him project. I'd felt him grab my light. Once his breakthrough came, he'd be able to take his customary position at the overachiever end of the bell curve.

"Gunshot," he announced.

I kept my voice neutral, because maybe he just needed to de-specify. Maybe he'd felt the impact and then filled in the rest of the pertinent details with assumptions. "Where?"

His brows drew together. He took in a breath and let it out slow, and then tentatively, he touched his chest. "Here."

Darn it.

I straightened up. My knees clicked. I shook out my sport coat and shifted my holster. "False hit—happens all the time. Go ahead and get centered—take your time—and see what else pops into your head."

He closed his eyes and thought harder, then turned to

me and said, "A stabbing, maybe?"

My poker face is pretty good, but he could tell he was getting colder. Obviously if he'd scored a hit I would've been excited for him, so my lack of expression was as good as calling him a loser. His face fell. "You're thinking too hard," I said. "You were having fun with it a minute ago. Focus on that."

A flicker of brick, a brief but hideous moment of impact, and the repeater disappeared. And then he was back again, gazing up. Jacob turned toward the wall and glared at the floor tile. So much for *fun*. "It's something weird, isn't it? Fire. Explosion."

"Now you're trying to read *me*. Forget about me. Think about the old repeater instead, him and his big mustache. Just him." The hitch in Jacob's brow smoothed. I waited a few seconds, then said, "Now—what's the very first thing that pops into your head?"

"Run over...by a wagon, maybe?"

I didn't sigh—I wouldn't dare—though I wanted to. Normally, Jacob's analytical mind was a great asset. Not at the moment, though. It was too busy with conjecture to let any extrasensory impressions come through.

"Try clearing your head," I suggested. "You know, think about not thinking. Focus on your breath."

I'm pretty sure hands-on-hips isn't a pose any of the New Age gurus recommend, but Jacob planted his arms akimbo anyway, and attempted to *force* himself to relax. No way was I about to point out the irony. He stayed that way for the duration of a few heartbeats, then opened his eyes and said, "Strangulation."

"Sorry," I said, and I truly was. Not having his way was so foreign to him, every minor delay in getting what he wanted felt like an insurmountable failure. "You want to salt this one, or leave him be and come back later?" I didn't care one way or the other. Even if I exorcised him, we'd find another.

We always did.

"Not yet," Jacob said. "Just...gimme a hint."

"Doesn't that defeat the purpose?"

"Okay, okay."

"Let's take a different tack." Maybe this thing he was trying to do—reading me, rather than the repeater—showed some promise. I pressed my fingertips to the back of his hand. I didn't shove white light into him, but I didn't shield myself from him either. Centered. Neutral. Open. Those things are pretty abstract concepts, and I don't do particularly well with abstractions. I was certain, though, that once we were on the same page, things would only get easier. I counted out a few breaths, then eased away from Jacob and said, "Getting anything?"

Maybe I was centered and neutral, but Jacob's frustration was still running away with him at a good clip. He turned back and glared at the floor, then the elevators, then a douchey businessman who was talking too loudly on his cell. I watched the talker nearly collide with a revolving door—and when I turned back, Jacob was glaring at the ceiling tiles. I was just about to call it a day and steer him toward the car when a massive heebie jeebie prickled through me, so visceral my arm hairs sprang to attention and my stomach did a flip-flop. He'd raised his hand to shield his eyes, and he was in the same position as the repeater—and I mean the exact same, right down to the tilt of their heads, the set of their shoulders and the slight bend in the weight-bearing knee.

Jacob wasn't watching my eyes, so he didn't see me taking notice. I went very, very still so his attention could stay where it was. The moment of impact hit—a mere flicker— then the brick appeared and the repeater broke his pose. Jacob snapped out of it at the same instant with a quick shake of his head. "Nope," he said disgustedly. "Nothing. Might as well salt it."

He seemed pretty set on being fed up with himself. I took in a deep, careful breath while I tried to figure out how to break it to him that his reception wasn't so shoddy after all.

# Everyone's Afraid of Clowns

## 1

Halloween is magical for some folks. Me, I mostly see it as a chance to sneak a big bag of candy into the shopping cart. Ghosts and monsters and things that go bump in the night don't need a special holiday to put me through the wringer. I deal with weird entities all year long. But there's weird, and then there's weird. I had it on good authority there'd be actual children at the party where we'd agreed to put in an appearance.

"We don't have to stay long," Jacob assured me. "An hour, tops."

I hadn't breathed a word about my lack of enthusiasm for this particular social obligation. Hadn't even rolled my eyes. Jacob, though...he knew. Maybe not in a telepathic way, but what difference did it make when he could read my thoughts in the set of my shoulders and the gaps between my sentences? I've got an obscure paper license behind my badge, one that declares *Victor Bayne - Level 5 Medium* is clearly too important to be expected to show up at social events. At least that's what my last few boyfriends made of it. But since I've paired up with another PsyCop, and a clever one at that, I'd need a more plausible excuse to play hooky when I wasn't in the mood for people. Either that or tag along for the ride and do my best to fly under the radar.

Sure, I'd daydreamed about weaseling out of this particular shindig, but I'd never thought it could actually happen. Being half of a couple isn't all easy kisses and inside jokes. It's occasionally doing things you'd rather not, especially when you'd prefer to stay home and half-watch scary movies you've seen umpteen times. Luckily, it was easy to take cues from Jacob. While I don't expect him to act as my crutch, when I need to navigate a social setting, being with him really is a valuable perk. For instance, I'd voted on bringing the extra wine in the back of the cupboard to the party, but according to him, wine wouldn't quite cut it. Halloween was one of those occasions where you were expected to be seasonally appropriate…even if you threw everything together last-minute, which due to our crushing work schedules, we typically did.

Only the truly prepared have time to drive all the way out to a suburban cornfield just to find a stupid gourd. It was a lot easier to hit the old lot on Montrose, the one that had been a car wash in its previous life. Maybe one of these days we'd plan far enough ahead to escape Chicago for a few hours and take a trip to the country. But not this year, not today.

The only thing worth looking at in this particular pumpkin patch was Jacob. Sure, he can rock a suit, but tonight he was a study of dark-on-dark, black hair, black goatee, black jeans and black leather jacket. Even though I'm pushing forty, I'm still as much of a sucker for a leather jacket as I've ever been. Sadly, even a vision of Jacob in leather looking dashingly intent couldn't elevate the lame-o surroundings. There was a fly-by-night quality to the lot's setup, and its flimsiness contrasted with my mental image of how "things" were supposed to be. Neat, square hay bales outlined a perimeter, and a puny scarecrow stood watch over bushels of apples and winter squash. Tarps covered the old blacktop, where pumpkins were arranged in clusters according to size and price. Streetlights shone down, obliterating any potential view of the stars. Shoppers were sparse. People bundled in winter coats milled around despondently. The single animated person there was a guy trying to pump up his kids' enthusiasm and get them to pick something out. They were too busy texting to notice.

Thankfully, Jacob wasn't invested in creating any memories. His family life has been as close to picture-perfect as a family can be, so he doesn't get all sentimental over things that might have been. Tonight we were on the same page—we usually were—and all he wanted to do was score a random pumpkin and get going. "Vic? What about those painted ones?"

"Sure." That way it would look like we'd put in some extra effort without actually having to carve something.

The painted pumpkins were stacked beside the register on a hay bale, perfect for grab-and-go shopping. But although I marched up with every intention of choosing one at random, I've always had a soft spot for Halloween, so I couldn't help but try to pick out something good.

I couldn't find anything.

All of them were smiling. Cats, ghosts, monsters too. All of them wore the same, identical gap-toothed leer. Seeing them all together like that, the attempt at differentiating one design from another seemed all the more half-hearted. Even the clown-painted pumpkins weren't scary. And everyone's afraid of clowns.

I doubt any of the foster families I'd lived with had enough means to hire a clown to traumatize us on our birthdays. My suspicion of clowns came from the movies, though not in the way it usually happens.

I'd started sneaking into R-rated films when I was way too young to understand them, but tall enough to pass for a burgeoning adult, which I'd been doing since I was thirteen. (Sometimes I think I'm still doing it.) Once in a while, the employee in the ticket booth would call my bluff and demand to see a driver's license. But most of the time, they couldn't be bothered.

The moldering second-run cinema a short bus ride from my high school had never once carded me. I think they just needed the business. They were always running gimmicks and promos, like guess the number of beans in a jar to win a free ticket, or free small popcorn to the first twenty customers, or half price Halloween double feature to anyone who came in costume.

I'm not big on advance planning, but that year, I was prepared—getting into the double feature meant getting out of the boring duty of accompanying the younger kids trick-or-treating. Most days I wore all black anyway, but that day I upped the ante with a black blazer, sleeves pushed up, naturally. After gym period, I gelled my hair into a cheesy widow's peak. Add a set of plastic dime-store fangs, and I was ready for my close-up. Okay, so I wouldn't be winning any vampiric costume contests, but it did save me $2.50 on my ticket.

Thanks to Patrick Swayze, ghost movies had started losing their edge by the early 90's, but gory, predictable slasher flicks were still a dime a dozen. This was good. Not because I couldn't appreciate subtlety, but because armpit hair and random boners weren't the only thing puberty had brought me. Ghosts. Sometimes movies get 'em right nowadays—especially the creepy Japanese flicks with English subtitles. But back before I figured out I possessed anything more than an overactive imagination, movies weren't actually that scary. Cinematic boogeymen were nice and blatant, hockey masks and chainsaws. And the characters who ended up minced and mangled had done something so stupid—opening that door, venturing into the basement, going off to have sex in the woods—that whatever those lamebrains got, they deserved.

I'm not sure why the dilapidated theater bothered opening its doors for a weekday matinee. Even with the half-priced Halloween double deal, attendance was sparse. By the light of the decaying snack bar promotion, the cavernous space with its rows and rows of stained seats felt hollow and forbidding. All the other moviegoers had spaced themselves out, ten or twelve seats away from their nearest neighbor. Was it some natural law, maybe a magnetic field that caused strangers to distribute themselves so carefully? Hard to say. That'd be an awful lot like physics, and I had trouble maintaining a steady C- in loser math.

It wasn't the fear of blocking others' view of the screen that sent me creeping toward the back of the theater. The place was so empty I didn't need to worry about getting in anybody's way. It was more that I'd developed an overall preference for slinking in at the last minute and sitting at the back of the room. Not the very last row, though. Those seats were up against the wall at a rigid angle. The second-last row, right in the middle. My seat. Really, it was. I'd carved my initials in the armrest and everything.

Just to be clear, my main reason for sitting all the way in the back was not the anticipation of an anonymous handjob. It only happened that one time. I could hardly call the handiwork anonymous, either, because I was fairly sure my five-minute friend was the kid with the braces who worked at the sub shop across the street. At least I hoped that was why he smelled like cold cuts.

Sitting all the way in back did make it harder for me to lose myself in the movie, since I could see the edges of the screen, the point where the projected reality met real reality and the glamour fell away. Not only was I there to indulge in some distraction, but I'd positioned myself to be distracted from the distraction itself, so I couldn't get sucked in too deep. Even that young, I'd had some high level avoidance techniques all figured out.

Film rolled. Same plot, same setting, and only nominally different actors. A group of kids in the middle of nowhere, and wouldn't you know it, the car breaks down and it's nearly dark. The very blonde girl is wearing heels, so we all know how she's gonna end up. And the guy who's too much of a smartass for his own good? He'll buy it ironically. They always do.

I was postulating this detail almost a quarter of a century later, of course. Other than tiny flashes of clarity that I tend to question, my actual recall is not nearly that good. Mainly I do remember sitting in my initialed seat, sipping from a can of warm Pepsi I'd smuggled in, and watching a movie that was supposed to be scary, but was actually comfortingly predictable.

It was entertaining enough until someone crept into the row behind me. That's when my memories start feeling different, less like something I've conjectured in my 20/20 hindsight and more like the physical, visceral experience of something that came surging right back, juicy with adrenaline and fear.

I remember straightening. I remember flexing my toes in my sneakers, like I could grip the tacky floor with them right through the worn rubber soles if I needed to make tracks fast. I remember the smell of fake butter-scented oil covering traces of scorched popcorn hull. I remember the horsehair-and-innerspring cushion creaking beneath my bony ass as I shifted my weight, trying to look casual. And I remember the thread of apprehension coiling like worms through my innards as I warred with the thought of leaving. Because I'd put actual planning and effort into my costume, dammit, and I wanted my half-priced movie.

I remember all that, the pissed off clench of high alert. And I remember rolling my eyes when the creep in the back row sidled his way across several seats and planted himself just behind my right shoulder.

In my dozen years as a PsyCop, I've seen enough gruesome shit to instill a better sense of self-preservation. But at that age I was such an ignorant twerp, I was all sneer and swagger. I turned around to confront the guy—probably with a brilliant remark like, "Excuse me?"

There was nobody there.

I remember it with utter clarity. I heard the guy. Knew it was a *guy*, even. Knew exactly where he was positioned relative to me. Except he wasn't.

Even though the rest of the sparse crowd was too busy watching the movie to be paying any attention to me, I hunched in on myself, feeling stupid. Apparently someone had used the narrow back row to cut across. No big deal. I settled back in my stiff, creaking seat, took a cautious sip of my warm pop, and stared straight ahead. In the movie, flashlights were dying, a storm was rolling in, and the soundtrack was starting to get spooky. Though I'd been jostled out of the moment, it wasn't exactly an intricate plot. I slipped right back into the experience of the film—at least as deeply as I ever allowed myself to—and I watched the smart-aleck guy fight with the snotty kid brother while the high-heeled blonde tried to make peace...and I saw movement out of the corner of my eye. Not up on the screen, but just over my right shoulder.

*Okay, asshole.* I vividly remember thinking that. *Now I got you.*

I held my head very, very still, and I looked only with my eyes. The guy behind me was leaning forward, sprawling across the seat-back, cradling his chin in his hands. Dozens upon dozens of empty seats, and he was right there in my personal space. If not for that fluke hand-job, I would've whipped around and told him to get lost. Instead, I continued to scope him out in case I might get lucky again. Pale. That was all I could see without turning my head. Angling for a better look, I scratched the nape of my neck so I could tilt my head, and finally, then, I caught a decent glimpse.

Not only was the guy behind me in costume, and not only was he at least a venerable forty years old, but he was dressed as a clown.

Even the potential of getting fondled didn't cancel out my revulsion. I stood up to move, and turned at the last moment to shoot the clown a dirty look for creeping me out of my own damn seat.

He was gone.

Clown or no clown, I wasn't about to put up with somebody fucking with me. I threw myself against the seatback, fully prepared to find him huddled down in the back row, dick in hand, snickering to himself. But other than a scattering of trash on the floor, the row was empty.

2

Heebie Jeebies—the gift that keeps on giving. A quarter-century later and I was still chafing gooseflesh off my forearms.

"Do you see something?" Jacob murmured. He gets off on watching me do my thing.

"No. Not really." I scanned the parking lot. It was clean. "Just thinking."

"Tell me."

Although Jacob was crowding me worse than a dead clown in a run-down movie theater, my barriers didn't shoot up. He was allowed in. Take that any way you care to. It was a comfort, actually, to have hooked up with the one guy who thinks *Hooray!* when the dead start bleeding through. "Not much to tell. It was a long time ago."

Jacob picked up a massive, ugly smiling pumpkin and headed for checkout. Twenty bucks—highway robbery—plus tax. The teenaged boy behind the hay bales needed to count my change three times. I'm guessing he would've preferred I put it on my card, but knowing what I know about electronic surveillance, I just can't bring myself to swipe it through a tablet. Everyone knows those things are only good for YouTube videos and solitaire.

Jacob handed me the smiling whatever while he beeped the lock and opened the car door, then took it back so he could settle it in carefully for the ride. I would've just thrown the damn thing into the backseat and let it fend for itself. Then again, I would've ended up scraping pumpkin guts off the upholstery after we took a sharp turn and ended up playing roller derby.

Pumpkin situated, we buckled ourselves in. He pulled into traffic, went a few blocks, and stopped.

Red light.

Not anywhere near us, more like two blocks up the street, but traffic was frozen for the whole stretch of road. Was it a clean intersection? I wasn't sure—I didn't drive this route often enough to have every haunted crash site memorized. I craned my neck to see if I noticed anyone wandering in and out of traffic...literally. But it was cold and dark and miserable out, and the only pedestrians were huddling in their coats, not rambling around hoping to get in the final word with the driver responsible for their current state of deadness.

"So," Jacob ventured, since it seemed we were settling in for a nice long wait. "This thing on your mind—the long time ago...how long?"

I considered how much emotional scar tissue surrounded the clown memory. Not much. I'd only had a glimpse, after all. He hadn't followed me home to lurk in my closet. He hadn't touched me. He hadn't even said anything. Any anxiety I currently felt was due to the anticipation of a house full of shrieking tweens, not the clown ghost.

My decision to go ahead and talk was based mainly on the knowledge that Jacob would really get off on hearing about it. And when he's looking all slick in a leather jacket, I can't resist. I eased my hand onto his thigh, dropped my voice down low, and said, "I was sixteen. It was a darkened movie theater. Typical nineties slasher flick. I was sitting there alone in the second-last row—"

"The one on Sheffield?"

"I dunno. Could be." I gathered my thoughts and put on that ghost story voice he digs so much. "So I was sitting there. Alone. In the second-last row...."

"It was that general area, though, right? Near the El? Or was it the one on Broadway?"

"Maybe." I struggled to keep the annoyance out of my voice. "It was a run-down, turn of the century, single screen theater with floors like flypaper, and horsehair hanging out of the seats. Does that set the stage for you?"

"The Mercury? Biograph? The Music Box?"

"I don't know. I was just a kid."

"But was it in Lakeview or New Town?"

"Lakeview. I guess. Probably." I paused to see if there were any more urgent questions. Apparently he had his bearings. I regrouped, imagined the feel of the darkened theater, gave his thigh a subtle grope, and said, "It was Halloween, and anyone in costume got in for—"

Jacob braked, a little too hard for the flow of the creeping traffic. "Halloween, to the day?"

"Whose story is this—do you mind?" Apparently, he did. In one of those decisive police driving moves that no one ever seems to question, he nosed out of line and swung a U-turn. "What are you doing?"

"If we drove past, maybe it would spur your memory."

"I remember the important parts." Damn it, who the hell cared which specific theater it was? Couldn't he tell I was trying to put on a sexy-voice? "What's the deal? Usually when I talk ghost, you stop and listen."

"I was listening. You were sixteen, it was Halloween, and you saw something." He swung around a poky driver trying to parallel park and high-tailed it toward Lakeview. "Whatever it was...what if it's still there?"

I spared a glance in the direction of the backseat. The ugly pumpkin grinned back at me. "I thought we were late."

"It's not that far out of the way."

No, not as the crow flies. But Halloween was as big a hindrance to traffic as a freak October snowstorm or a Bulls NBA championship win. Despite Jacob's assertive driving, it took us nearly forty-five minutes to traverse three neighborhoods. And once we were in a spot where I could've used some extra time to get my bearings, traffic picked up while I tried to fit together my jigsaw puzzle of a memory. We were zipping down Broadway when I finally spotted it—a tall, narrow building with a green awning where the marquee used to be. I checked the opposite side of the street. An old McDonalds. The kid who gave me a cheap thrill hadn't smelled like salami after all. It was fries. I felt the pieces fit into place with a satisfying snap, and said, "There."

"The coffee shop?"

"It wasn't a coffee shop then."

In fact, it could hardly be called a coffee shop now. It looked more like a catch-all meeting place for every obscure group from Boystown to Wrigleyville. We crept by it four more times in search of parking, and each time I scanned the gaps between the handbills plastering the windows to determine if the overhead lights were even on. On our final lap, I saw someone at the door usher in a few guys with a flashlight, money changing hands, so I kept my mouth shut while Jacob pulled another U-ey to grab a spot opening up just across the street.

"How's that for parking?" Jacob said. I was gracious enough not to mention I could hear him muttering a little bit louder each trip around the block. "And they're open, too. Perfect timing."

With whatever renovations had occurred over the past few decades, the façade didn't feel quite like the old theater to me. And yet there was a sense of deja vu as I approached, where if I really concentrated, I could feel myself swallowing spit around those cheap plastic fangs. Before I could get too self-congratulatory about finding the place, it occurred to me that I was barging into a big old building that was probably haunted, with no antipsyactive drugs, not even a packet of salt in my pocket, and I grabbed Jacob by the elbow before he could barrel on through the door and charge right into who-knows-what. "Hold your horses, mister. Let me get my bearings."

Jacob stopped and looked at me, dark eyes sparkling with eagerness. I'm still putty in his hands when he gives me that calculating leer. Unfortunately, before I could bask in his approval, he turned his attention toward the door. Sure, he got off on the idea of me being a medium. But when it was all said and done, he was way more interested in the ghosts.

I considered saying it was a long shot we'd find anything at all based on a single glimpse I got back when I only needed to shave once a week, but why rain on his parade? We hardly ever had the chance to go out together, and wasn't ghost hunting preferable to a Halloween party full of strangers and their kids? That was probably overly optimistic on my part. I do still have a healthy fear of ghosts. Seeing what I've seen and knowing what I know, of course I do. In all likelihood, though, if we found anything at all, it would probably just be a repeater. Those things were tame, more like a smattering of leftover death energy than a ghost. I could disrupt the signal, Jacob would get all hot n' bothered watching me do my thing, then he could take me home and do *his* thing. Win-win all around.

Or it could be seriously haunted.

I ignored Jacob's eager body language and shifted my awareness.

White light. It's not really light, and it's probably not white—but since the shorthand works, that's good enough for me. I visualized it streaming down from the heavens, surging in through my third eye. And I felt it filling me with the mojo that allows me to break the death barrier. This power source isn't tangible and it's definitely not measurable, but that's just because no one's come up with the right equipment to see it just yet. I've tapped it enough times to trust it's there, and to know with certainty that in some clumsy or rudimentary way, I'm able to use it.

If it's awkward for me, it's twice as bad for Jacob. He can't see this stuff like I can—but I've learned the hard way he can suck up my white light without batting an eyelash.

He moved to take my hand, and regretfully, I had to step away. "You had your shot back in the car. Look with your eyes, not with your hands. I'm charging my batteries now."

"Sorry." He cocked his head toward a rainbow flag. It felt natural to be grabby in Boystown. "Habit."

I was wearing my black wool peacoat, and those pockets went deep. I stuffed my hands in to keep from discharging my light into Jacob, and also hoping I might find some prop I could call upon in case we were blundering in on something scary. The more I searched—and the more I came up with nothing but spare change and gum wrappers—the more spooked I felt. Jacob was raring to go, holding open the door, and it occurred to me that I'd grown phenomenally blasé if I was willing to face off with a freaking *ghost clown* just to give him a few jollies. Blasé, or stupid.

I headed in.

3

It was dark inside, except for emergency exits and flashlight beams. I dug deeper into my pockets looking for a pen light, but it was in my work overcoat, so I didn't even have that. A guy in an old-timey carnival barker costume with a wooly fake mustache told us, "Ten dollars." Jacob paid the guy, who handed him a pair of plastic wristbands, and said, "Down the hall and to the right."

We headed down the darkened hallway, me trying to place it in my memory, Jacob with a flashlight out. Of course he had his flashlight, even in his leather jacket. He's nothing if not prepared. He flicked it over the wristbands and read, "Men 4 Men Haunted House."

"Huh. Guess I can't say you never take me anywhere."

"Tonight's the last night."

"Yeah, they'll need to start putting out the Christmas decorations soon as they lock up behind us."

Jacob passed me a wristband and I took it, careful not to brush fingertips but now regretting that we'd ended up at some big gay Halloween thing and couldn't even touch each other. I fastened the band and scanned for something familiar in what little I could see. "I'm not sure this is even the place."

"Slow and steady. I've got your back."

I was on the verge of surrendering to the obvious smartass reply when Jacob pushed through the swinging double doors and a jolt of memory hit. Me, shouldering through the lobby doors and smelling that intense fake butter popcorn smell, then wishing I had a few more bucks to buy a popcorn, even a small one, and hoping no one searched my backpack for the contraband carry-in Pepsi.

Yeah. This was definitely the place. Luckily the doors hadn't changed, because once we were through them, the darkened lobby looked nothing at all like it had in my high school days. The concession stand was covered with espresso machines and pastry displays. The arcade games were ancient history. And the old smoking lounge off to the side? Now it was a makeshift stage with a big chalkboard on the wall inviting everyone to next Thursday's open mike. The secondhand tables and chairs were deliberately mismatched, and stilted art that screamed "local" crowded the walls. It felt crappy and cluttered, but only five years' worth of clutter and crap. Not twenty-five.

"This way," a chunky guy in a skeleton T-shirt called out, gesturing with his flashlight for us to stop drifting toward the empty cafe and go through the balcony doors. I'd never been up in the balcony—I'd always presumed it was in total disrepair. Not sure what had me more spooked, the thought of digging up a ghost or my fear of falling through a rotten floorboard. But Jacob plowed on ahead, and I tried to tell myself that if the floor could support his bulky gym-rat physique, my skinny butt would make it through unscathed. Despite my attempt at a positive, can-do attitude, the farther in we got, the more my blasé confidence leached away. My heart fluttered as the passage narrowed, turned, and narrowed again, and I felt like a steer being prodded through the processing plant. It was dark and close and warm and musty. I opened up my internal valve and let white light surge in, then pushed out a protective membrane to cover both Jacob and me, straining so hard to do it that I broke a sweat. We approached a final door, lit by a single red bulb. Jacob gathered his courage and reached for the doorknob.

The door flew open and a figure burst through. "Bewaaare!"

I jumped back, grabbed for my sidearm and came up with a handful of nothing. Lucky for the guy in the zombie mask I was off duty—although it was quite possible Jacob might deck him right through the fake rubber skin.

"You are about to behold sights and sounds that would drive a lesser man insane. You will be called upon to reach down deep and connect with your primal masculine nature to navigate the horrors within. Are you ready?"

When it became apparent that Jacob was too busy keeping himself from smacking the guy to answer, I muttered, "Sure."

The guy handed me a restaurant pager. "Only when you receive the mystical signal may you progress to the next ghoulishly diabolical level."

I stared stupidly at the piece of plastic. It flashed red and buzzed.

"Step up to the gaping maws of terror—and proceed."

Jacob shot the guy a nasty look and strode through the door. As I followed, the guy quietly added, "In the event that the overhead lights come on, follow the instructions to the emergency exit."

Lame. My adrenaline ebbed, and I shifted my attention to pulling down more white light. Maybe the douchebag in the mask was just a guy, but with live people wandering around in costume, I reminded myself, the dead ones would be a lot harder to spot. Our flashing plastic disc urged us forward, and we trooped down a short hallway and passed through the door at the end marked SECOND CLASS CITIZENS. I was steeled against the probability of some poor schlub of a volunteer leaping out in front of me, yet poised to scan the room for something scary, when a light flashed so brightly it blinded me. Not metaphysical white light, either. A strobe, aimed right in my face.

"Fuck." I turned aside and knuckled my eyes. Technically I should be able to see spirits whether or not my retinas froze. It's not like I see them with my physical eyeballs. But I've got to navigate all the planes of existence at once, and I needed my physical sight to at least get through the damn room.

"You okay?"

I gave Jacob a disgusted "pff" and blinked for all I was worth. "If you can still see anything, make sure no one gets the bright idea to jump out and grab me."

"It's okay. We're alone."

I blinked harder and forced a few deep breaths, but the relentless strobe kept the spots from clearing. I closed my eyes and just listened, then, and the room's soundtrack swelled around me. What had first sounded like crackly, worn speakers was actually the recorded sound of a fire. And the sirens in the distance weren't real, either. Shielding my peripheral vision with cupped hands, I slowly opened my eyes. Still strobing. But I could see, sort of. The balcony had received a major remodel sometime in the last few decades. The seating was gone, the floors were leveled, and it had been closed off from the auditorium below to create a long, narrow room. Sheer nylon "flames" hung from the ceiling, rippling in the breeze of a few small fans. They probably didn't look like much with the lights on, but in the suffocating red light punctuated by the white-hot flares of the strobe, they were practically alive. Not exactly like flame—but creepier, like the way things from the other side are no longer exactly alive. The soundtrack welled around us, crowd sounds threading through the fire sounds, and behind it all, someone called out, "Women and children first! Women and children first!" Over, and over, and over... and the lights strobed, and the nylon flames danced, and all the while I struggled to determine if that voice was actually on the recording at all, or if we were walking directly through an auditory repeater.

A dry ice machine gasped out a cloud that looked eerily substantial in the strobe light. It was the perfect place for some kind of fucked-up entity to hide. "I need to get out of here," I said.

Jacob tends to play by the rules—except when he

doesn't—and he wanted out as much as I did, whether or not he had permission from the flashing piece of plastic. "The door should be on that wall." He strobed between the fake flames, I followed, and between the two of us, we located the door just as the stupid vibrating puck lit up.

We crowded into an antechamber. When the door closed behind us, the crackling flames and sirens fell silent. The building may have been old, but it was a theater, and the acoustics were deliberately engineered.

"This was a bad idea," Jacob said. "Let's turn around and go back."

I almost slid an arm around him, but in the interest of keeping my white light to myself, I couldn't. Which meant I'd need to articulate something that would've been so much easier to convey without words. "Just a few colored lights. Big deal. It's fine. We're fine."

He took a breath and nodded, and I crossed the empty, darkened space to the far door, which had CASTRATION STATION painted on it in drippy glow-in-the-dark paint. The room beyond was dark—at least until Jacob broke out the flashlight. Good thing. I narrowly avoided caving in to my gut reflex of grabbing his arm and discharging the light I was hoarding. Even with the flashlight beam, the room was plenty creepy. The scent of institutional antiseptic was strong, and my gut said "hospital" before my mind even registered the beep of a heart monitor playing in the background. Given my less-than-savory history with the medical profession, the room had "panic attack" written all over it.

"That's enough," Jacob said. "Turn around."

"No, I'm good." That wouldn't be the case if the soundtrack played the metallic clatter of a gurney, but for now I just gorged on white light and repeated *not real, not real, not real.* "There's the door, straight across. Let's keep going."

4

A few steps in, Jacob snarled and batted at something. The flashlight beam bounced around the room, disorienting me. And then I felt it, the whisper touch against my cheek. Annoyance spiked, not fear. If a ghost was pawing me, I'd damn well know it. Something was hanging from the ceiling, that's all. That cottony fake cobweb stuff? Or maybe sewing thread.

I stretched my awareness for anything that might truly raise my hackles, anything lingering on the wrong side of death, and came up with nothing. I stepped around Jacob to lead the way. "Keep going, just ignore it."

And again I was looking in exactly the wrong place when the room flooded with light. An activation strip of some kind was stretched across the middle of the room, and I'd marched right up and stomped on it. "Sonofabitch." I tried to blink away the spots, but all I could see was the afterimage of a bank of lightbulbs. I did my best to fix the room's layout in my mind—the split second I'd glimpsed between all the strobes—and groped my way toward the far wall. I reached out with more than just my hands. My psychic feelers were out, too. But other than the fact that a bunch of really stupid special effects had thrown me for a loop, nothing had the kind of supernatural wrongness I associate with spirits lingering where they shouldn't, tricking death.

The stuff dangling from the ceiling thickened, brushing my hair and my shoulder. I ducked my head and opened my eyes just a crack, but it wasn't enough to really see what was going on, just erratic strobing that revealed a field of dangling stuff. Pendular. Like dozens of hairy potatoes hanging from the ceiling in stretched-out pantyhose legs. If the group running the house was something a little more innocuous, like March of Dimes, I'd figure my own sick imagination was the reason I felt like I was wading through a field of testicles. But Man-On-Man, or whatever these jokers called themselves? It had to be intentional. Maybe most people would only get their hair ruffled, but lucky me, tall as I was, the fake balls kept bopping me in the face. I'd never been teabagged by a haunted house before. Can't say it was anywhere near as fun as it might've sounded.

Jacob gave an exasperated huff and began batting the danglers out of his way. "Could you stop aiming them at the back of my head?" I asked.

"Damn it." He swatted a scrotum. I ducked and hopped forward to make sure it missed me on its return trip…only to trigger another pressure-activated mat. The strobing stopped, the room plunged into darkness, and the screaming began.

White light. I sucked it down like an ice cold fountain drink, and I reassured myself that if there was anything impinging on us from the other side, I'd see it whether or not the lights were on. But even knowing what I know, the canned screaming—combined with the meaty sawing noises and the bleeps of an EKG—had the back of my shirt soaked through with sweat and my heart rate climbing like I was attempting to tackle a Stairmaster. A single small, high-intensity light reappeared, Jacob's flashlight. It lit on the door at the far wall. "There," he said. "Go."

Before he could forget the touching moratorium and short-circuit my white light, I went…right across yet another floor trigger.

The room lit up red, and a pair of animatronic figures burst into motion right beside us. *Fake*, I told myself, *all fake*. Of course it was fake. I could hear the motor whirring beneath the soundtrack of the screams.

But fake or not, the scene made my brain start pumping out panic-juice.

It was a patient and nurse scenario, played out by a couple of secondhand department store mannequins. The nurse had a rusty, blood-covered saw fixed to her hand with clear tape, wound around her wrist at least two dozen times. She was on some kind of mechanized belt that made her whole body tilt forward and back between the legs of another mannequin. The male patient was splayed on his back, hospital gown rucked up around his hips, arms and legs out stiffly...in restraints. The restraints had been made for sex-play, and not very vigorous bedroom hijinks at that. Even so, freakout mode hurtled toward me, threatening to not only take my carefully gathered white light, but my dignity. The last thing I needed was a debilitating panic attack with a football team's worth of testicles swinging around my head.

I made myself look with my third eye. Nothing there, nothing dead. I put one foot in front of the other, and I forced my way to the door. The plastic disc hadn't given me permission to go, but just let it try and stop me. I spilled out into a hallway, a small square passage where we could gather our wits. In front of me, the next door was closing. I heard a group of guys laughing together. They were having *fun*.

Jacob joined me, the door on the nightmare castration hospital closed, and everything went quiet except for my pulse pounding in my eardrums. His flashlight beam traced the emptiness of the hall. I scanned too. My sixth sense saw nothing. "We should go back," Jacob said. "It's not worth it."

I visualized what I remembered of the theater, its layout, the angle of the balconies. Right, center, left, each connected by an angled hallway. "No, this has got to be the last balcony coming up. It'll be faster to go through."

"I guess." Jacob shone his light back toward the door we just exited, then sighed. "Castration? Seriously? If this is the new kink, then I'm getting old."

"Good thing. I didn't find it even remotely hot." Call me a stick-in-the-mud, but I like balls just as nature intended, firmly planted between a pair of hairy thighs. I focused on my white light, on reinforcing the protective membrane around us both, and I caught my breath in that calm pocket of silence.

The puck lit up. Oh joy.

The word PRISON was stenciled on the door to the third (and hopefully final) room. A fake cell shouldn't trigger a panic reaction from me, not like a fake hospital ward. Though you never know. I hadn't ever landed myself behind bars, but as a PsyCop, I had introduced my share of residents to the system.

My inner eye told me we were all clear, so I went on ahead. The first thing I noticed was that the lighting was a lot calmer. It wasn't exactly steady—it rose and fell to illuminate one part of the room, then another—but it didn't flash in my face and blind me. Behind some bars made of wooden dowels, one wall was muraled with hangdog men in orange jumpsuits. Since this *was* Boystown, I expected at least one of the inmates to be getting his jollies in the shower with a hunky, tattooed convict. But no. All the poorly-drawn prisoners just gazed out through the bars looking pitiful and morose.

A two-dimensional cutout of a prison guard whirred toward me, set to roam back and forth along the bars on a simple parallel track. Not the musclebound type of guard you'd find in a tasteless gay prison porno, either. A woman...a woman who looked like she'd dressed as a slutty prison guard for Halloween. She stood in profile with her back arched and her pouty lips slightly parted. Her skirt was so short you could see her butt cheeks peeking out beneath the hem, and the shadows her perky nipples cast against her tight, skimpy uniform top had been painted with excruciating and deliberate attention.

Jacob passed me cautiously so as not to brush together and discharge the juju, scanning the room with his flashlight. Me, I was fixated on those lush nipples, baffled, watching the 2-dimensional guard glide back and forth, back and forth, while the prisoners gazed straight ahead. Once I could tear my eyes away from the figure, I gave the room a scan. No ghosts. Just some cutouts and murals, with a soundtrack of clinking and clanking chains. And on the wall behind us, a bunch of photocopied handbills. That must've been why the lights weren't strobing, instead fading tastefully in and out—to give people time to get a look at the writing. Jacob was right up against that wall, reading intently by the beam of his flashlight. As I approached him, I passed a speaker with more high-end than the others. The whisper, "falsely accused…falsely accused…" came clear, looping through the clank of chains. Maybe if I wasn't so juiced up I would have taken it for a repeater. But my white light was shining bright, and it was obvious there was nothing in that old balcony but a bunch of weird paintings, flimsy bars, a soundtrack, and some amateur animatronics.

What a relief. I'm not the most social guy, but I was more than ready to write off our Boystown date as a bust and get to our obligatory party when Jacob grabbed a handbill off the wall and whirled to face me. "Whoever's in charge of this *event*—he's answering to me. Now."

Okay. Or not.

I backed up a couple paces to give him room to charge through the exit, then surreptitiously pulled down another handbill before I followed. It was a wanted poster—not the Photoshopped old west party-gag type, either, but the sort we'd see posted at the precinct. Nope, no gag. This one was authentic. The guy was wanted for aggravated sexual assault. And the word INNOCENT had been stamped beneath his photo in inch-high red letters.

I'd been so focused on keeping an eye out for the clown ghost, I'd totally missed what was really going on. Second-Class Citizens…Castration Station…Falsely Accused…. These Men 4 Men bozos had nothing to do with leather chaps and rainbow flags—their sole mission was to hate on women. No wonder the haunted house was a total turn-off.

Jacob banged through the door, leaving me to fumble along behind. Old ghosts could wait. He had fresh horrors staring him in the face.

Sometimes I feel like I'm nothing more than a bundle of baggage, and anything can set me off. The sound of a gurney, the sight of a restraint, a whiff of antiseptic. But I don't suppose anyone lives this long without knowing things they'd rather not know, without developing a sore spot. Jacob's put in a lot of years working sex crimes, so he's seen a lot. Maybe too much. And he's just as haunted by his ghosts as I am mine.

By the time I made it off the balcony and down the far stairwell, Jacob had his rage under control. He asked the worker in a perfectly nice, perfectly reasonable tone to speak to the manager. And either he was so charming—or the guys running the event were so oblivious—that maybe they even thought he wanted to pay his respects and congratulate the guy on a job well done. The worker led us to a long, narrow room that buffered the old theater from the concession stand, a disused staff break room crammed with plastic furniture stacked halfway to the ceiling, plain chairs too unhip to populate the new bohemian coffee shop, clunky tables beginning to warp and yellow, all of it peppered with old graffiti and cigarette burns. One corner of the room had been cleared and set up with a single set of table and chairs. The open laptop looked weird on the furniture of my misspent youth. And the guy tapping at the keys didn't quite fit, either. He was Caucasian and mid-thirties, maybe a handful of years younger than me, average height and weight. Not bad-looking. His hair was neat and his clothes matched.

He didn't seem like the type of guy who'd be involved with an anti-woman cult. He looked so...normal.

When Jacob interviews someone, his attention doesn't waver. He tractor-beamed this guy in and began asking him questions in a tone that was very, very interested. And when Jacob's interested, who can help but be flattered? Good-looking guy like that, nailing you with those shrewd, dark eyes. Maybe a straight guy wouldn't find himself squirming in place as desperately as I had. But no one's immune to the charm. And once Jacob had the guy right where he wanted him—bragging about their membership numbers, reveling in the haunted house's attendance, taking credit for the theme of the displays—once the guy was firmly planted in the casually laid snare, then Jacob picked up the strings, and pulled.

"And this statistic...." he produced a handbill from his pocket and smoothed it onto the yellowed plastic tabletop. His voice stayed even, but its friendly tone took on a cautionary chill. "*Three in five reported rapes are false accusations.* From which credible source did you draw that?"

The guy froze up as he realized the adulation he'd been basking in was nothing more than bait, and he'd fallen for it, hard. "Well. We have a reference sheet." He started shuffling papers that looked mainly like menus and random receipts to me. "A handout. A pamphlet. Somewhere." His hands started to tremble as Jacob's cool, collected gaze bored into him, unflinching. The moment stretched, awkward and increasingly painful. Or satisfying, depending on who you were. I personally enjoyed watching the creep squirm. "Well, I can send you the resources if you give me your address."

"You do that," Jacob said, voice like silk. With deliberate, slow, precision, he pulled out his badge, dropped it open in front of the rapidly paling woman-hater, and extracted a business card from a pocket in his ID. There's nothing on his badge the guy would recognize, and nothing on his card to indicate which agency he actually works for. But it all looks very important and vaguely threatening, just like Jacob, when something rubs him wrong. When he handed his card over, the guy flinched as if he was worried Jacob might take him out in a stunning papercut ninja-move. "And if I don't hear from you by the end of the business day tomorrow, I'll be in touch."

The guy shuffled it into his stack of scrap paper. "Sorry, I'm all out of cards."

"That's fine." Jacob poured on the sinister charm. "I have a database."

I presumed he'd made up that database thing to spook the guy. But then I realized something like that probably did exist—and even if Jacob didn't have the clearance to scan it himself, he could at least put in a request.

Jacob delivered a long, uncomfortable look, a look that was in itself a threat. He was utterly still, while the haunted house guy fidgeted and squirmed, and a sheen of sweat broke out across his upper lip. Better to let the creep imagine what he'd been caught doing—and to worry about what the consequences would be—than to spell it all out. Jacob allowed the lingering badass look to stretch a moment more, then finally turned away before the guy's head exploded.

I tried to catch his eye for a subtle show of support. We locked gazes. Only briefly, but that was plenty. The control I presumed came so naturally? It was hanging by a thread. If the sweating guy was stupid enough to rally with a parting shot, he might end up with a black eye for his troubles. Then Jacob would be the one suffering consequences.

I shifted into their line of sight to put myself between them, and gestured toward the exit with my chin. "Let's go. We're already late."

Jacob snapped around and strode out the door. To most people, he might have seemed agitated. Ticked off. Miffed. But to my surprise, I was actually pretty fluent in his body language. His posture was too rigid, his footsteps too forceful. He wasn't merely annoyed—he was furious.

I've got a pretty good long-legged stride, so I was right behind him in the hallway when the punch he'd been holding back finally landed. I didn't feel the physical impact, but it jarred me nonetheless. It was only my mundane sympathy at work, though, nothing physical, and nothing psychic either. No one actually felt the blow but Jacob…not unless the shabby wall had developed some kind of consciousness.

I grabbed for Jacob's hand, but he angled away from me and shook it out. "I'm fine."

Uh-huh. "We should put some ice on it."

"It's fine."

I thanked our lucky stars he'd whomped paneling and not cinderblock. Otherwise our night could've ended in the emergency room. "At least run it under cold water." As I suggested it, my shoddy memory offered up a glimpse of a bathroom that should be close by. We'd delved pretty deep into the bowels of the building tracking down management. But if I recalled my exits correctly, there was a side door not far from us, and beside that, restrooms.

Jacob's knuckles must've been smarting pretty good, because he let me herd him down another hallway instead of charging out toward the car. I was rifling through my mental rolodex, trying to figure out who I could call about these Men 4 Men assholes, when we strode under a bank of black lights and I lit up like someone had just trod on my motion sensor.

"What the hell?"

My entire front was glowing. And glittering. Glowing *and* glittering.

Fucking pumpkin.

5

Jacob turned and got a load of me, then glanced down at himself. There was a single smear of glowing glitter on his leather jacket, which he buffed off neatly with the heel of his palm.

I swallowed back a groan.

"I have some napkins," he offered.

"Don't bother. You'll just grind in the glitter."

"Not if we're careful."

"But, your hand…."

"It'll just take a second. C'mere."

I rolled my eyes and eased into the alcove beneath the UV bulb, where a poster proclaimed in luminescent letters, *Men's Rights Are Human Rights!* Maybe it was best for him to take a stab at cleaning me up in case there'd be black lights at the party. After all, he couldn't make it much worse—plus, if he was focused on my peacoat, he wouldn't need to dwell on his throbbing knuckles—or the poster's stupidity.

Jacob pulled out a napkin, hunkered down in front of me, and dabbed.

My heart skipped a beat, and my field of vision went white.

There was no big boom, no smell of ozone and crisped hair, no dancing afterimages, but it seemed like there sure as hell should have been. At least Jacob felt it too, the energetic smack when the white light I forgot I'd been hoarding arced from me to him, and he lit up brighter than a well-positioned strobe light. He gasped and staggered back, and then he gave a long and heartfelt shiver.

Well…that was one way of distracting him from his shitty evening.

He resettled his jacket with a shrug and rubbed the back of his neck. "I can't believe I…I'm so sorry." He shifted around as if he was suddenly uncomfortable in his own clothes—or, heck, maybe even his own skin.

There weren't really words for this energy swap phenomenon—not yet, anyhow, since the field of Psych is so new. The give-and-take routine is uncharted territory. Whatever Jacob does, he's strong. But even so, I worry that someday I'll channel more juice than he can absorb. Maybe the overflow would just go back wherever it came from—maybe not. I haven't overloaded Jacob's mojo-receptors yet, but I wasn't keen on testing our limits when we had no idea what the consequences might be.

"Are you okay?" I asked.

Jacob took a deep breath and let it out slowly. "It tingles."

I'm visual, he's somatic. The energy I label as white light feels effervescent to him. "C'mere." I opened my arms. "Pass some of it back."

It was as good a time as any to experiment. I'd generated a bunch of protective energy, and the only scary thing in that old theater was the fact that the people in it actually believed their own idiotic hatespeech. He reached toward me, just one hand, and we pressed our fingertips together. And waited. The sixth sense can be elusive. Unless I've got a visitor from the spirit world chatting with me, everything feels subjective, and frankly, somewhat made-up. It seemed as if I could feel the energy teeming beneath Jacob's skin, but it also felt like a figment of my own imagination. He scowled at our point of contact, and he tensed. But all the physical straining in the world wouldn't channel energy. I watched, less invested in the outcome. I'd been dealing with my "gift" for a good hunk of my life and was nowhere near as motivated to prove anything.

It was when I acknowledged my relaxation that everything shifted. It's like looking in through a window on a sunny day, that moment where you stop seeing your own reflection and get an elusive glimpse at whatever lies beyond the glass. My barrier shifted, and some of that energy Jacob had grabbed flowed back in. Not through my crown chakra, but through my fingers. I saw it glow—and I felt it. Kind of.

Or maybe I just imagined that I did.

Jacob gazed deep into my eyes with a look so tender, I suspected he felt it too. Especially when he redoubled his efforts at transferring the charge back to me. "Hey, c'mon." I enfolded his punching-hand in both of mine, drew it up to my chest and blew on his knuckles. We both shuddered. "Keep some for yourself. I'll find more."

Here's the thing with energy—it can make you a little loopy. When I pulled Jacob up against me, our bodies sparked together. Maybe I was just imagining the fireworks... but I don't think so. Suddenly we were grappling together, and he crushed his mouth to mine so decisively it was as if he was trying to replenish not only my energy, but my oxygen. As if all the air had gone out of the world, and the only thing left to do was pass the last breath back and forth between us. No, we didn't need to worry about wasting the energy. Most folks go their whole lives without even feeling this psychic current. Jacob and I, we had plenty.

"Do you feel it too?" he murmured against my lips. I nodded. "Is it always like this?"

"Only with you."

Jacob wedged a hand between my legs and stroked me. Aggressively. Like everything he'd held back when he was talking to the manager was now straining at the seams. Me, I was a goner even before we'd started snowballing the white light. His intensity does that to me, creates a feedback loop of need. Now I ached to be touched, humping myself into his hand like a horny teenager getting his rocks off in the second-last row of a crappy afternoon matinee.

Theaters are full of oddball passageways, places for actors to make their surprise entrances, or ushers to skulk through in search of rule-breakers to terrorize. I tore my mouth from Jacob's and picked out a door painted to match the wall with a yellowed STAFF ONLY sign hanging crookedly at eye level. Lucky for us, whatever staff currently used it was too lazy to lock up behind themselves. We spilled through it into a darkness that felt so still, so vast, it could only be the auditorium itself, with three-story ceilings and an utter absence of light. The rest of the building felt as if it was cycling through a revolving state of decay and repair, but in the auditorium, time stood still.

Maybe I was still sixteen after all, and maybe the guy cramming his hand down my pants was some stranger from a fast food joint across the street. Maybe the last twenty-five years were a wacked-out scenario I'd invented to kill some time during a tedious study hall.

And maybe somewhere over my right shoulder, there was a ghost clown taking the whole thing in.

"Wait," I whispered.

Jacob paused, and whispered back, "What?"

I listened. Or looked. Or whatever it was I did with that elusive piece of my brain that connected with the dead.

Nothing.

My caution threatened to kill the mood—and me with a raging hard-on that really needed some attention. Telling ghost stories from the safety of the car was one thing. But barging into a haunted theater on Halloween? "Just making sure we're...alone."

Lucky for me Jacob's got some majorly screwed up turn-ons. My back slammed up against God knows what, and his tongue subdued my mouth. He worked at my fly, groping hard, while I fumbled with his belt buckle. The huff of our breaths attempted to punctuate the dark, but they were no match for the smothering acoustics. We grappled together in the suspension of time and place, sight and sound, and my awareness filled with the wet slide of

Jacob's mouth against mine, his lips and his tongue, and the insistence of his urgent stroking. That would've been enough to bring me off—not only the feel of his mouth and his hand, but the force of his arousal. But Jacob doesn't do anything halfway. Before I could think too hard about the mundane horrors lurking on the theater floor, he knelt.

If the kisses and strokes were intense in the muffled darkness, his mouth was capable of short-circuiting my brain. The sensory deprivation knocked my perceptions out of balance. I'd been reduced to a single neural pathway—and Jacob was working it for all he was worth. I tend to waffle about whether to murmur words of encouragement or simply keep my trap shut, but in that rare and strangely condensed moment, I felt free to simply lean back and enjoy the sensation while he gave me head. Vaguely, I noticed the soft friction of his hand pumping his own dick, and the occasional grunt where he throated me especially deep. And maybe I uttered some sounds, but mostly I was caught up in the climb. The teetering brink. The delirious release.

I grasped ineffectively at his short hair when I came, and he squeezed my ass hard enough to leave a pattern of fingermarks behind. Jacob doesn't just get off on ghost stories, he gets off on getting me off. I'd even go so far as to call him an overachiever, not that I'm complaining. I cradled his face against my groin and shuddered while the last few twitches played out, and I counted my blessings. I'm lucky to have him. I'm fully aware of it, too.

I sighed, and said, "I'll finish you."

"I'm good," he assured me—and not like he needed to wait 'til later, either. Oh well. The auditorium floor was no stranger to a little DNA. I knew that for a fact.

Only once we'd gotten ourselves tucked away and straightened out did I start feeling all turned around, wondering where we actually were in relationship to the rest of the room, and what I'd been propped up against while he gave me my jollies. "Lemme see your flashlight," I said, and Jacob pressed it into my palm.

When I hit the light, I saw shapes. Not ghostly forms—but not anything I'd been expecting, either. Like the rest of the building, the auditorium had been repurposed. Currently, from one end to the other, it warehoused towering stacks of carpeting rolls. No wonder sound wasn't carrying right. The entire room had been drinking up the acoustics. And now that I had a visual on our surroundings, I registered the peculiar odor of man-made fibers and glue. I wouldn't say I was saddened—after all, when I knew the place it was already well into its decline—but I did feel kinda melancholy. At least back then it was still entertaining people other than a group of sorry men with self-esteem issues.

I sought out the second-last row, but with the seating gone, I couldn't quite place my reserved spot. I scanned the far wall, the ceiling. Murals, too dark to make out, and some fancy plasterwork more or less intact. "Carpet storage?" I said. "That sucks."

"You'd think someone could do more with it in a location like this."

Who's to say why some things thrive while others decay? At least the theater was still standing, I supposed. Maybe someday, a new owner would revive it and do it justice.

On Jacob's request, I aimed the beam toward the floor. No spilled drinks or popcorn were there to camouflage our evidence, so he swabbed up after himself with the napkin he'd used to clean up my peacoat. He wasn't being all that thorough. But if anyone did a walkthrough with a UV light, maybe they'd see some transferred glitter and presume the fluorescing smears on the floor were just craft paint. He tucked the napkin into his pocket and said, "Let's get out of here."

With pleasure. I slipped back into the hallway, already calculating the quickest route to the party, when Jacob snagged me by the sleeve and stopped me from storming out through the lobby. "Line of fire." He pointed toward my feet. By the black light, my jeans showed a telling splatter mark glowing purple across the hem. "Sorry."

It really looked nothing like craft paint.

6

"There." Jacob pointed out the old restroom I'd half-remembered. It looked as disused as the rest of this far corner of the theater, but as long as the plumbing still worked, it would do. We ducked in. It was dark, and the overhead lights took another second to flicker to life. The room must've last seen regular use in the discount cinema heyday. It had a vaguely 80's feel, but with everything more scuffed, chipped and discolored than I remembered. I paused at the sink, briefly considered taking off my jeans entirely, then decided that plan held way too much potential to take a mortifying turn. I hauled my foot up to sink level instead, belatedly hoping I wouldn't pull a groin muscle.

At least the tap worked. And if I didn't manage to get my pant leg entirely clean, I could at least disguise the evidence well enough to blame the painted pumpkin if anyone noticed me fluorescing inappropriately. Beside me, Jacob ran his knuckles under a stream of cool water. They didn't look too bad. Guess he'd experienced a last-moment whiff of common sense and pulled his punch.

"You'll live?" I asked. He nodded ruefully. "Don't worry. Maybe we don't personally have the resources to target their knucklehead group. But one of us is bound to know someone who does. First thing in the morning, we'll make some calls."

Jacob's shoulders slumped. "I guess that's the downside of digging around, looking for trouble. You might not like what you find."

"It's a shame, though. This place. It wasn't all that stellar back in high school, but at least it wasn't full of carpet rolls and misogynists."

"Especially with the location," he agreed. "I could see a place like this going to pot in an iffier neighborhood. But here?"

I was still scrubbing off his spooge when Jacob shook the water off his hand and went looking for somewhere to dispose of the sticky napkin in his pocket. He tried one door, then another, then another. Of the dozen stalls, only one wasn't locked from the inside. Easier for the cleaning crew, I supposed. While he rattled a toilet handle, he started making those grumbling noises he makes when he's trying to park the car. I reached for a paper towel to blot my shin dry. The dispenser was empty. Of course. And I was too soaked to just shake it off.

I joined Jacob by the stalls and said, "Pass me some toilet paper."

"Hand some over here too, while you're at it."

I jumped at the sound of the stranger's voice. Jacob didn't. Good thing. Otherwise I would've probably stuck my hand over the top of the stall without verifying whether I was dealing with a corporeal being…which, judging by the fact that it was locked, not to mention the pair of big transparent shoes visible beneath the toilet door, I was not.

I took the wad Jacob handed me, set it on the floor, and edged it under the door with the toe of my shoe. A transparent hand reached down and grasped for it, then passed right through. And then, a heavy sigh.

As calmly as possible, I murmured, "We're not alone."

Jacob stopped rattling the toilet and turned around with exaggerated care. I opened my internal spigot wide and called down as much white light as I could picture. I also edged away from Jacob so he didn't brush up against me and siphon it all off.

"If you want to talk," I told the bathroom ghost, "we can talk." With a curt hand gesture, I motioned for Jacob to fall back to the row of basins so we'd have more room to maneuver. I followed, crouched, walking backward with my eyes fixed on those ghostly shoes. "But don't try anything funny."

"What the heck is that supposed to mean?"

"It means that talking is talking, and that's all. Not touching." And definitely not an invitation to slip inside and take my body for a joyride.

"Oh." The ghost stepped through the stall door and into the aisle—in costume. And makeup. "Here I figured you were being a weisenheimer."

I backtracked as fast as I could.

As he squared up with me, I noted his shoes were at least a couple sizes too large. He wore gigantic trousers with bright patches sewn on the knees, wide suspenders, and a penciled in five o'clock shadow that followed the curve of a painted frown. He was bald on top, but what hair he had left stuck out sideways, and a tiny bowler was perched at a jaunty angle on the curve of his smooth pate. Now that I got a good look at him, I could see his makeup looked more like the pre-painted pumpkins than a circus clown's. He wasn't a clown per se, more like a vaudevillian hobo. I wouldn't have known the difference when I was sixteen, but even if I had, I would've figured that no matter how you slice it, a clown's a clown.

"What's it doing?" Jacob asked.

"He, it's a he. Just talking."

"So if the both of you are lit up like a night game at Comiskey Park," the hobo said, "why is it that you can see me, but the other one can't?"

"Different skill sets."

"Huh. Whaddaya know? Mesmerists, table rappers, mind readers—I've seen every kind of mentalist you can imagine. Figured it was all some kind of schtick."

"Probably not all of it."

"I guess not. So, you got some history with this dump?"

"Not as much as you, I'll bet."

Jacob said, "Does he know he's...?"

"Dead?" The hobo pulled an exaggerated, wide-eyed

look of shock. He patted down the front of his costume and said, "So that's why I've been walking through walls."

"He knows—and he can hear you just fine."

Jacob put on his best reasonable authority-voice and said, "Everything's okay, we'll work it out, just stay calm."

"He's plenty calm," I said.

"And if there's something you need to say, now's the time. We're listening—and we'll do what we can to help."

Jacob was making an awful lot of promises he had no way of knowing we could keep. Or was he? He's notoriously slick about doling out no more of the truth than is absolutely necessary, and I supposed "do what we can" is all anyone ever really does.

"I knew you fellas were good eggs when you told off that creep in the office." The ghost took a couple steps forward in his oversized shoes and I motioned for Jacob to back up toward the door. Sure, the ghost wasn't wailing or rattling chains or blasting us with cold spots. He wasn't chanting a phrase over and over or regaling me with the details of his death. But he was still a ghost. And mediums can get bumped right out of their own driver's seat if they get careless around the dead. "But there ain't nothing you can do for this old place, not unless you know the Mayor. You don't, do you?"

I didn't. Jacob might have shaken his hand a time or two, but that probably didn't matter. The Mayor would be less likely to invest his influence in protecting a single building nowadays than he would have in vaudeville times—back when a cup of coffee cost a nickel and nobody had yet uttered the words Wikipedia or Facebook. Things were complicated in this brave new millennium. Sure, PsyCops were elite. Yet we were so specialized, I doubted we even had enough influence to shut down a bunch of blowhards like Men 4 Men.

"Sorry, no. Real estate's completely out of my league.

Maybe you should just go toward the light."

The spirit glanced up at the cruddy light fixture.

"Not that. The *white* light." While I had no personal experience with whatever lay beyond the veil, I've seen my share of ghosts cross over. Stuck spirits tended to cheer up once they took the leap. "I'm sure you've got a lot of good memories invested here, but it's not the end of the road."

"The good old days? Maybe. Once. Hard to say. All's I can think about is what a knucklehead I was. My pal Bernie owned the joint, and these wiseguys would come by three, four times a week and shake him down for protection money. And finally I says to him, Bernie, you gotta go to the cops with this. If you don't, I will."

"And whoever was shaking him down, they found out you reported them?"

"And how." The ghost crammed his hands in his pockets and schlepped toward the basins. I put an arm across Jacob's midriff—just short of touching—and backed us both out of its way. "After that, the payments doubled. One for the wiseguys, another one for the cops in their pockets."

Ouch.

"So Bernie started putting in more hours, booking racier burlesque acts. I doubled up on my shows for the same pay. It didn't help. We were working ourselves into the ground and the only ones to benefit were the dirty cops and the mob. I was on my way to try and convince Bernie to sell, get out while he still could, when all them bouts of angina finally caught up with me." His eyebrows twisted together and his hand fluttered across his chest. "The long hours. The drinking. The wondering about who would come sniffing around next, looking for another handout."

"Do you know what happened to Bernie?"

"He sold. Without me helping him book the acts and keep all them crazy actors in line, he barely rode out the final month. Last I heard, he'd made tracks for Florida, scoping out some properties in the Everglades."

Damn. I was hoping maybe this Bernie guy was still lurking around so I could dig him up, negotiate some kind of reconciliation between the two of them and herd them along to their afterlives. But Bernie was long gone, and the thing that tied the hobo to this godforsaken theater was his own regret.

"Hanging around here, thinking about what you could've done different…it's not gonna change the past. It's time to move on."

"I'll go find some salt," Jacob said. But I caught him by the sleeve and gave my head a subtle shake. Laying a mindless repeater to rest was one thing. But a ghost with free will—one who wasn't doing anything worse than moping around and second-guessing a decision he couldn't unmake? I'd feel like a grade-A jerk if I tried to force it to cross over before it was ready.

"Cops aren't as crooked nowadays," I offered. Maybe that would make him feel better.

"Yeah? Then how is it the numbskulls in the back office get away with charging ten smackeroos for a traipse through the balcony?"

"Well…I didn't say the police were perfect. Just that they're not *all* on the take." I thought about how different the theater was from the movie house of my teens. Then I imagined how much it must have changed since the time of snappy hats and unfiltered cigarettes. "Things change. No amount of regret's gonna make a bit of difference. What good does it do for you to watch the place backslide?"

Before the hobo could answer, I realized maybe it wasn't random bad luck that this prime piece of real estate was being used for open mics and carpeting storage. I said, "Ever stop to think that maybe the savvy type of developer—a prospective buyer who'd really spruce up the place—decides to take a pass 'cos the theater gives him the willies?"

"What're you getting at? Other people besides you can see me?"

*See* would be an awfully strong word. But *sense*? On some level, some deep and subtle level, absolutely. "It's notoriously difficult to sell a haunted property," I told him. "Even if most folks'll tell you they don't really believe in ghosts."

"I never thought of this place as...haunted."

The last thing I wanted to do was give the poor guy more regret to wallow in. "Look, I'm not big on making promises, but one thing I'm sure of is that the next step, whatever it is—it's good. Maybe you can resolve things there, or heck, maybe it'll be enough to get the long view and see how it all works out. But first you've got to let go."

Did he shimmer? Or was that just my own wishful thinking? I cranked up my internal faucet and flooded myself with white light. If he'd been a mindless repeater, I would've strengthened my light armor and given him a good hard shove. But since his personality was intact, it just didn't feel right. He'd need to cross over himself.

Though that didn't mean I couldn't help.

I glanced at the door and lit up the whole thing in my mind's eye. The room around me, the row of basins, the spotty mirrors, all of it went a bit dimmer. And although that doorway led to nothing more than a dingy little hall that smelled like a thrift store, it glowed. "It's easy," I said quietly. "Just as easy as walking out that door."

He gazed at the exit. It was difficult, but I did my best not to oversell it. And just as I wondered if maybe I really should send Jacob to find some salt—after all, there'd be plenty in the cafe—I saw the ghost was most definitely shimmering. He took one step, then another. Reached for the knob...then glanced back over his shoulder, at me. "If you think of anyone looking for an investment—artist, architect, I'm sure a guy like you knows plenty of them *types*. Put in a good word for this place, okay?"

A guy like me. Huh. "Okay."

With a shrug and a wistful smile, the hobo ghost turned, and in his oversized shoes, walked through the glowing door, and was gone.

My shoulders relaxed. Jacob, as tuned in to me as ever, widened his eyes. He was dying to start asking questions, but he contained himself and waited for me to speak.

"We did it," I said. I didn't need to open the door and make sure the ghost wasn't lurking out there in the hall. I'd felt the shift when he crossed, like a change in the barometer. Given the way Jacob started fidgeting around, like he was trying to resettle himself in his own skin, he'd felt it too—or maybe he was just trying to will away some goosebumps.

We headed out to the car in silence, part companionable, part stunned. Connecting with a supernatural entity is a game changer in itself. Add to that the glimpse of another era that feels nearly as visceral as time-travel, and you've got yourself one hell of an experience. I slumped in the passenger seat, slightly buzzed, but mostly worn out, and wished we could skip the party. What I really wanted was to go back home, kick off my shoes, order a pizza, and process everything that had happened. Just Jacob and me.

He may be no telepath. But he can read me like an open book.

At first I worried it was wishful thinking when the route Jacob chose didn't lead toward the party, but pretty soon it became clear it wasn't just some shortcut, and I'd successfully dodged an awkward night of social niceties and small talk. All it took was a trip through a truly horrifying haunted house and an exorcism. He pulled up in front of our place. My hand dropped to his knee, and a shiver coursed through me and into him as my surplus white light redistributed itself between us. Carrying around too much mojo is a strain. It felt great to finally allow myself to relax.

He covered my hand with his. I tactfully ignored the bright scuffmarks on his knuckles. After a moment's consideration, he said, "What did he look like?"

"The ghost? Caucasian. Fiftyish, maybe. Hard to tell—he was in a clown costume."

"We were talking to *a clown ghost*?"

"Or a hobo. More like a hobo."

Jacob shuddered. "You're fearless. You acted like it was nothing."

"It wasn't nothing. I was watching to make sure he didn't try anything...funny."

"See? You can even joke about it. If I didn't know you better, I'd worry."

But he did know me. And he knew that I was plenty cautious. I wasn't exactly fearless, either. A good part of my current state of relief came not from laying a ghost to rest, but knowing I wouldn't be expected to fumble through a bunch of awkward chitchat.

He gave my hand a squeeze. "So...was the clown ghost confined to the bathroom, or could it see what else was going on in the theater?"

What was he talking about—the balcony atrocities, or the hummer? I gave him a sidelong glance. "We're totally busted."

Jacob quelled a smirk.

"Don't even think about developing any new kinks, mister," I warned him. "Ghost exhibitionism is not a thing."

He quelled harder. And didn't quite succeed. "You're sure? That he saw us, I mean."

"He mentioned something about me probably knowing artist-types, so yeah. I'm sure."

Jacob sighed. "I wish I could've heard both sides of the conversation."

Maybe someday he could. Back when I'd first glimpsed that ghost in the last row of the theater, most people thought psychics were doing some kind of act—Mesmerists and table rappers. And only a few years later, science gave its blessing and put us psychs under the microscope. They've already developed drugs that can dampen or boost psychic talent. Unpleasant, sure. But they exist. Maybe someday those pills will be as safe and common as penicillin and aspirin. I wouldn't be surprised if it happened in our lifetimes.

We unbuckled our seat belts and leaned in for a kiss. Who's to say which of us initiated it? As different as the two of us are, more often than not, we're in synch.

We even flinched in unison when we glimpsed something leering at us from the backseat. I cut my eyes to the floor.

Fucking pumpkin.

I fixed my attention on Jacob, brushed my lips across his, and murmured, "I'll get it." I'd only held the damn thing for a few seconds, but I knew it was heavy. It would feel phenomenally satisfying to haul it to the alley and pitch it in the trash—plus it would be a great way for me to show my appreciation for skipping the party without coming right out and saying it.

Besides, it wasn't as if it could do me much more damage.

I was already covered in glitter.

# Waiting Game

"If you'd just sign here, ma'am, we should have the car ready by tomorrow afternoon."

*No, you won't. And that's miss, not ma'am.*

Lisa scrawled *LM Gutierrez* across the line at the bottom of the form without reading it. While she wasn't keen on being car-less for—two?—no, three days, there really was no better option. Victor would probably—yes—let her borrow his if she drove him to work in the morning. So the only problem that remained was getting herself home. Was anyone at the cannery now? No. A text to Vic, then.

*can u pick me up at jeffers brake & lube - car dead*

Once she sent the text, she wandered into the waiting room. She plugged a coffee pod into the machine and emptied her mind as the hot water surged through the grounds with a satisfying hiss, and a stream of rich, dark coffee shot into her travel mug. Good stuff. Even the fourth cup out. A quick glance at the magazines told her there was nothing in any of them worth reading. No worries. She blew on the coffee and inhaled the aroma, lingering, then took a tentative sip. The stuff at home was so gritty and sour, she'd never dare drink it black. Vic seemed oddly attached to his coffeemaker, though, and Lisa was just a guest. She could get her own...those pod-things were pretty neat. No. It would be perceived as a threat, somehow. Even the best damn cup of coffee in the world wasn't worth undermining a relationship. Anyway, with enough cream and sugar, anything was drinkable.

Lisa glanced at her phone. Text notifications were on. A text to Victor would either get a reply seconds later, or hours, depending on what he was doing. Paperwork, seconds. Scouring a crime scene...maybe you'd hear back from him that day. Maybe not. Kind of like car repair.

Although...it was late enough in the afternoon that he might even be done for the day. Yes. But had he seen her text? No.

Jacob, then. She sent the same text to him. Sipped her coffee. No reply.

Are they together? Yes. At home? No. Good—because then she could ease her mind away from the obvious reason they'd be together and not responding to her texts. She wasn't a prude. It was a matter of respect, of personal privacy. Plus, she preferred to be the one running her own mind, not the sí-no. Though the talent did have a way of insinuating itself...basically everywhere.

She sipped her black coffee. Beyond the plate glass, traffic streamed by. Cars, SUVs. A bus. Maybe that bus would take her close enough to...no, not really. Another sip. Another glance at her phone. No reply. Fine. Another opportunity to put the details of her current situation aside, sit her butt in a chair, and practice being present while everything else—the situation, the repair shop, the car—faded into the background. She sat. The vinyl seat squawked loudly, and a bickering couple entered the repair shop, both of them nasal and shrill, growing louder and louder, like they were trying to out-whine each other. Living in the now wasn't always as great as it was cracked up to be.

Time for a cab. She pulled up the keypad to dial

information when her phone chimed an incoming text. Before the sender's name appeared on the screen, she already knew. Victor? Yes.

*On our way 5 min.*

Good thing. The whiny couple was now launching into a loud accounting of who did the dishes more often.

Lisa drained her coffee and went outside, and a few minutes later the black Crown Victoria eased into the lot. She would've been happy enough to hop into the back seat, but Jacob climbed out before she could avoid the awkward door-holding moment. "How long are they keeping it?" he asked.

"They said the end of the day, but...."

"How long, really?"

"Two, maybe three."

"Are they waiting on a part, or is it a matter of scheduling?"

Scheduling? Yes. "They've got the part."

"I can talk to them," Jacob said. "See what they can do to move it up."

It was sweet, the way he enjoyed playing the knight in shining armor for her, but it wasn't necessary. Being without her car was an inconvenience, but fair is fair, and she was willing to wait her turn. She glanced through the shop window and saw the whiny couple gesticulating at each other. Just so long as those two didn't get shuffled ahead of her by virtue of being annoying....

Yes. Yes, they did.

"Ask them," Lisa said. A look of satisfaction crossed Jacob's face before he even charged into battle, then he thumbed something from the corner of his mouth as he turned toward the door. He and Vic had probably been out grabbing dinner somewhere—no.

Not surprising. It was just past five, and they usually settled down to eat closer to eight or nine. She climbed into the back seat and Victor turned and said, "Hey."

"Hey." She was about to ask him if they could stop at the store on the way home when she realized he was blushing.

"So that sucks. Cars. Is it the muffler? Because last time, my muffler fell off when I was on a hill. Then I ended up chasing it down the street so it didn't cause an accident. And then this other time, it was the belt."

She'd wanted to drop it, this matter of what they were doing when she sent the text, honestly she had. But now Victor was blushing and babbling. His shirt was bunched funny around his holster, too. And, now that she thought about it, Jacob had been looking particularly self-satisfied.

She didn't picture it, exactly—in fact, she didn't even really ask. Nonetheless, her precognitive talent supplied her with the scenario as a string of narrative with only the barest hint of sís and nos in between the lines: flirting, escalating. Jacob pulling over and shoving Victor against the passenger door so he could go downtown. Victor would be anxious, yes. Excited, too. Jacob's head bobbing. Victor grabbing hold of it, doing his best not to attract attention from people on the street.

She looked at the ceiling. Now she was blushing, too. "We're out of detergent," she said, to save him from dredging up more embarrassing car stories and hopefully allow them both to stop out-blushing each other.

"Oh. Okay. We'll make a pit stop."

They watched the shop door in silence for just a moment, and then Jacob came striding out. He looked especially well-pleased with himself. "They'll take care of it first thing tomorrow morning," he said as he climbed into the car.

Victor, blushing all over again, turned toward the passenger window as if the parked cars on that side were fascinating.

Lisa bit the inside of her cheek to keep from smiling. It was cute, the way they were so into each other, going at it in the car like a couple of horny teenagers. They hadn't met until they were, what, in their forties? She was only twenty-seven. Seeing the two of them together gave her hope that somehow, somewhere, there was someone special out there waiting for her, too. Wasn't there?

Sí.

# On the Road

Jacob whisked past me in the hallway, carrying a teetering mountain of stuff. Holy crap, was that his luggage, plus mine, plus the ten-ton audio system we got his parents for their anniversary? "We're not late," I said to his back.

"Just packing the car."

"We're not late," I repeated, though I suspected that other than any well-hidden surveillance devices, there was no longer anyone there to hear it. Jacob walks fast when he's got a goal in his sights.

We weren't late. We'd probably be early. I knew this because my discomfort around other people provided me with an uncanny knowledge of how long it took me to get from point A to point B. Showing up late is awkward as hell—everyone looking at you when you walk in—but showing up too early is just as mortifying, leaving you sitting there with the host, or the staff, or even standing there entirely and utterly alone, trying not to look like a big dumbass. On time, minus five. That was how arrival should be done. Fat chance, with Jacob handling the details.

The cannery door banged and Jacob swooped past me again, heading in toward the kitchen now. "Heat's turned down, calls forwarded, GPS programmed, map printed…

anything else?"

"Nothing left to do but drive there." I congratulated my-self over not adding "phenomenally early." And if it carried through in my tone...Jacob was way too focused to take any notice.

I was wondering how subtly I could get away with drag-ging my feet when a plastic grocery bag whapped me in the chest. "Garbage," he said.

Right. Nothing like coming home to a house full of fruit flies.

Even my jaunt to the alley couldn't buy me much valu-able time, and if I was too obvious about trying to slow Jacob down, he'd only drive faster. I chucked the trash, braced myself, and headed for the car. A long weekend with his parents, I could totally do. I was even looking for-ward to seeing them. His sister and her kid, though, not so much. When you do the long-term relationship thing, I guess you've got to take the good with the bad. God knows Jacob puts up with his share of ups and downs from me.

In the meticulously packed car, I found him thumbing in an alternate route into the GPS. Or maybe, in his go-mode, he was finding us an alternate to the alternate. With great effort, I forced myself not to sigh. Don't get me wrong, I freaking loved him being all capable and in-charge. But eventually I found all the checking, re-checking and triple checking a tad bit neurotic.

"All set?" he asked.

Hopefully that wasn't code for, *Are you sure you've gone to the bathroom?* Even my patience has its limits. "All set."

The drive itself wasn't bad. Not only am I accustomed to holding it, since you can't always drop everything to tin-kle when you're on the scene of a homicide, but I'd limit-ed myself to a single cup of coffee to ensure I didn't add any more stress to the trip. Once you get out of the city, the scenery is great. And once we got past all the tolls and construction, Jacob could finally un-tense his shoulders and relax.

At that point I figured I could even get away with teasing him. Just a little. He asked me to hand him some gum, but the pack in the glove compartment was empty. "If I report this, will the Boy Scouts revoke your Preparedness badge?"

"Oh ye of little faith. Back seat."

I should have known. Jacob wouldn't miss shopping for a road trip any more than I'd pass up a slice of cold pizza on a lazy Saturday morning. I snagged the plastic bag and reached in, prepared to eat crow along with my cashews or Pringles, when I realized the bag had something damp inside. Paper towels. At first I thought my better half had chosen obnoxiously healthy road-food, like freshly washed apples or grapes. But then I hit a layer of egg shells. And coffee grounds. And chicken bones. And then I realized the beige plastic grocery bag looked uncannily like the one he'd had me toss on our way out the door. Same brand, same weight, same size.

"I'm thinking you don't want to chew on this." I held up my hand and gave him a little wave with my coffee-crusted fingers.

He cut his eyes to me, glanced down at the bag, then planted his gaze firmly on the road ahead. "Napkins—glove box. Hand sanitizer in the center console."

I de-coffeed my hand without comment, though now all I could smell was garbage. Jacob, too, judging by the way he cracked his window even though that meant listening to the wind whistle through the gap.

If ever there was a moment ripe for a snide comment, this was it. But what was the fun in teasing him when he gave me such obvious ammunition? We all make mistakes.

Even Mr. Perfect.

# Wood

Here's the thing about being in a long term relationship. There's more involved than just inside jokes and shared mortgages, objectionably healthy things in the fridge, or discarded socks that never find the laundry hamper. Back when a horny, shape-shifting, mirror-shattering entity exploded in Jacob's apartment and left him with nowhere to sleep that night, I'd suggested he stay at my place. And when we outgrew that place, we found a new one. Together.

That fateful decision didn't just score me a boyfriend. It earned me a family.

It's not too big, as families go. Jacob has one sister, and she's always pissed off about something. Her kid is no gem, either. Both parents are still alive, and grandma too, though I think she's pushing a hundred-fifty. But Jacob's uncle Leon is the one who shared a special bond with him. He'd taken Jacob to his first concert at age twelve: Weird Al Yankovic. He bought Jacob his first soldering gun. Apparently this was a big thing in late 1970's Wisconsin. He probably would've been the one to teach Jacob to drive stick, too, if his right arm hadn't been torn off in an industrial accident years before.

I like the guy. I may not have the history Jacob's got

with him, but he's easy to talk to, and he always acts excited to see me. Missing arm or not, he could count on our help to put together his new furniture. No doubt Jacob's dad could've handled it, but it gave us an excuse to drive up for the weekend without centering our trip around seeing Clayton play soccer or looking at Clayton's latest science diorama or sitting there uncomfortably while Clayton looks daggers at us. Okay, he only does that to me, not his beloved uncle Jacob—but the point is, I was kinda looking forward to being the youngest guy there in the male bonding session for a change.

Leon greeted us at the door with the standard greeting, asking us how the drive was. The missing arm greeted me with a wave. I nodded at them both while Jacob handled the amicable banalities.

I eased past into the living room while Leon launched into a tale about a certain legendary local speed trap. Even though I'd only seen Leon's place a few times before, the new remodel startled me with its striking difference. Nothing structural had been changed, but the mishmash of furniture styles was gone. Now there was a theme of sorts. Big, inviting leather couch and chairs, and walls painted various coffee colors, and a sleek flatscreen mounted above the mantel. I thought I'd miss the white walls, but with the monochrome muted palette and lack of clutter, there was a warmth and simplicity to the new setup that I liked. Plus, you gotta hand it to someone willing to remodel at his age. It's pretty optimistic if you ask me.

The only thing left to handle was putting together the bookshelves. My fingers were itching to tackle the massive stack of cardboard boxes marring the interior wall of the living room and get those cluttery books they contained in some kind of order. My actual preference would be to drop them off at the local Goodwill, but I've learned to pick my battles.

"So where are the shelves?" Jacob asked, once the driving chitchat had been exhausted.

"Delivery guy left 'em on the back porch. Wouldn't even think about bringing them inside." His tone was only moderately annoyed, but his ghostly arm gave a little jerkoff motion to tell me what he really thought. *What kind of tool leaves a one-armed guy to fend for himself?* Can't say I disagreed.

Luckily he had Jacob. And me. 'Cos no doubt Jacob could bench-press those boxes with one arm tied behind his back, but they'd be awkward to wrangle through the screen door alone.

Jacob strode out first, then stopped so hard I had to backpedal to avoid ramming him. "I thought you were getting the shelves from Ikea," he said with his words, though his tone clearly announced, *What the hell?*

Leon scoffed, "I'm gonna drive all the way to Minneapolis when they got the same stuff right down the road?"

Hardly the same. I'm no furniture connoisseur and even I know the difference. But Jacob picks his battles, same as me, and he wasn't about to give his favorite uncle a hard time over something that'd be a royal pain in the ass to return.

As for me, I felt a comforting pang of nostalgia from the box's tacky green and white graphics. It had been so long since SaverPlus sank money into updating their look that it was practically retro-cool again.

We set to work dragging the oversized boxes inside. Once they were in—and this was no mean feat, given the angle of the screen door and the location of the cabinets around it—Jacob and Leon popped open a box and started puzzling over the instructions. The shelves looked pretty slick in the photos, ladder-like things that leaned into the wall on brushed metal poles. While they were less utilitarian than the white pressboard stuff I usually chose, I'd assembled so many cut rate SaverPlus specials in my time, I had an edge over everyone else. I knew that furniture like I knew which donuts in the corner store had the best jelly inside. The instructions sound like they're written by a drunk man. There's always a mysterious extra part in a little plastic baggie. And the Allen wrenches included in the box really hurt your hands.

"Heavier than I thought," Jacob huffed as we wrangled the shelf pieces out of the box.

"That's primo particleboard for ya," I agreed.

While he paused to scope out the bookshelves' future home, I took a moment to catch my breath. When we first came in from the cold, Leon's house felt toasty warm, but now that we'd been exerting ourselves I was sweating up a storm. I mopped my brow with the hem of my T-shirt. Once I was done blotting, I found Jacob gazing at my bare stomach like it contained the secrets of the universe.

If the two of us were alone, I'd blurt out, "Hey, mister, my eyes are up here." Because, come on, what a hokey thing to fixate on. But as much as I liked Leon, he didn't know me well enough to tell I was being a total smartass. Plus, it was dangerously like flirting. And flirting and family should never mix.

I thought I felt my man's gaze on me while we got all the pieces and parts lined up and counted. Especially when Leon announced, "Good thing it fit through the back door." Not only did Jacob glance at me, but a tiny smile quirked the corner of his lips.

Evidently being around his family brought out the teenager in him. And I had to admit, there was a certain charm to it that drew an answering smirk out of me.

Leon was too busy looking meaningfully through the reader part of his bifocals to notice. "All right. First things first, get the foundation together. One of you hold it up by the base."

Say what?

"Now find the shaft. The big one."

Uh oh.

"Aim it at that hole."

Seriously? SaverPlus Instructions Guy wasn't drunk the day he wrote up these particular how-to's. He was horny.

I *held the base.* Jacob met my eye and gnawed hard on the inside of his cheek while he leveled the *shaft* at the *hole.*

"Okay," Leon said. "Screw it in."

I squeezed my eyes closed and bit down on my tongue a few times. When I opened my eyes again, Jacob's mouth was clamped shut tight with the effort of squelching laughter.

While Leon was occupied with the instructions, I murmured, "You're really good at screwing that big shaft in."

Jacob cuffed me on the shoulder. It would've been funny, if not for the fact that I happened to be holding a screw. It flew out of my hand and rolled with great purpose to the heater vent halfway across the floor.

Leon was closest. He dropped the instructions and dove for it, both arms grabbing. I suspect he might have even caught it if the non-corporeal arm had any effect on the physical plane. Unfortunately, the screw was on an escape trajectory and even a ghost arm couldn't stop it.

All three of us went still and listened to the sound of it pinging down the ductwork for a good minute. "That won't end up lodged in anything important," I asked, "will it?"

"Furnace is at the other end of the basement," Leon said. That was good, I supposed. A furnace sounded like a big-ticket item, not the sort of thing you'd want to grab on impulse from SaverPlus.

Leon re-counted the remaining screws and shook his head. "We had just enough of that size. Why couldn't it have been one of the big ones? There's three extra."

Not very surprising. That's SaverPlus furniture for you.

Leon hauled out a yellowed cigar box full of nails and

tacks and washers and screws from under the kitchen sink. All three of us sifted through it for a good several minutes before we had to concede, the one that got away was an oddball size, which didn't surprise me either.

Leon grabbed his jacket. "I'll run over to the hardware store before they close and pick up some more of these. You want pizza? While I'm out I'll grab a pizza too."

I was about to offer to help, but judging by the neat stack of Towne Pizza boxes next to the green plastic recycling tub, Leon could single-handedly wrangle his pizza just fine.

While Leon forged out to gather supplies, I set about putting away the stuff we weren't currently using anymore, since that's how I roll. Besides, no one wants to step on a wayward tack. I began shoveling everything back into the cigar box, which wasn't as easy as you'd think with a big guy leaning over my chair, mashing himself into my back and pressing his goatee against my ear. "Gimme a hand," Jacob purred. "I need you to hold the base."

I laughed it off, since really, who gets turned on by something so cheesy? Except I think I might have squirmed. Minutely. And Jacob never misses anything. He said, "I'll show you my big shaft if you show me yours."

He ran his fingertips down my forearms and trapped my hands in both of his, lacing our fingers. I tried nudging him off me with my shoulder blade but didn't quite succeed. "Keep your pants on, mister. We're in your uncle's kitchen."

"And?"

"And…it's your *uncle's kitchen.*"

"Leon's not here. Even if the right screw is sitting on the hardware store counter waiting for him and the pizza's ready-made, he'll be gone twenty minutes. At least."

Good point. Especially since Jacob could pop my cork in less than five if he set his mind to it. And my cork was feeling pretty frisky, what with all the shafts and the holes and the screwing.

I reached behind me and fondled him somewhere random—the hamstring, I think—but it was enough to signal that his cheesy pickup line was working. Once Jacob had my blessing, he dove right in for the kill. He clamped onto my neck like the true predator he is. I'm such a sucker for the neck. He knows it. And he knows I know he knows… which makes it all so much hotter when he goes for it.

Screws and washers pinged to the linoleum as I struggled to my feet with him glommed onto my back, a chair between us and both my hands trapped in his. The chair tipped when I extricated myself and turned, and the two of us staggered toward the fridge where I mashed him up against it and planted a deep, needy kiss. A few plastic magnets popped free, and a sticky note with a phone number on it transferred itself to my forearm. I ground the fronts of our jeans together, and my burgeoning hard-on was met with one just as promising.

Jacob squeezed his hands between us and started working open my fly. "Wait," I gasped against his wet lips. "Not here." Not where his uncle could just walk in on us if he turned back because he forgot something.

As one, we cut our eyes to the tiny half-bath off the short hall to the dining room. I made it there first, and Jacob squeezed in behind me and pulled the door shut. He stared at it briefly. No lock. So he spun me around to use my body weight to anchor it shut.

A door-mounted towel bar prodded me mid-back, and I replayed some memories of another time and another bathroom. The layout wasn't like the can at my ex-partner's basement. Too cramped. Plus the frosted window let in a different kind of light. But there was still an old-man-bathroom feel to it that evoked a pleasant deja vu.

Jacob wasted no time shoving my jeans down, then his. He was about to kneel—I know his body language by now, and I'm well-versed in most of his moves, too—but I stopped him by cupping the back of his head and pulling him into another kiss. I eased a hand between us and grabbed his dick. Stroked it. Not feverishly, not like we'd wreckingballed our way through the kitchen. Slow and steady. Like I had every confidence that we'd get where we needed to go, and we'd do it in the few stolen minutes we had. Because I wasn't done kissing him yet, and that's what I wanted. To savor the rasp of his whiskers against my lips, and revel in his sheer bigness pinning me to the door.

While we kissed, he grabbed me and started stroking, matching my pace. My back arched and my hips flexed, like my whole body wanted to get in on this thing we were doing. So simple, nothing more than a quick grope. But so right.

Moisture kissed the edge of my forefinger as it met a drop of precome, and I stole my hand away, just for a half second, to give my palm a nice lick. Jacob grunted, then spat into his palm and mimicked the gesture. A rush of giddiness surged down to my groin when he grabbed my dick with a wet hand and stroked me hard.

"Who would have thought?" Jacob murmured into my hair. He'd been revisiting bathroom memories of his own.

I love it when we're on the same page.

I paced my strokes a little faster so I could enjoy the huff of him breathing against my scalp. Closer now. Me and him both. My free hand had fallen to his shoulder. I cupped his head again and teased the bony ridge at the base of his skull with my fingertips. He jerked me off harder and gnawed my earlobe.

"It's good," I said.

His breath flickered over my ear and he rooted deeper into the crook of my neck—and oh yeah, there it was. My own personal hotspot. *No hickies.* I don't need to say it anymore. He knows there'll be hell to pay. But he's figured out exactly how hard he can go at it without leaving much of a mark. Each of his moves built on the other—the hand on my dick, the mouth on my throat, the sound of him grunting encouragement as I jacked him off too. I surged toward orgasm with the confidence of someone who'd been brought there innumerable times before by this hand, this mouth, this man. I came first, shoving him back at the last minute with the realization that against his black sweater, my jiz would stick out like a sore thumb. We both laughed breathlessly as I semi-successfully detoured and shot mostly on his bare thigh, then together we fumbled at his cock, sticky-handed, until he clenched all over, shuddered, and peaked into my fist, jiz oozing out between my fingers. He sagged against me. I couldn't say who was holding up who. I pressed my lips to his forehead and basked in the moment, and listened to the sound of him breathing into my flannel shirt.

"It is good," he sighed. Eventually. When he had his words again. And even though we knew there were a few dozen obvious clues on the kitchen floor just waiting to announce our shenanigans to Jacob's uncle, we lingered there for one more moment, and held each other, and savored the feeling of wanting and being wanted. Loving, and being loved.

For all that I wasn't particularly comfortable jammed up against a door, I wished we could have lingered even longer. But before Leon returned, there were nails and tacks and screws and washers to gather up off the floor, and several magnets that needed re-sticking. He'd probably wonder why we'd moved the magnets, if he was the type to notice that sort of thing. Given that Jacob came from his gene pool, it was a fair bet. And that couldn't be helped. If the topic came up, I'd let Jacob field it. He's way better at lying than I am.

Turned out we hadn't needed to rush. We got everything

back together well before Leon showed up with a couple of pizzas, a baggie of extra screws, and a can of WD40. Lube—like we needed one more thing to make us laugh.

It's hard to please a native Chicagoan with pizza made anywhere else, but pizza's a lot like sex. I'd stop what I'm doing even for mediocre pizza. So we sat down around that kitchen table, pushed the cigar box aside, and enjoyed our okay pizza while Leon spun a tale about Jacob forgetting his tree-lines in a third grade Arbor Day play.

And eventually we did get back to those shelves, with their perplexing directions and slightly misaligned holes. The world's dirtiest directions seemed a lot less pornographic now, though occasionally the word *shaft* would earn me a quick glance and a naughty half-smile from Jacob.

In the end, it was a good thing we had two sets of hands and three sets of eyes. Otherwise we would've missed the importance of the final pegs in back that kept the whole structure from skewing diagonal and wobbly. "That's it," Leon announced triumphantly. "Pound it in and show it who's boss."

Jacob made a choking sound, then covered it with a few coughs. Me? I was too busy being distracted by a washer that dropped out of a fold in my flannel, pinged to the floor, and spun around on its edge a few times before settling to a dramatic, clattering stop. Hard to say if it belonged somewhere in the now-complete(ish) bookshelves, or if it was a spare part I'd picked up while Jacob was mashing me into the kitchen table.

I flipped the washer into the air, caught it, and tucked it away in my pocket. "I wouldn't worry about it. SaverPlus furniture..." well, it's a lot like a good relationship. "It might not be fancy, but once you pull it all together, it's surprisingly solid."

# Off the Cuff

Jacob fiddled with the radio until he found a nineties indie rock station playing something I half-recognized. He turned up the volume, then settled back into his heated seat, eyes on the road. I was occupied with trying to work a nasty kink out of my neck. I did notice, though, that as he approached our side street, he coasted right past the turn without even slowing. "Aren't we going to stop home and change?" I asked.

"We'll miss our reservation."

Really? He'd picked me up from the Fifth Precinct the second I got off work, and it wasn't even dark out yet. We never ate before sundown. "Oh. It's just...I've been running around all day. I wouldn't mind changing my shirt."

"It's fine."

"And my work shoes. They're kinda schleppy."

"No one will notice."

Says him. He always looks like a million bucks, morning, noon and night. "I could at least drop off my sidearm," I said. "Nothing says 'look how classy I am' like a holster bulge."

He dropped his hand to my thigh, grabbed down, and gave my leg's inside meat a few slow kneads. "Don't worry about it."

I slid a look in the direction of his profile. He was being awfully casual, I realized. Maybe a little *too* casual. "So we've got reservations—freakishly early reservations—that we can't possibly bend. But it's okay if I show up in my frumpy work shoes and my holster plastered to my side with sweat."

"Your clothes are fine. It's no big deal."

"But—"

"It's fine. Really. Besides, we're already here." While he pulled into a lot, I scanned the neighborhood and tried to pinpoint the restaurant that was so important. Only I couldn't find one—not the type of place that took reservations, anyway. There was a diner on the corner and a storefront bodega that sold menudo across the street. That was it.

I pondered the lack of fancy restaurants briefly, and then pieced that observation together with Jacob's evasive non-answers. I came to the same logical conclusion anyone else would draw. Clearly, my partner was leading me to a room where a bunch of my friends and a drug counselor would all be sitting in a circle on some flimsy folding chairs, waiting to confront me about my prescription drug use.

"Hold on a second," I said. Although Jacob had cut the engine and opened his door, I made no move to get out.

He looked me in the eye, finally, and said, "Everything's fine."

"Whatever this is, we don't need to do it."

He sighed. "Okay, you're on to me." His eyes softened, and he smiled. "It'll take fifteen minutes. Twenty, tops. And it's my treat."

Either I was still hazy on the definition of the word *treat*, or I'd read the situation all wrong. My gut was telling me that if he'd been planning an intervention, I'd be able to pick out some telltale tension around his eyes, or maybe some stiffness in the set of his shoulders. Since there was none, I stood down my internal red alert, resigned myself to enduring whatever it was he had planned, and climbed out of the car.

Jacob rounded the long black hood, buttoning his jacket. As expected, he did indeed look like a million bucks. And maybe slightly chagrined, but not like he was leading me to the chopping block. I played it cool in the hopes that I might deduce how all the cloak-and-dagger would culminate, but I was still in the dark when he marched me to a narrow door I would have otherwise missed, and nudged me up a worn staircase.

The door at the top read *Cecil Matthis, Tailor* in chipped gold paint. It looked like it had been lettered somewhere around the Hoover administration. While I gawked, Jacob reached around me, turned the knob and gave the door a push. It opened to a cluttered room stuffed with rows and rows of garments in drab menswear colors, gray, black and navy suits along one wall and pale broadcloth shirts another...and I realized that I actually had just been roped into an intervention after all. A phenomenally mortifying intervention.

I'd frozen in my tracks, which I didn't realize until Jacob nudged me. Twice. "I promise," he murmured into my hair, "Cecil doesn't bite."

Maybe not. But the thought of some stranger grabbing me by the inseam was a lot creepier than I'd imagined it would be—at least now that it was such a distinct and palpable possibility. As I forced myself over the threshold, a wizened old man with a measuring tape draped across his stooped shoulders shuffled out from the back room. His pate shone through his scanty combover, but his nostril hair was lush and thick. His horn-rimmed glasses were about as antique as the lettering on his door. On a hipster, they would've looked obnoxiously retro, but on him they just looked old. He nodded at Jacob, planted his hands on his hips, and peered up at me through the scratched lenses. He smelled like Aqua Velva. "So. This is the one." He subjected me to a critical once-over with a funny little smile wrinkling his face. "Well. We got our work cut out for us tonight, don't we? Go ahead, kiddo. Change."

He nodded toward a garment bag. My garment bag. Which was already hanging from a rickety changing screen over in the corner. "You owe me, mister," I muttered to Jacob, who bit the inside of his cheek to keep from smiling.

The suit waiting for me was an off-the-rack number I'd ordered at the Big & Tall shop. That transaction had been awkward enough, me reeling from sticker shock while they swiped my credit card. And no one there had been fondling my junk, either.

I suited up and marched out to meet my fate, telling myself I could endure pretty much anything for fifteen minutes, but dreading it nonetheless. The groping started right away, with Cecil drawing chalk marks on me as he pinched my shoulders and tugged my cuffs. Short, businesslike yanks. Regardless, I hate being touched, however briefly or chalkily. He circled behind me, grabbed the hem of my jacket, pulled, and prodded me in the back a few times with the chalk lozenge. "This needs to come in," he declared. I must have sighed louder than I thought, because he added, "Trust me, it'll hang better, and you won't miss having all that extra fabric in your way."

He tugged and chalked his way around to the front, and I braced myself for the question I'd been dreading: which way I "dressed." Because the state of my dick was no one's business but my own. "You plan on wearing this suit to work?" he asked.

That made a difference? "Yeah."

"Okay. So, which side?"

I felt my cheeks color. "The right."

He plucked at the side seam of the jacket just beneath my ribs. "Shoulder holster, or belt?"

I processed the question for an awkwardly long moment as it dawned on me that he was talking about my *sidearm*. "The other right," I said. "Shoulder."

"Maybe you should put it back on," Jacob suggested.

"You got your gun with you?" Cecil cried. "Well, go get it."

The shop's phone rang as I handed my jacket to Jacob and went to retrieve my holster from behind the changing screen. Cecil was a loud talker—his hearing was probably starting to go. He set an appointment at such high volume that all his neighbors would know what time his next customer was coming in. Jacob, on the other hand, had a talent for pitching his voice so that only the intended recipient can hear it. "Were you thinking what I *think* you were thinking?" he asked me while I strapped on my Glock.

What exactly had I been thinking? Who knows—I was probably baffled by the idea that a guy might reposition his wang based on the day's agenda...which would bring a whole new meaning to *Casual Friday*. "I'm getting a suit tailored—it's a logical enough assumption. If I'd known you had a guy who was experienced at fitting a holster, you probably could've talked me into this before now. And with less coercion." I buckled the strap and shrugged the sidearm into position. "But I gotta say, I'm relieved he didn't cop a feel."

Jacob held up the new jacket and I slid back into it. Across the room at his cluttered desk, Cecil finished jotting his appointment in a yellowed ledger, then threw his arms in the air to indicate his approval of my holster.

I'd figured I was home free when Jacob leaned in and

whispered, "Sorry to break it to you," his voice dropped even lower, mock-sultry, "but the serious molestation comes later. When he fits your pants."

"You totally owe me," I grumbled. "Big time."

# Locked and Loaded

"You forgot your gun," I murmured.

Jacob huffed a short sigh through his nose and narrowed his eyes. By this, I took it to mean that he was seriously pissed off, and any disbelief I was voicing would only serve to darken his mood. "Look," he whispered, "you're the one who saw something, so you tell me. Would it matter if we both had physical weapons or not?"

"It was just a glimpse." I edged sideways down the alleyway and thought about calling in for backup, but let's face it, I see shit all the time. If I carried on like the sky was falling every time the bloody wreck of a human wandered through my peripheral vision, I'd lose whatever small credibility I still possessed.

I drew my sidearm, then opened my crown chakra and sucked down a torrent of white light. Power crackled through my subtle bodies, and I felt its echoes in my physical shell—numb lips, tingling fingers and toes, and a metallic buzz in the hinge of my jaw. Locked and loaded. Nowhere to go but forward.

We crept past a bricked up coal cellar and a line of recycle bins that were clearly stuffed with something far more pungent than sorted glass, plastic and paper. Slipped around the corner, senses prickling on high alert, searching a back alley jumbled with old pallets and crates with my sidearm at high ready. Maybe nothing. Probably nothing. My shoulders relaxed marginally and I was about to drop into a more relaxed stance when Jacob bellowed, "Police—let me see your hands!"

A scrawny figure shifted in the shadows and a length of electrical conduit clattered to the ground. "I din' do nothing! I din' do nothing," the guy insisted.

"Hands on your head," Jacob barked. Once, twice, three times. It took a few tries since the guy was so scared he apparently couldn't tell his knuckles from his scalp. But eventually, shaking from head to toe, he complied. "Easy, now," Jacob said. "Step toward the light."

The shifting shadows resolved, and our trembling wreck of a guy turned out to be covered not in gore, but paint... unless he bled orange. But judging by the smears of drywall dust that accompanied the colorful wounding—plus the fact that Jacob could see him too—not only was our target alive, but hale and hearty.

"I was just looking for copper," he blubbered. "They pay good money for copper at the scrapyard."

I lowered my aim while Jacob ran through a few basic questions to determine our trash-picker lived nearby, and appeared to be doing exactly what he said he was doing: saving a little scrap from the landfill. The sidearm was easy enough to holster, though my psychic ammo wasn't quite so easy to put away. The tingling in my fingertips faded to an unnatural chill, but thankfully, at least there was no goopy leak of ectoplasm. Maybe my psychic sense can discern a paint-streaked dumpster diver from an earthbound spirit faster than my logical brain could process the difference. I was just happy I wouldn't have to deal with slimehand.

Shaken, the trash picker went on his way, and Jacob and I resumed our trek toward the movie theater. No doubt the film would be nowhere near as thrilling as our pre-show detour, but at least there'd be popcorn involved, and Good n' Plenties if I really wanted to punish my teeth. My adrenaline was ebbing, and my tweaky mojo was, too. But Jacob's annoyance? Hard to say.

He grabbed our tickets from the kiosk while I stood on the sidewalk and replayed the event in my mind. Between the stance and the voice, he'd nearly made our target soil himself, even without a gun in his hand.

A loose crowd milled around the entryway, some coming, some going, and it was only the residual heightened alert in me that noticed a motion that was slightly too repetitive. Carried out by a guy who was slightly too transparent.

Bullet wound. I didn't see the bullet and he blinked out before I could gauge the wound, but people only jerk in that particular way when they're stopping lead. Plus, now that I was looking right at it, I vaguely remembered the news coverage from a few years back. Whoever pulled the trigger was stamping license plates in Joliet these days, so there was no reason for this guy to keep getting shot. I reached for my weapon—not my sidearm, but the powdery spectral neutralizer that showed up on command when I thought about it hard enough. Whether I created it myself by synthesizing it from white light with my stubbornness and panic, or I simply gathered it from the environment, I didn't know. But a quick dusting and a mental shove was all it took to send my gunshot repeater on his way.

By the time Jacob came out to get me, I was holding my slimy, cold hand in a loose fist, and debating whether or not to hide it in my pocket or just sit tight until I could veer into the bathroom and rinse all psychic evidence down the drain. Jacob wasn't paying any attention to my hand, though. He was busy ruminating on our alleyway encounter.

"I didn't *forget* my weapon. I'm off-duty, and there was

no reason to think I'd need it tonight."

Heck, mine wouldn't have been on me either if I hadn't come straight from work. Now I'd be stuck with a sweaty holster against my side for how long? Two more hours, minimum. "Look at it this way. You stopped a guy by pointing your finger at him. Pretty badass."

He grunted. Not ready to joke around about it, not yet. Maybe not ever.

It was a fluke I'd been carrying, though I don't have a tendency to go entirely unarmed. By whatever freak of nature spawned my abilities, I was never without my non-physical weapon. No shutoff valve existed, just antipsyactives with more side effects than they were worth.

But I wasn't kidding about Jacob stopping someone with a finger. It was his tone, his stance that the guy had reacted to, not the presence or absence of a sidearm. If the mind is our best weapon, then I can guarantee, Jacob is someone you do not want to butt heads with. I slid my hand into his—yeah, *that* hand—and watched his expression shift into one of startlement, and surprise, and finally wonder, as the ectoplasmic chill seeped into his palm. I pressed my lips to his ear and said, "You're right. You didn't need your gun tonight. Between the two of us, whatever this crazy-assed world throws our way...together, we're ready."

# Inside Out

*A year, four months and eight days before Maurice Taylor retired from the Chicago Police Department...*

"Honestly, Jacob. A meeting is a meeting. It's nothing to get worked up over. Believe me." Carolyn flipped down the passenger-side visor and gave her subdued peach lipstick a quick check. "Seriously. It's like watching paint dry. Probably even more tedious than that."

"But this is a *PsyCop* meeting—my first one. That's got to count for something. And if it's so dull, why'd they keep the Stiffs in the dark for so long?"

"Who knows? Maybe someone in brass just realized it can count toward your continuing education credits so it saves them the expense of paying for a class."

Jacob reached for the handle to open the car door, but he noticed Carolyn didn't. He paused.

"Did you talk to Keith?" she asked.

The lie came to him first—*I left a message.* He'd never considered himself a liar, but the very first conversation he'd had with Carolyn was a real eye-opener. Over the past few months he'd been trying to mend his ways, but it was a work in progress. No doubt everyone lied—to spare people's feelings, to avoid coming off like jerks. But everyone didn't work with a telepath.

"He's still mad," Jacob chose to say. That was true—and a strong enough assertion to divert Carolyn's attention from the fact that he hadn't admitted his reluctance to try to patch things up with Keith. It was over between them—Keith had made it pretty damn clear. He'd hung up his badge, but they still worked out at the same gym. They had the same friends. They were bound to run into each other sooner or later. No sense in being childish about the way things turned out. It was nobody's fault.

"I'd hate to be in your shoes," she said. "It's hard enough to deal with this job, let alone doing it while you're trying to keep your personal life personal. It's easier to just tell the truth. If people are going to find something to hate you about, they'll manage to do it anyway, no matter how you try to paint yourself to satisfy them. But in this case, I don't think telling the truth is an option."

"Sarge knows. You know."

"And I think you'd better leave it at that. Why should it be any of the other cops' business who you sleep with?"

Jacob waited with his hand on the door. They were in the car together at least an hour a day, sometimes more. Did she really need to analyze the ramifications of being gay and being on the force at that very moment—when Jacob was on the cusp of his first official inter-departmental PsyCop meeting?

Evidently so. She had her phone out and was scrolling through her pictures. "If you're positive that you're not going to patch things up with Keith—"

"I'm positive."

"—then my neighbor knows this guy."

"You're trying to set me up?"

"It's not like that."

"Really?" She'd said as much, he figured, so she must have believed it was true. "Then what *is* it like?"

"It's just...meeting guys on the force is probably not your safest bet. He sent me a picture—take a look before you decide you're not interested."

Jacob planted his elbow on the center arm rest and peered down at Carolyn's phone while she scrolled. "Wait a minute." He covered her hand with his before she could flip past—because a flash of color caught his eye, and because the sudden tension in her shoulders told him that scrolling past the picture that piqued his curiosity was exactly what she wanted to do.

She shifted her grip and kept scrolling, to a shot of a guy with a soul patch and artsy tortoise-shell glasses. Handsome enough. If you liked that sort of thing.

"Go back."

"Never mind that, this is Neil. He moved here from Boston last month."

Jacob supposed he wasn't going to get his way until he heard her out. "Uh huh."

"He's forty-two. Just bought a brownstone in Lincoln Square. And he's a jazz flautist."

"A *what*?"

"A jazz flautist."

"Yeah, I heard you." Jacob tilted her hand so he could get a look at this Neil character without the glare bouncing off the side-view interfering. Neil half-smiled back at him from a publicity shot. "A *jazz* flautist. How many different kinds are there?"

"I don't know. He could be part of an orchestra, I guess. This is one of those snap-judgements of yours, isn't it?"

Jacob considered lying. Again. Instead of assuring her it wasn't, he shrugged.

"Isn't he a good-looking guy?"

"What," Jacob said, "you can't tell?"

"By your standards."

"My homo standards."

"Well...yes."

It wasn't much fun arguing with Carolyn, since she couldn't exactly defend herself when you nailed her. Jacob sighed and looked more closely at the snapshot. "Neil, the jazz flautist" looked like a smug bastard, was what he looked like. "It's not that he's unattractive. He's just not my type."

"So you're attracted to someone more like Keith. More masculine."

When Jacob tried to take the phone from Carolyn, she held for a moment, then reluctantly released. Jacob scrolled back to the previous photo, and stared. Carolyn herself was in the shot, Carolyn in bright red lipstick—with a bleached-blond guy who looked like he'd just stepped off the set of a music video. He'd stretched out his arm and snapped the shot while they were toasting each other with a margarita at a run-down Mexican restaurant, in a plastic booth Jacob never would have imagined Carolyn sitting in without wiping it off first. And she didn't even look awkward with him, like she usually did, with everybody else. She was laughing.

"This guy is hot. Who's he, your gay neighbor?"

"No, that's my stylist."

She tried to take her phone back, but Jacob held onto it. "Does your stylist have a name?"

"It's Crash."

Crash. Jacob could totally see it. He had a neck tattoo—from the angle, he couldn't make out what it was supposed to be, but what difference did it make? It was a *neck* tattoo. "I'd take *his* phone number."

"I don't get it," Carolyn said. "He's kind of, uh...swishy. Which probably sounds more insulting than I mean it to be, since I'm crazy about him. But you're total opposites." Were they? Jacob could say the same thing about Crash and Carolyn, her with tasteful pearl earrings, him with a silver hoop through his nostril—but look how she sparkled while they were together. He had a broad smile that looked like it got a lot of use. No stuffy half-smiles there. "What's wrong with Neil?"

"I don't know." Was that a lie? Possibly. But maybe it was a nebulous enough lie that Carolyn didn't need to point it out. "I just don't like him."

And that was the truth.

"Neil isn't your type—but Crash is? Why?"

Jacob caught himself before he denied knowing why, since that wouldn't have been entirely true, though saying Crash had a gorgeous smile was more information than he wanted to dole out. "Lots of reasons," he said, one of the ways he answered her without lying, but without really answering, either. A black Crown Victoria pulled up beside them, a pair of female PsyCops from Rush Street, and he added, "We can talk about this later. I want to get a good seat."

"The clairvoyants are already sitting in them." It was more a statement than an argument, as Carolyn already had her phone stashed and her most inscrutable designer sunglasses on. They locked the car and walked at an efficient clip to the Twenty First Precinct building, where a squinty-eyed rookie at the door pointed them toward the meeting.

As conference rooms went, the room in the Twenty First was unremarkable—a bit shabbier than the meeting room at the Seventh, but big enough to hold all the PsyCops without rubbing auras. Jacob eyed the other detectives as well as he could without being too obvious. Some, he'd met: Valdez, precog, Midway area...Blaine, clairvoyant, South Loop. Those were the only two he recognized. As for everyone else? He couldn't tell the Psychs from the Stiffs. Not by simply looking.

Carolyn edged between a pair of bulky middle-aged guys who glanced down at her well-toned glutes while stepping aside to let her get at the snacks. It was subtle, not quite the type of ogle she would have gotten if she'd walked by a bunch of construction workers—but it was still noticeable. She had that effect on men. Sure, she might be able to read their minds, but as most straight men saw it, she was still a hot blonde. Jacob could hardly find fault with the detectives. They hadn't been particularly lecherous about their staring…they just couldn't help themselves. He himself was no better, checking out every other detective he hadn't met, and wondering if they were a Psych or a Stiff.

Because with something that important, it seemed like you should be able to tell just by looking. Although usually you couldn't.

Carolyn picked up a banana. She considered how green it was and put it back. When she then reached for a yogurt and found that it was only an empty container, she couldn't censor the observation, "The food at these things is pathetic."

A young detective who'd approached from the opposite end of the table lifted a donut out of the box, scattering sugar. He peered at the small hole in the side of the dough, and said, "I know. I can't even find one decent custard-filled—" as if it heard him complaining about it, the donut disgorged enough strawberry filling to top off an evidence bag, straight down the front of his lapel. "Sonofa—" he waved the donut, scattering still more sugar, and now jelly, then dropped the half-squashed pastry in the donut box's lid. "Swear to God, of all the fucki—" he glanced at Carolyn, "er, sorry…."

Jacob pursed his lips to stop himself from laughing—because, come on. Such an absurd amount of red goo had squirted out of that donut, it looked like there'd been a props master off to the side pumping it out through a special rig.

Then he recognized the detective pressing a wad of napkins into the hand of the jelly-covered detective and realized it wasn't just any PsyCop who'd been slimed. It was Victor Bayne in the flesh—and his partner, Maurice Taylor, who Jacob had known for years, but not well enough to say more than "How's it going?" and "Is the guy in custody?" and "How many bullet holes did they find?" And that had been ages ago, when Maurice was a regular plainclothes cop, and Jacob was still in uniform.

Of course Jacob had heard of Taylor's Psych, the Chicago Police Department's only medium, but they'd never actually met.

He hadn't imagined Detective Bayne would be so tall.

Bayne reached for a bottled water, overshot, and knocked it off the table. It landed with a hard thwack between his feet and Carolyn's, rupturing in a spray of water. "For crying out loud," he snapped, and knelt to swab Carolyn's shoes with the handful of napkins he should have used on his own jacket.

"It's fine," she said. "It's only water." She sounded embarrassed.

If the whole "all-thumbs" act was really an excuse to grope Carolyn's feet—and get a good look at her legs—it was a very well-executed drop. But when Bayne straightened up, he seemed too flustered to have orchestrated the maneuver. Plus, he backed away from Carolyn like he was an empath on psyactives who couldn't bear the sting of her annoyance. He'd been in a spot to look right down her blouse. And he hadn't taken the bait. "I'm really sor—"

"I said it's fine," Carolyn snapped. "Stop apologizing."

Bayne mopped at the front of his blazer with the now-soggy napkins, which began to disintegrate, shred and pill. The napkin shreds stuck in the jelly. He sighed. "Hand me that other water," he said to Jacob, who held his tie against his abs to stop it from dragging through a splatter of jelly as he reached past the green bananas for a bottle of tepid water. "Thanks." Bayne took it without making eye contact, then turned back to Taylor and said, "Now I'm gonna be sticky all day, unless we stop at SaverPlus."

Taylor handed him a larger pile of napkins, and made a noise in reply that didn't sound like either a yes or a no. Jacob supposed it sounded sympathetic. Maybe a repertoire of ambiguous noises would help him navigate his Carolyn conversations, though he supposed if his ability to make such noises hadn't developed by now, his chance of spontaneously picking it up was pretty slim.

Before Jacob could say hello to Taylor in hopes of striking up a conversation with him and, by extension, his mysterious but sticky PsyCop partner, a florid guy in a pinstripe suit told everyone to grab a donut and find their seat, since admin wanted to make sure there was enough time for Q&A after the PowerPoint was done.

All the seats with a good view of the door were taken, as Carolyn had predicted. So were the seats by the dubious snacks. Jacob chose one that would normally have gone empty in a room full of cops, the chair that left his back to the door as an irresistible target for any axe-wielding mass murderer who might have slipped by every other cop in the precinct and headed straight for the conference room because their uncanny crazy-guy sense told them there were still a few squashed donuts left.

It just so happened to be the chair across the table from Taylor and Bayne.

The lights went low and a laptop projector with a loud fan flicked on. A piece of clip art appeared on the screen of a man with rays shooting out of his head. Someone really should have come up with some better psychic clip art by now. "The rights and responsibilities of a PsyCop are as close to those of the rest of the force as we can make them. But let's face it. You're playing by a different set of rules." The title Psychic Evidence and the Court System swooshed in over the stock art.

Jacob had hoped the presentation would be a bit less dry. A new psych talent, maybe. Or a twist on the old methodology. Or a roster of all the city's PsyCops—with precincts. And phone numbers. Because wouldn't it make sense to share intelligence among themselves? Working with a telepath was nothing like working with an empath, for instance. All Jacob had needed to do with his old partner, Warren, was keep himself on an even keel to make sure his own inner dialog wasn't read. What might it be like to work with a precog? Or a telekinetic?

Or a medium?

Across the table, Bayne kept fussing over his jacket without even pretending to pay attention to the PowerPoint. Taylor settled back in his chair, sighed, and shut his eyes. Jacob recalled Maurice had never been much of a go-getter. How he'd ended up landing one of the coveted PsyCop positions, Jacob had no idea. Maybe he knew somebody.

Light from the projector glinted off Taylor's wedding band as he got comfortable by folding his hands over his stomach. Jacob's eyes went to Bayne's left hand. No ring. Not that it meant anything; plenty of cops didn't wear a band on duty. They caught on things like gloves and fences, and could result in some pretty nasty injuries. Everyone on the force knew someone who knew someone who'd lost a finger to an unfortunate wedding band incident.

Although Carolyn wore her ring. She'd said flat-out that it was the uniforms' job to vault over a chain link fence in pursuit of a suspect, not hers. And she'd said it right in front of Sergeant Owens, who likely would have preferred she phrase it with a little more tact.

Jacob scanned the opposite side of the table. The precog Valdez had been looking at him, but looked away before he could read anything into the glance other than casual curiosity. Bayne's hand came down on the table. Jacob's eyes went to it again.

No ring.

And he'd passed up the opportunity for a high-angle view of Carolyn's cleavage.

What if...?

While he didn't strike Jacob as gay, neither had Keith. Not on duty. It wasn't until Jacob spotted Keith on the leg press at his gym, a primarily gay gym—glistening with sweat, in a flimsy tank top that was more armhole than fabric—that he realized he wasn't the only gay cop at his precinct.

But Bayne was probably straight. To hope otherwise would just be wishful thinking. He probably just had Keith on his mind, was all, since Carolyn had been asking about him in the car. And the *jazz flautist*, whatever his name was. And Carolyn's new hairdresser with the neck tattoo—as well as her question about what his "type" was. As far as Jacob knew, he didn't have a type. He just knew it when someone rubbed him wrong. Like the jazz flautist.

Bayne scowled at his blazer and picked bits of napkin from his lapel, flicking them onto the floor. Jacob knew he shouldn't stare. If he got caught, it would come off as some kind of macho challenge he'd never intended. Even if Bayne might be gay—or at least single, and open-minded enough to experiment—Carolyn was right. It wasn't safe to date someone on the force. Look what happened with Keith.

The speaker stretched a convoluted explanation on the importance of recording sixth-sensory impressions, no matter how bizarre they might seem, into a mind numbing half hour—when five minutes would have sufficed. One of the PsyCops from Rush Street then asked it if was absolutely necessary for her to capture more than one form of documentation, and pointed out that if she was expected to do more work than her NP colleagues, she saw it as a form of discrimination.

The room turned bluish as the PowerPoint slide changed, and Jacob looked up to find Valdez now staring at Detective Bayne. The precog looked at Jacob again, gave a little flinch, and looked away.

Weird.

Taylor's pager went off as the presenter answered her question by repeating a few lines from the presentation that were dull enough the first time around, and the PsyCops from the Fifth Precinct slipped out of the room, leaving two empty coffee cups, a greenish banana peel, and a few rolled flecks of damp napkin behind. Jacob stared at the spot where Victor Bayne had been sitting, wondering if his seat was still warm.

*Bad idea. It's not like he's even gay.*

But his bad-boy scowl had ignited all sorts of urges within Jacob, where the jazz flautist's tepid half-smile had definitely not.

A few more questions, then a mandatory evaluation form which nobody filled out with many details, and the PsyCops began filing out in twos and fours. Jacob stood to intercept Valdez as he passed the remains of the donuts. "Jacob Marks," he said, offering his hand. They'd been introduced before, maybe two years ago, so he figured it couldn't hurt to remind him. "Twelfth Precinct."

"Oscar Valdez." He shook Jacob's hand, but released it quickly. He looked Jacob in the eye, then looked up at the ceiling, then down at a spot on Jacob's chest.

Jacob glanced down to see if maybe he'd been jellied and hadn't realized it. Nope. "Carolyn's the telepath of our team."

"Yeah, I know. I've seen her before. Must be…interesting… spending so much time with someone who can read your mind. A partner like that, they'd know you inside out."

What an odd thing to say. Especially coming from a precog. "It's not exactly—"

"Anyway, gotta run. Good to meet you."

Carolyn approached, holding a green banana she looked none too thrilled with. "He just took off like I insulted his mother," Jacob told her. "Doesn't anyone network at these things?"

She steered him toward the door with a subtle shift of her shoulder. "Of course not. We're Psychs. We're too awkward to mingle. Especially with each other."

Jacob held the door for her, and she slipped through and walked briskly toward his car. While Psychs did tend to be incredibly awkward, Jacob was an NP, so he didn't count; someone should want to talk to him. They got in the car. Jacob fit the key into the ignition, but instead of starting the engine, he said, "I think Valdez saw something... about me. And I think it spooked him."

"Why do you say that?"

"He wouldn't look me in the eye. If he saw me winning the lottery or something, I don't think he'd be acting so funny. What if he saw me...getting hurt...in the line of duty? What if he saw me getting killed?"

Carolyn thought about it. Most partners would have blithely insisted that everything would be perfectly fine. But instead she said, "I can track him down and ask him. But before I do, you'll need to decide. If he saw something bad, and there was no way to prevent it—do you really want to know?"

Jacob considered. If Valdez had seen him meet his maker, chances were he didn't know exactly when the dire deed would occur. A month. A week. A year? It seemed like an awfully inexact amount of time to sustain a high level of panic. Ideally, Jacob would envision himself living every day as if it were his last day on earth. He'd write a big check to the local food bank. He'd skip the gym for just a night and sit on his roof to watch the sunset. And he'd tell all his loved ones how much they meant to him.

But those were things you couldn't really do every single day, or else you'd end up broke and flabby. And your family would think you'd finally started to crack under the pressure of the job.

"How accurate is Valdez?" he asked.

"Hit or miss. I think he's level three."

Jacob started the car and stared down at the steering wheel, working his jaw.

Carolyn went on. "Don't you think he would have said something if he'd seen you getting injured? Seems to me he would have, as a courtesy. I'll bet it's something else that he wouldn't feel professionally obligated to disclose."

"Like what?"

"Something personal, maybe. What was going through your mind during the meeting? Did you think about Neil? Because maybe you're right, and Neil's not really a good match for you. And maybe Valdez picked up on something as simple as that."

Jacob frowned. "How...specific do you think his precog skills are? Like, vague feeling? Or full-on homoerotic imagery?"

"Please tell me you weren't thinking gay thoughts at work in a room full of certified Psychs."

"*Gay thoughts?*"

"Jacob...."

"Should I have borrowed a straight brain before I showed up at the meeting?"

"That sounded a lot worse than I meant it. You know what I mean."

Unfortunately, he did. The middle aged guys who'd been ogling Carolyn's glutes were probably fine thinking whatever it was they thought, even in the company of precogs and empaths, because people thought things like that about the opposite gender all the time. But given the way Keith had been railroaded out of their precinct...Jacob probably would have been better off not entertaining an extended analysis of the reason Detective Bayne hadn't snuck a peek down Carolyn's blouse while he had the chance.

"It wasn't racy. I was just wondering if maybe Victor Bayne—"

"The skinny guy who just doused himself in *jelly*?"

Jacob pulled out of the lot and headed back toward the Seventh. "That was pretty wild. It was like...a dozen donuts' worth of jelly inside."

He gave an amused sniff, and Carolyn echoed it, then said, "He never says anything at those meetings. That's the first time he's ever spoken to me. I don't think he's married or anything...but he doesn't seem...."

"What?"

"Well...I just think that if he was gay, he wouldn't have been wearing that awful sportcoat."

Cliché. But true.

"Besides," she went on, "I thought we established that it was a very bad idea for you to date guys at work."

"He's in a totally different precinct."

"Jacob. Remember Keith."

He sighed. "Okay. You're right. And he's probably straight anyway."

"You're dangerous when you're single," Carolyn said as she held up her phone and snapped a quick photo of his profile. "I'll see if Crash wants me to give you his number."

# Witness

## 1

I'll say one thing for the Fifth Precinct: at least I knew where everything was in relationship to everything else. No matter how many times I tried to get the lay of the land at my new job, I always managed to take an unscheduled detour and show up five minutes late. Laura Kim looked up from her desk and greeted me with, "Oh good, you're here." She'd ensconced herself in an office as far away from the FPMP's resident repeaters as she could possibly get, and I wondered if she'd also had some kind of aversion whammy placed on the door. Because I always found myself checking out the records room or the cafeteria in response to one of her summonings.

Apparently that Friday afternoon I wasn't the only one at the Federal Psychic Monitoring Program who'd been summoned. Super-buff empath agent Jack Bly stood at the window, hands in pockets, daylight gleaming over his severe buzz cut as he gazed out over the railyard. And the Super Stiff who'd shamelessly bribed me into eating *quinoa* for dinner last night by shoving his hand down my pants?

He was ever so casually checking out Laura's bookshelf, doing his best not to look smug, and failing miserably.

Laura stood, planted her hands on her desk, and said, "Since Agent Bly has wrapped up his current investigation and Agent Marks has completed his verbal de-escalation course, you're all available to take part in a technical workshop this weekend."

What? Now that I'd graduated from the Chicago PD I was supposed to have weekends off. I'd been building up my Netflix queue all week, and a new pizza place down the block just slipped a drool-worthy menu through our mail slot. I was about to say *thanks, but no thanks* when a quick look from Jacob informed me that Laura wasn't asking me to give up my weekend, she was telling me. And any protest on my part would just make me look like the dumb FPMP rookie I was.

Fine. I didn't complain. But I might have sighed. Quietly. To myself.

Laura fanned three sheets of paper across the desk and said, "Due to the particular nature of this training, we'll require a signature on this waiver form." Each of us picked up a form and read. Or at least tried to, in my case. The legalese was so thick, they'd lost me after *Waiver Release and Assumption of Risk*. My eyes defocused as I thought about the Carnivore Special. Ground beef, Italian sausage, Buffalo chicken...was that it?

"Question about item four," Bly said. "Is it absolutely necessary?"

Four, that's right. Four toppings. And what was that fourth topping?

Laura said, "Think about it. You'll get more out of the training."

Bacon. Yes. I might as well run the pizza through a blender and inject it directly into my arteries—and I could barely wait. Between the quinoa and the working weekend,

Jacob totally owed me whatever indulgence I could possibly dream up. Sunday night would be greasy food, TV, sweatpants, and—

"Drugs?" Jacob said. "It's a lot to ask."

Wait, when did we start talking drugs? Because scoring random pills from the friend of a friend in a shadowy gin mill was one thing. Having a governmental agency medicate me? That was a flat-out *no*.

I scanned the consent form in a panic. Four, four... where the hell was four? Bad enough I couldn't find section four, I started doubting I even remembered what the number itself looked like. I was too busy imagining a bunch of musclebound apes strapping me down to a gurney while someone shoved an IV into my arm....

"There." Bly reached across and pointed out a paragraph. The paper was trembling. I took a deep breath and somehow managed to quell the impending freakout. Barely. I found number four on my consent form and read it more closely. *I understand there are general risks with any medication, including: sedation, dizziness, nausea, vomiting...*fucking hell, was it too late to go crawling back to Sergeant Warwick with my tail between my legs? *Cold hands and feet, suicidal thoughts and behavior, memory loss and death.*

I'd never had any illusions my stint as a federal agent would be a walk in the park. But death? I preferred the threat of dying to come from the barrel of a gun or a few decades of questionable diet, not some dangerous and untested drug that had no business coursing through my system. I was just about to slap my consent form down and make a big stink when I saw a word I knew all too well: Auracel. One tab, twice daily.

Well, fuck. I could do that standing on my head. In fact, when I went grocery shopping, I'd take that dose anyway to spare myself the sight of the intersection repeaters.

Bly penned his signature. Jacob was watching me. I gave

in with a shrug, and the two of us signed away our weekend. Laura co-signed the forms, tucked them away in a locked drawer, then pulled out bottled waters and dosage cups, each cup containing a single pill. As I scowled down at the Auracel, I realized I wasn't the only one who'd hesitated. The other two official psychs were eyeballing their pills with dread.

"Wait a minute," I said to Jacob. "You'll be sick as a dog if you swallow that."

"It's Neurozamine," Laura said calmly. Neurozamine was Auracel's wimpy cousin—and it didn't do squat for me. "You're the only one cleared for Auracel."

Jacob said, "If one psych is forced to take a stronger medication, it invalidates the entire experiment."

Laura assured us, "That might be a consideration, if this were an experiment. However, it is not."

"But you are sending us off with our talents compromised," Jacob insisted.

"It's a training exercise in witness interview techniques."

A single Auracel—essentially, no big deal. It might be strong enough to knock most psychs on their ass, but I'd built up so much resistance I could stomach three or four. A normal dose wouldn't even leave me with its signature behind-the-eyeball headache hangover. Did I trust Laura Kim? As much as I trusted anyone, I supposed. And in law enforcement, training was as ubiquitous as paperwork.

I did my very best to staunch the Camp Hell panic as I tipped back the pill—what if it only looked like Auracel, but was something worse, a new psyactive, maybe. Or a tracking chip disguised to look like a pill. But my tongue recognized its old frienemy immediately, the shape of it, the smooth coating—and as I paused just a moment too long before I swallowed, the pervasive, eye watering bitterness.

I swallowed. And if Bly felt me panicking, he wouldn't get to revel in that sensation much longer. He and Jacob both downed their pills too.

"Agent Powell will see you to your transport," Laura pressed a button on her phone and a forgettable Caucasian guy in a black suit opened the door, then stood beside it, hands folded, waiting blandly. But as I turned to follow Jacob and Bly, she added, "Agent Bayne, a quick word?"

Now what?

Once we were alone, she said, "Obviously I'm not sending you into a haunted training facility."

"Okay."

"But it would look bad if I made an exception for you. Understand?"

"Sure."

"Even though there wouldn't be any natural reason to compete among you—I mean, your talents are so completely different that they complement each other—I think that an ability as strong as yours is bound to spur some rivalry. And what I want you to focus on here is gleaning as much as you can from the workshop. So, the Auracel."

"Right. Got it."

"Good."

As I rejoined Jacob and Bly, I puzzled over the fact that Laura was attempting to mitigate jealousy. Over my mediumship. Laura Kim might be one of the smartest people I'd ever met, and I had no problem taking an Auracel for the sake of humoring her. But this idea that anyone found me threatening was patently lame. After the horrific exorcism the three of us had done together—formaldehyde, plastic sheeting and a thrashing corpse—I'd bet money that neither of my colleagues envied my abilities. Plus, it didn't sound like we'd be training our psychic abilities this weekend, only our mundane skills. And no fellow officer has ever found me threatening.

Creepy? Sure. But never a threat.

2

By the time we reached the parking garage, I felt a gentle buzz. Maybe it was all in my head. Auracel is pretty fast-acting, but I doubted there'd been much chance for it to hit my bloodstream quite yet. The chemical cocktail in my brain knew what it could look forward to, though, so I was already approaching that floaty wave as the generic agent led us out to our transportation—not a gleaming Lexus sedan like every other car in the lot, but a van. Not a soccer mom Lexus van, either. An armored van.

A look shot through the group as we climbed in. Armored vans might look cool on TV with SWAT teams pouring out the back doors, but in real life it was dark and claustrophobic, all metal and no windows. Luckily I didn't suffer from motion sickness. Hopefully neither of my fellow agents did either.

The van turned left out of the parking ramp, and within a block I was completely lost. We endured the ride in silence. The van was probably bugged. Besides, what was there to say? There was city driving, then highway driving, then something that felt suspiciously like the hypnotic two-lanes we take to visit Jacob's family up in Wisconsin. But only an hour had elapsed when they cut the engine and opened the doors, so wherever we were, it was unlikely anyone in a Packers jersey would try to lure us into a dull conversation about the weather, hunting, or sports.

When we offloaded from the close darkness of the van, the sun felt too bright. We were in a parking lot surrounded by trees and a few plain cabins. The sky was crystalline, and the nip in the air smelled sweet. Normal city sounds like traffic and gunfire were absent, and birdsong filled the empty spaces. It was the perfect place to murder us all and hide our bodies under a snowdrift.

A bearded guy in a parka strode out from the biggest cabin, checked a clipboard he was carrying, and said, "Welcome, you must be the Chicago group."

What gave it away, the fact that we were all glaring at the scenery like we were waiting for the trees to attack us? Maybe, since his talent was so subtle, Jacob felt more like himself under the influence of antipsyactives than the rest of us. He was the first to shift back into pro-mode, put on his calmest voice and take point. "We are. And this is...?"

"Integrated Dynamics, where Tactics Become Habit." He handed Jacob a manilla envelope. "We do things a little differently here—no names, please. It's all part of the program—impartial treatment for egalitarian learning. You'll find more detailed instructions with your room assignments. Once you're settled and changed, join us in the Convergence Hall for your debriefing."

He turned on his heel with a jaunty half-wave and strode off, leaving us to stand there looking bemused. It was so weird when adult civilians played Secret Agent.

A few yards away, the idling van ground into gear, and Agent Whatsisname rolled away, leaving us stranded, out in the middle of nowhere.

Jacob opened the envelope. Inside, smaller packets were labeled with our names—first initial only and no titles, with a two-digit number below it. I took the V. Bayne envelope and tipped out a key.

"Cabin numbers," Bly said. Automatically, Jacob and I glanced at our numbers, then checked each other's. Same cabin. What a stunning relief. We trooped over and located our accommodations, 8x12 shacks covered in snow. Bly was across the way. He headed in with a look of resignation. Jacob unlocked our door, though I suspect if he leaned on it hard enough it would have fallen right in.

I stepped in behind Jacob and my eyes adjusted to the gloom. What the heck? The armored van had felt one step shy of sending us out with bags over our heads and duct taped wrists. But instead of Guantanamo, we'd ended up at a family campground. The interior was rustic, with log walls and a pair of antlers hanging over the electric space heater. Entertainment consisted of a weather radio and a few battered board games. The Auracel had definitely kicked in, because my innards swam with relief. There was a table and two chairs in plasticky indoor-outdoor resin, and...I stifled a laugh. Because, seriously? Bunk beds?

I poked at one of the pillows. "Top...or bottom?"

Jacob raised an eyebrow.

"Bunks," I said innocently.

He let that one go with an eye-roll and approached the neat piles of clothing folded on the bottom bunk. "It gets even better: uniforms."

From the psych ward to the police force, I've worn enough uniforms to know my current outfit wasn't too bad. A navy T-shirt and hoodie, and lo and behold, sweat-pants. All of them printed with the word INVESTIGATOR in clunky block letters, across the chest, the back, and down the right thigh. And to top off the look, cheap nylon jackets in blaze orange, with a flocked lining to keep out the worst of the cold. Normally, going around so ill-equipped would be courting pneumonia, but we'd been in the midst of a warm snap that would surely come back and bite us as a freak snowstorm come April.

Once our suits were hung up and our new getups were donned, we reconvened outside the cabin. Jacob and I were quite the pair in our orange jackets, blue sweats and black leather shoes. Bly looked the same, though without the structure of his suit, it was easier to imagine him like I'd known him years ago, a PsyCop schlubby with paunch, before the FPMP hid him in plain sight with an extreme haircut and the world's most motivated workout regime.

It might be above freezing, but if we were going to stand

around and complain, it would be better to do it indoors. We power-walked to the biggest shack—the *Convergence Hall*—to embark on our surprise weekend adventure. While I wasn't exactly eager, I figured the sooner we got started, the sooner I could loaf around in my new sweatpants. In a bunk bed.

The folks from the FPMP weren't the only ones converging in the Convergence Hall. A couple dozen unfortunates were wearing the same wardrobe we'd been assigned. They looked like law enforcement, square and young and fit, though the word INVESTIGATOR emblazoned on all those muscular chests and thighs had helped me form that opinion. Since I don't suppose a bunch of random fitness buffs had any reason to be out in the middle of the woods learning interrogation, I was probably right. We took a seat, and the man who'd greeted us strode to the front of the room. "Nowadays," he said, "surveillance equipment has been advancing by leaps and bounds. Cameras are small enough to tuck into a lapel pin. Listening devices will synch right to your cell phones ten yards away."

And if you're lucky enough to have the FPMP interested in your private matters, psychs can do all that and more.

"But even with all this new technology, an investigator's biggest asset is still...his brain."

Rustic beard guy launched into some convoluted explanation about how we'd divide our days: an hour of lecture followed by an hour of mock interviews. Our subjects would be the bored-looking twenty-somethings standing up against the wall. All of them were dressed identically, just like us, but they'd be a lot harder to spot outside. Their windbreakers were gray and their sweats were winter camo, emblazoned with the word WITNESS. Using whatever technique we'd just been lectured on, we'd question the kids in camo until they coughed up some kind of evidence.

When he held up the visual example of said evidence,

the energy in the room shifted palpably. I'm no empath, but I know a bunch of hypercompetitive macho types when I see them. Heck, I live with one. The evidence—a diagram of a handgun, maybe a Browning .22—was the size of a playing card. And from baseball cards to Garbage Pail Kids to Pokemon, cards were something everyone in that room had been raised to covet and collect.

"These cards contain key pieces of evidence that can be assembled into various scenarios. Piece together your crime based on the evidence, write up your report...." Report writing. The part of law enforcement no one warns you about.

Anyway, digest the lectures, collect the right cards, jot down the right thing, blah blah blah, and maybe you'll prove you have the biggest dick.

Beard guy dismissed the WITNESSES, and an academic type took the floor. He launched right into a spiel about building rapport. It held my attention for about two minutes, until he broke out the statistics. And then the sound of the baseboard radiators pinging hijacked my attention, and I became transfixed by the patterns in the old linoleum floor. The twelve-inch tiles had been printed with a design to make them look like smaller tiles, but they weren't fooling anyone. Each tile was made up of sixteen printed squares. Three gray, eight white, five blue. And they might have formed a regular pattern, had they been installed all facing the same direction, or at least all rotated in a consistent way. But the installer had either gone according to a cunning scheme only he was privy to, or he'd been completely random. Over by the window, the gray squares were rotated toward each other so they looked like they were clumped together, whereas around our table, there was a wider gap between them. And over by the door, a string of five tiles all faced the same way, with the gray squares forming a repeated row in front of the threshold.

"...and by mirroring the tilt of the witnesses' heads," the speaker was saying, "the amount of useful information gained in the interview is increased by twelve to fourteen percent. Any questions?"

Yeah. How can you break down "usefulness" into a statistic? I wondered, but I didn't ask. My curiosity was overruled by my desire to get on with whatever was in store for us next, get through the day, finish out the weekend and go back home. Besides, in my experience, questioning someone's stats just results in a fresh barrage of terminology I don't understand.

Beard guy reappeared and told us, "The twenty witnesses will be stationed throughout the facility. Question as many as you can. And when you've properly demonstrated the technique..." he held up a crime scene trading card. "You've got three hours. Time starts...now."

Maybe I missed the part about which way I was supposed to tilt my head, but I could still glean something from the INVESTIGATORS' body language. The kids who were eager to prove themselves were the first ones up and out the door. The seasoned pros knew that basic attendance would be enough to fulfill their departmental requirements. They lagged behind, chatting. And my team? Bly and Jacob both looked like they had something to prove. "If you take the north end of the camp," Jacob told Bly, "I take the west and Vic grabs the area behind the cabins, we won't be competing for the same witnesses at the same time."

Bly considered the plan. "But what if witnesses are more concentrated in some areas? We should rotate our territories so we all have a fair chance at the same number of cards."

"You guys do what you need to do," I said. "I'm not gonna step on your toes. I can...observe."

"But you won't get any cards that way," Jacob said.

"That's a sacrifice I'm prepared to make."

He looked at me as if he couldn't quite comprehend what I was getting at—much like me and anyone who tries to impress me with a statistic—but after a moment's consideration, he treated me to a shrewd smile. His nostrils gave that little flare they give when he's intrigued by something, and his eyes sparkled. When we turned toward the door to go locate our witnesses, he bent his head to my ear and whispered, "Game on."

He thought I was playing him to get ahead?

Seriously?

3

I tromped out into the woods with all the other INVESTIGATORS. Some of them had located witnesses and begun to question them. I poked around the buildings while I waited for one of those witnesses to free up. But the other law guys seemed just as eager to score some cards as Jacob and Bly, and they weren't letting any of the WITNESSES get away, so eventually I picked out a random trail and wandered off.

Aside from the odd overgrown lot, there's not much nature to explore where we live. And frankly, the thought of an idyllic campground out in the woods intrigued me. There hadn't been the money to send any of us in foster care to something like this, actual cabins, where kids learned songs and made crafts and swapped completely made-up ghost stories. In fact, my main exposure to campgrounds was in the slasher horror movies I loved so much in high school. So seeing one up close and personal was, dare I say it…interesting.

Trails were easy to follow in the packed snow, and my cop-soled shoes provided adequate traction. I looped around the office, meandered past a snow covered tennis court, and threaded my way through some trees on a path that led to a ramshackle amphitheater. The corner of one wooden bench had been cleared, and on that corner perched a girl in a gray windbreaker, smoking furtively. Her camo hoodie was pulled up snugly but the ends of her hair stuck out, blondish and damaged, like she'd dyed and permed it a couple years ago then realized keeping it up was more trouble than it was worth. Her cheeks were broken out, which was accentuated by her cold-red nose. She looked like she'd rather be anywhere but there.

I turned to leave her to her smoke when the snow

squeaked and revealed my presence, and her head jerked up.

"Sorry," I told her.

"We're not supposed to smoke," she said, without making any move to get rid of the incriminating cigarette. "But they're making us work, like, four hours with no break. Four hours. I could probably report them for that."

"I guess. If you could find anyone to listen."

"It's minimum wage, y'know? And no breaks?"

"Bosses will get as much out of you as they can." I ambled over, cleared a spot halfway down the bench upwind of the smoke, and sat.

We both gazed off into the trees. I could see a few yards in before visibility ended at a stand of pines. I asked, "Where are we, anyway?"

"Don't you know? Blankley. Population 1200."

That meant nothing to me. I shrugged and asked, "What do you do when you're not hiding from guys in windbreakers?"

"I work at the grocery store. Part-time. Took a semester off to save up some money and somehow never got back to my degree. We had some family stuff going on. My sister...."

A shockingly red cardinal dropped onto the top row of benches, hopped a few feet, gave off a sound like a miniature car alarm, then launched up into the treetops and out of sight. We watched it fly away. I wouldn't go so far as to say I had a camaraderie with my new acquaintance, but it wasn't too awkward. "I'm not exactly sure what this whole exercise is all about," I admitted.

"Oh my God," she said. I looked at her. She was sizing me up. "You're doing it and I didn't even realize."

"Doing what?"

"That mirroring thing."

Well, true, we were both sitting on a low bench with our elbows on our knees, canted forward with our hands dangling down between them...but there are only so many ways to sit on a snow-covered bench. "Not really."

"Here." She handed me a card with a picture of grass blades and the word *scene* printed on it. "You a cop?"

I almost admitted to it, but at the last moment, I realized I no longer carried that particular stigma. "Not anymore."

"Oh. Well, you're good. I thought we were just, y'know, talking."

I'm pretty sure that's what we'd been doing, but I accepted the card just the same.

Once she finished her cigarette, it was time to head back inside for yet another lecture. I found Jacob and Bly ensconced at the same table we'd occupied before. Territorial lines had been drawn, I suppose. It seemed like everyone had become accustomed to their "spot" and returned to wherever they'd randomly sat the first time around. The lecturer came back out, called up his PowerPoint, and proceeded to tell us all we needed to establish rapport. I was guessing they weren't telling Bly anything he didn't already know, only he did it by digging around in the heads of his witnesses. When I questioned anyone with him around, they couldn't *wait* to tell us a story.

The lecturer clicked to a slide of a guy talking to a cop. They both looked pretty stilted to me. "Witnesses with greater rapport experience more accurate recall."

I meant to listen to him, but I've always been averse to people telling me things that are basic common sense. I thought about the card in my pocket. Knowing Jacob, he'd amassed a good handful in the time it took me to score one. Bly, I wasn't so sure of. How many cards had he racked up so far? Probably a dozen. Although...if he was on Neurozamine, maybe not.

While the lecturer went on about the importance of active listening, I pondered what Laura might have intended by sending us off into the woods with our talents on pause.

For me, it was a matter of people versus ghosts. When I'm on Auracel, I needed to focus my investigation on living witnesses. The others? Jacob was no longer inscrutable to psychic suspects, and Bly couldn't predispose people to trust him.

Sending us on this stupid excursion did make sense, like night-training at the shooting range. For them, anyway. Not for me, not really. Ghosts were anything but reliable, so I had plenty of practice talking to living witnesses.

Once the dull PowerPoint was done, we were served a simple catered meal of sandwich, chips, and cookie. Bly muttered, "Carb explosion," and went to talk to the staff about hooking him up with some salads in the future. He even had to forego the cookie. Poor sap.

There was an optional "icebreaker" afterward, but it looked pretty lame, a bunch of twenty-something straight guys prancing around looking burly and macho, and a few women looking equally as macho.

After the first five minutes, I grabbed an extra soda with an eye to making my escape, when Beardy McBeard waylaid me just shy of the exit. So close. "Chicago crew—I've got special orders from your boss." He gave me a pointed look that could only mean "pill." He gestured to Jacob and Bly and said, "Let's head to the office."

He must not have been accustomed to pilling his trainees. Not only did he lack the tiny paper cups, but he didn't have bottled water on hand, either. It took several minutes of fussing and futzing while he dug up some coffee mugs and tried to figure out who got which dose. We watched him impassively, each of us with our own brand of PsyCop patience, and when he finally got his act together, we swallowed our pills and waited blandly for our dismissal.

"First search starts at 0800 hours," he informed us. "Stop here afterward for another dose." And even I could hear the part he didn't voice: *I don't know what this is all about, and I'm guessing I don't want to, but it's kind of titillating anyhow.*

The camp was small and the cabins weren't far from the office, but with the sun now set and a thick, oppressive damp settling in, I was eager to wrap up in a blanket and do my best to catch up on my sleep. A few Reds would have been the perfect chaser for my Auracel, but even if I had one in my hot little hands, I wouldn't have taken it. The thought of some habit-demon pulling my strings sucked out all the enjoyment.

"Have any luck out there today?" Jacob asked casually.

"Hardly." I plunked down into a plastic chair. "You?"

"I found five witnesses, stationed about twenty yards apart. Where were you looking, exactly?"

I made a vague gesture in the general direction.

"By the snowshoe trails? By the bonfire pit?"

"Out in the trees." I sighed. "I don't see the point, anyhow. Collecting cards is great, for a twelve-year-old. I just can't get worked up over a nonexistent crime."

"Look, new agency, new job—your performance matters. Even in a simulation."

So this was how working with Jacob was going to be. His *gung ho* to my *ho hum.* He hunkered down in front of me, draped his forearms across my knees, and asked, "The tree line at the north end, or the one closer to the warming station?"

"Are you strategizing, or are you trying to poach my witness?"

He gave me a sharky grin and walked his fingers up my leg. I angled my hips, and he tugged my new sweatpants down around my knees. If the two of us both knew he was trying to manipulate me, did it still count as manipulation? I tried not to think too hard about it. It was a good thing, him finding his groove again at the FPMP, trusting Laura enough to take the pill and get with the program. Even since Laura took over, he hasn't known where he fits in. And if Con Dreyfuss had made him uneasy, Laura had him feeling downright leery.

Then again, the fact that he was trying to get a rise out of me didn't really prove he was relaxed. We fucked loud and often under the FPMP surveillance. Hell, I think we made a special point of being raunchy to defy whatever random black-suited guy was listening in. I wouldn't exactly call being monitored an aphrodisiac, but I'd be lying if I said it didn't heighten the senses.

Jacob teased his way up my inner thigh, trailing moisture with his tongue. His breath played over the finer hairs and sent courses of shivers through random branches of my nervous system. The tingles arced down my leg to my toes, then back up to my ballsack, which shifted in anticipation. He worked his way higher while my body vacillated between turned on and ticklish, and I clutched at the squeaky plastic chair arms to force myself to keep still and endure that initial ambivalent sensitivity.

"Stop teasing and suck me off," I said, and he gave a huff of satisfaction against my balls that made every last one of my hairs stand on end and my dick fatten up in anticipation. Things were so much simpler for that dumb hunk of flesh between my legs. It didn't care *why* Jacob's hot, wet mouth was rooting around in its proximity, it just wanted to shoot its wad inside. And maybe, when it came right down to it, the rest of me didn't much care either. Fake witnesses and zero crime. Nothing to get worked up about. Nothing but…. "Yeah. Fuck, yeah…do it."

I threaded my fingers through what I could of his short hair, and reveled in the feel of his jaw working as he took me deep—so deep, so good. Sucking hard. So good. Yes. The peak was coming fast, and he knew it. Not with his talent, but with his standard five senses. He knew me inside and out, the way I shifted or went still…the way I breathed, or stopped breathing, eager for that final nudge to send me spiraling into that velvety black pit of satisfaction where everything melts away but the sweet relief.

My back arched and I hovered for just a single, shining moment, unburdened, and then I came. I emptied myself into him, all my ambivalence, all my vulnerability. Maybe I would never trust anybody one hundred percent, but I knew how far the borders of my trust with Jacob spread. And that perimeter was so vast I might never find all the edges.

Maybe the type of trust you hear about in schmaltzy songs doesn't even exist, not in the real world. Jacob sat back and looked up at me, and even now, after all this time together, I was a total sucker for those smoldering dark eyes, that pleading look. The chink in the armor. The notion that I wasn't the only one venturing into some scary trust territory.

I trailed my fingers down his cheek and considered my options. If we tried to slot ourselves into that bottom bunk together, I'd brain myself on the top bunk for sure, so I dragged the mattress off and threw it on the floor. It was more of a cushion than a mattress, just a thin, waterproof pad. A couple of daddy longlegs staggered away from the commotion like a pair of drunks at closing time, and Jacob brushed them toward the door, grabbed the top mattress, and added it to the pile.

"Not exactly a five-star hotel," I said.

Like Jacob could care less. His eyes were dark with need, and the word INVESTIGATOR on his thigh was distorted by the prominent tenting going on up front. He settled back and dragged me down on top of him. Our breath was coming fast as we jockeyed for position in the narrow space. I knelt between his legs and pulled down the sweats, and his meaty cock thwacked his stomach, ruddy and thick. I found it with my mouth while he clutched my head, and despite our desperate scrambling, we managed to fit ourselves into place without anyone losing an eye.

I jammed down hard. The hugeness filled my mouth, my throat, my whole awareness. Fake witnesses, silly playing cards, even mandatory Auracel, all of those concerns shrank down to pinpoints of light I could ignore if I simply unfocused my attention. The only thing that mattered was the massive cock plunging in and out, in and out, and the taut, muscled body arching up into me, trembling with the need to shoot.

I slipped a hand under his sweatshirt, reached up and raked my fingers through his chest hair, toying with one nipple, and then the other. Beneath me, Jacob squirmed and moaned, and nudged my hand down to stroke his balls while I blew him. As I wrangled the sweatpants out of my way, I found my hand caught up in the wrong side of the pocket. That was when I noticed a telltale hardness a heck of a lot smaller than the one pummeling my throat. More significant, too. Because if I know anything, it's pharmaceuticals. And that little bulge I felt through the pocket's fabric was the exact shape and size of a Neurozamine tablet.

It was easy enough to put my body through its paces. When to suck, when to ease off. Where to tug and exactly how hard. What sorts of throaty sounds of encouragement would hasten the big finale. I could do these things with one hand tied behind my back—or with most of my conscious thought occupied with wondering what Jacob had hoped to accomplish by ditching his meds.

I had no doubt he'd tried Neurozamine before. Heck, Auracel too, for that matter, though we'd never specifically discussed it. I didn't know how much antipsyactives disagreed with him, and whether or not he could even tell that his shielding capabilities were compromised. Maybe he had serious concerns about traipsing through unfamiliar territory at a disadvantage—or maybe he just wanted to make sure he collected more cards than anyone else. Either way, he hadn't seen fit to let me in on his reasons. And so, as he shot down my throat and I quelled my lazy gag reflex and allowed myself to swallow, I decided that two could play at that game. I'd keep my discovery to myself.

My tactical advantage was shortlived. I still had his dick in my mouth when a knock at the door sent us both flying. I leapt to my feet and yanked my pants up in a single fluid move, and Jacob followed suit—but as he did, a certain little pill launched out of his pocket and landed on the plastic matt between us. "Who is it?" I called out.

"It's Jack." Apparently Bly thought we were on a first name basis. "You busy?"

"Nope," Jacob called very, very casually. He picked up the pill, gave me an inscrutable look, and stuck it back in his pocket. "Just a sec."

While he tossed the mattresses back onto the bunk bed, I patted down my sweatshirt and wondered exactly how obvious it was that I'd just been sucking cock. I stuck my head into the closet-sized bathroom and mashed down the hair that, mere moments before, Jacob had been ruthlessly pulling. My lips looked swollen and ruddy. Not collagen-injection swollen, but noticeable enough if you were checking for that sort of thing.

But why would he?

Unless being on Neurozamine made Bly especially observant, and he was trying to fill the void where he usually picked up the feelings everyone around him thought they must be hiding.

Bly came in and sat on one of the plastic chairs. His pale gray contacts were out and it was disconcerting, seeing his old eyes in his new face. Between that and the sweatsuit, he looked less like an actor playing a g-man in a low budget thriller and more like a regular guy. "I found an old map of the campsite in my cabin, tucked into one of the jigsaw puzzles. I think if we team up, we can crack this thing."

"Why?" I didn't see the point of going all overachiever if no actual crime had been committed. "Is someone keeping score?"

Bly said, "Someone is always keeping score."

"We can pool our cards so one of us finishes first." Jacob suggested.

"Right," Bly said. "But they'll probably hold back the key piece of information until tomorrow. That way, nobody finishes the exercise too early. So we'll need a rendezvous point. And a plan."

"We'll meet up after the last lecture and piece together the narrative as a team," Jacob said. "Whoever has the most cards gets the win."

"Agreed." Bly stood and stretched, and his gaze fell on the top bunk mattress—which was pointedly askew. I can mask my thoughts well enough in front of a telepath with jingles and nursery rhymes and obnoxious catch phrases from TV shows I don't even watch. But masking your emotions in front of an empath is another thing entirely—and I was suddenly convinced he knew we weren't exactly playing Yahtzee when he stopped by.

But if he really was privy to my embarrassment, he didn't show it. He tipped the mattress into alignment with an absent shove on his way to the door. "I'm gonna turn in early. We'll touch base tomorrow."

We waited until his footfalls receded, then Jacob pressed his mouth to my ear and said in a voice so low I could barely hear it, "Did he actually take that pill?"

He must have, because I was embarrassed enough to make a porn star blush and it hadn't registered with him. Though for all I knew, that only proved Bly was really good at hiding his reactions.

## 4

We started our day with another brisk trek into the woods. While I was burning to know why Jacob was cheeking his pills, we both knew better than to discuss it inside the cabin, which was probably bugged. But the good part about the compound was that there were lots of places electronics couldn't live. Not for long, not with exposure to the weather. If we broke our own trail through the thin, brittle snow crust, we could find pockets of space where no one had been since the last snowfall, or maybe even all winter. My ankles were none too pleased with me for veering off the beaten path, but I was willing to endure clammy socks for the sake of privacy.

And so we struck out early to have a little chat. Even running my lines to put myself to sleep in that lonely top bunk, I still hadn't come up with anything very bright. "What the heck?" I whispered.

"You seriously thought I'd walk into an unknown situation with my single advantage blocked?"

"First of all, stop fishing for compliments, you've got every advantage and you know it. And second, it's not an unknown situation, it's a training exercise. Laura said."

Jacob's response was a single raised eyebrow. Trust between the two of them didn't run deep. Once he'd discovered Laura's sidearm was Roger Burke's murder weapon, any chance of the two of them being chummy evaporated, even if it wasn't really Laura who'd pulled the trigger, not exactly. Even when she was herself, Jacob couldn't trust her. Funny thing was, given that I fully believed her when she said she wouldn't send me into a haunted situation on Auracel, apparently I did. Huh.

"Maybe we should stick together so I can keep an eye on you," Jacob said. "If you're on Auracel...."

"Then a ghost is gonna leap out of the trees and hop on for a ride? That makes zero sense. It was psyactives that made me boundary-challenged. Not Auracel." If anything, I was safer from getting hijacked while my talent was dampened. But then I caught that predatory gleam in Jacob's eye, and realized his logic was working just fine. He didn't seriously think I was vulnerable to possession—he wanted my cards. "Nice try. See you at breakfast." I turned toward my designated witness-gathering territory and tromped away.

I fully intended to find my spot, stay there and bide my time, but let's face it, without landmarks or street signs, trees and snow look as similar to one another as the hallways of the FPMP headquarters. I followed a trail comprised of all kinds of boot tracks, some ATV tires, paw prints, and the occasional yellow dribble dimpling the snow. When I looked up, I found I'd somehow circled the woods and popped out on a snowmobile trail. And there, hunched on an ice-covered bench, was a familiar WITNESS. She cringed a little at the sight of me emerging from a side trail, then recognized me and allowed her shoulders to relax, and said, "Hey."

"Hey." I joined her, figuring my butt probably wouldn't conduct enough heat to melt the ice if I kept my visit brief. "You're here early."

"Whatever." She shrugged. "I need all the money I can get. Dropped my phone last week and the screen totally shattered."

I nodded. I wasn't particularly kind to cell phones myself.

"You got a name?" she asked.

"Vic."

"Not Officer So-and-So or Captain Whatever?"

I hadn't quite imprinted on Agent Bayne. Not after all the years I'd spent as a homicide detective. "Just Vic. What about you?"

"Allison."

"Allison," I repeated. Sometimes it helps me remember, sometimes not.

"I used to get hand-me-down phones from my sister. She'd save up her paychecks and upgrade the second the new model came out. She even camped out in line for the last one."

We sat together in silence and watched our breathing stream in and out, pale in the early morning light, and I said, "Cell phone cases are supposed to withstand all kinds of damage. Apparently not falling off the roof of your car, then being run over by a garbage...truck." I turned my head to find her holding out a card marked *weapon* that showed a drawing of a hunting knife. "It's okay, you don't have to feel sorry for me."

"Yeah, right. You just hit the three rapport-building skills we're supposed to look for this morning—give me your first name, let me go off on a tangent, and take a personal interest."

Weird. Now if only I could score cards for playing solitaire on my phone or picking paint off a windowsill, I'd be in business. I tucked the card away and shifted down a few inches to stave off the inevitable wet butt.

"Aren't you gonna run off and find another witness?" Allison asked.

"Nah. I'll let my partners have 'em." They were the ones with something to prove, after all. Not me.

In a few more minutes, I had to report and take my pill, anyhow. What did it say about me, that I went along with the program while Jacob skirted the rules—that I was going soft? Or that he'd never been as much of a Boy Scout as I'd always presumed?

The thing that bothered me the most was the idea of being played for a sucker. But if I was on to the fact that taking meds on command was a sucker thing to do and I played along because I was biding my time for the sake of building up a veneer of trust, that was actually clever.

Right?

Maybe. Or maybe it was just easier to go with the flow. When pill time came, I watched Jacob and Bly around the rim of my coffee cup. They both appeared to be swallowing their meds, although if anyone thought to shine a pen light in Jacob's mouth, he'd be busted. But no one did. He hid the Neurozamine all the way to the dining hall, until he could wipe his nose on a paper napkin, palm the pill, and jam it in his pocket. Given that Bly went right for the coffee, I'm guessing he'd swallowed.

So had I—but not because I'm a sucker. If I carried an Auracel this far, I'd be tasting it for the rest of the day, and I was in no mood for pill-mouth. That's all. I would've told Jacob as much, given half a chance. But breakfast went right into lecture, and lecture led to another wild goose chase as INVESTIGATORS dashed off in search of more trading cards, and I regretted the fact that tromping through the snow would pretty much kill the single Auracel's floaty kick.

Outside, there were a couple of people in WITNESS sweats chatting by the side of the building, but I could see by the way the male was leaning against the siding like a cool guy and the female was batting her eyelashes that any intrusion on my part would be less than welcome. Besides, making an actual effort to obtain cards would imply that I cared about this fake crime scene. Which I didn't. I liked to reserve real concern for real problems in the real world. Heck knows there's enough of them to worry about.

I circled the building aimlessly a few times, then decided to go see if there was still any coffee to be had. Allison must've had the same idea. I found her trying to tip the last bit of coffee out of the urn while pressing the spigot and holding her cup underneath. Without an extra pair of hands, she wasn't having much luck. I held the urn at an angle while she coaxed out enough for us each to have most of a cup. She handed mine to me and said, "Someone told me they don't clear down right away, so I figured…." She pocketed a bagel. I decided it wasn't such a bad idea and did the same. It must've put her at ease when I helped myself, because once I did that, not only did she stash away three more, but she grabbed a big bran muffin to wolf down on the spot.

Voracious appetite? Maybe she had a metabolism more like mine than Bly's, and she could carbo-load all she wanted. But given the deteriorated state of her sneakers, my guess was that she needed to save food for later. Sad, but you can't go around giving people money. They tend to take offense. Same for advice. All you can do is not judge, and I like to think I'm okay at that.

I took a cranberry muffin so she didn't have to eat alone, and said, "Take your time. If anyone bothers us, I'll say it's part of the interview."

Her shoulders slumped, and she relaxed. "My mom used to make us breakfast. Not anymore."

Social skills aren't in my repertoire, but even I could see there was a big story behind that statement. Whether she actually wanted go through with telling me about it was another matter entirely. And so I pretended I was really interested in picking out walnuts and let Allison speak, or not, as she saw fit.

I picked. She ate. We both drained our coffees. And as I started searching for a good exit line so I could disengage and leave the poor kid alone, she said, "Two years ago, Sarah—my sister—left. Up and left. Not a word to anyone. Just…gone."

My stomach sank. "You're sure she…?"

"I don't know. Not really. But the sheriff checked out her boyfriend and he was just as upset as anyone else, plus he was at work the whole time. So that's their best guess, that she moved away. Dad was so upset he started sleeping all the time, like fifteen hours a day. Lost his job. Mom says it's just a matter of time before we lose the house."

Maybe Sarah really had moved away, for love or drugs or a dozen other reasons. Or maybe her raped and beaten body was rotting in a shallow grave. Whichever it was, I doubted either answer would bring her family much peace.

Even so, *knowing* is better than not knowing. Wasn't that the big reason my latest Auracel prescription was just sitting there in our medicine cabinet untouched?

To swallow or not to swallow when my next dose of Auracel came…my apprehension was beginning to overtake my urge to lay low. But with the missing girl, all the baggage attached to being a good little soldier and following orders felt like a much bigger burden.

Lunchtime rolled around. Whatever Bly told management must've made some kind of difference. Salads and fruit had appeared alongside the sandwiches and cookies, though he still stared longingly at my chocolate chip. I don't see what harm a single cookie would've done him. Unless…I shifted my vision to see if anything noncorporeal was behind that sugar craving. Nothing I could see. Not on Auracel. Though it was interesting the antipsyactive didn't dampen my impulse to try.

Jacob was in hyperfocus mode, scoping out the room. He and Bly spoke in low, overly casual tones about who among the other trainees had the most cards, and where they'd been scoring them. I tuned out, thinking. Neither of them noticed.

I probably couldn't get the driver to swing by Allison's house on our way back to Chicago, not without making a big fuss over something that might turn out to be a bust. Besides, I wasn't even sure Sarah had still been living at home back when she went missing. Plus, if there was a spirit, if she even was dead, it was probably lingering wherever she'd been planted. Or wherever some sick bastard had grabbed her. Or where he'd taken her and...I pressed my knuckles into my eyes and tried to erase the disturbing mental images I'd conjured, though I didn't have much luck.

Midway through lunch, I abandoned my turkey on rye to go to the can. Ostensibly. But somehow I found myself lurking around a window that faced the parking lot where the sweatsuited WITNESSES were getting orders. A deck of cards was being passed around, phony clues tucked away in fleece pockets, and the herd was divvied up and deployed. Allison went in the direction she'd been pointed until she hit the tree line. Then she picked out a small, overgrown path and slipped away. When I received my official lunch dismissal, I followed.

I found Allison maybe a hundred yards down the trail, perched on a tree stump. She tried, and failed, to light a cigarette. I ambled over, opened up my coat, and provided additional windbreak for which she was profoundly grateful. She handed over the latest card she'd been given without even bothering to do a fake interview. This one had a frowny face drawing and the word *depression*. I tucked it away with the other two. "Sarah taught me to ski up here." Oh. So that's what the flat lines on the trail were. "She was sixteen and I was twelve. You can walk here from our house if you're willing to cut through some brambles. We felt so grown up the first time Mom let us come here by ourselves."

I'd had free rein as a teenager too, but I think that was due to neglect, not trust. It makes you self-sufficient, though, to not have to answer to anyone hovering around you. And it makes it less likely that you'd run off and not tell anyone just for the sake of proving a point.

Allison said, "I'd show you a picture, but it's stuck in my damn phone."

"They can usually transfer that stuff."

"I know. It just sucks. Wait a minute..." she rifled through her pocket and pulled out a set of keys with a cascade of decorative keychains attached. "I do have one. Here."

She held up the tangle of metal and plastic, and there among the tchotchkes was an acrylic heart that contained a picture of two young, smiling girls in puffy ski jackets. One was Allison. The other one looked a heck of a lot like her. And both of them looked happier than I'd ever imagined Allison being. I touched the fob and a shiver traveled down my arm. That couldn't mean anything good.

Maybe I could drive up next weekend. Have a little visit. Stop by for coffee. Check out Sarah's favorite haunts.

Right. That wouldn't seem weird at all.

"Hanging out here, we weren't big jocks or anything. It's just a good place to come and think. Well, it used to be." She sighed. Cigarette smoke and the vapor of her breath streamed away. "Now all I can think about when I'm in these woods is how much I miss her."

My heartbeat sped, like my body had figured out something my brain was too cautious to grasp. "Because you spent a lot of time together here."

"I dunno. We spent a lot of time together in a lot of different places." Allison gave an uncomfortable shrug. "There's just something about these woods."

5

If we were back at the cannery and I wanted alone-time to check something out, I could invent half a dozen reasons I urgently needed to dash over to the store. Jacob might think of a few things to add to my phony shopping list, but unless my absence screwed up other plans, he wouldn't think much of me leaving. But here? In the dark, in the dead of winter, with no car and nowhere to go but some cross country trails or the dining hall? No way was he going to buy that I wasn't up to something, and no way would he let me comb through the woods alone.

"Maybe we could go for a walk," I suggested.

Jacob, crammed into the bottom bunk, looked up from the training handouts he'd been re-reading with an expression that said, *Yeah, right.*

Fine, I'd give him a reason. He knew me well enough that I couldn't point to excess post-dinner cookie consumption as an excuse to undertake voluntary physical activity. So, what might be more plausible? "The log walls in here, they're kind of claustrophobic. So brown. So much... wood."

My reason must've resonated. He got up and pulled on his overcoat.

The grounds were eerily quiet in a way that didn't happen in Chicago, even in the dead of night, but when we ducked into the trees, my hearing shifted. The sound of snow and gravel felt overblown, and the trees made various shooshing, rustling or squeaking sounds depending on whether they were winter-bare or covered in needles and snow. Even the sound of my own breathing, my own heartbeat, grew distracting. No wonder people in horror flicks went on stir-crazy murder sprees.

Hopefully that was just in the movies.

It was also just in the movies that you could navigate by a full moon once your eyes adjusted. We flicked on our flashlights. Jacob aimed his at the ground and I shone mine up ahead, and even still I wasn't sure of what I was seeing. After dinner, I went back and forth a dozen times and ultimately decided to take that last dose of Auracel. Now I was doubting the wisdom of that choice, but the drug was deep enough in my system that sticking my finger down my throat wouldn't accomplish anything.

"About the Neurozamine," Jacob said. I sighed. My breath made a dramatic plume in my flashlight beam. "For all we know, Jack's getting a placebo, and he's here to monitor us and report back to Laura."

"He's an empath. What's he gonna tell her, that you're way too into card collecting and I think the whole thing's pathetic?" Laura's no dummy, she could've figured all that out on her own.

"The training's not over," he said. "We don't know what's going to happen tomorrow morning."

I was pretty confident I did. More muffins, more flat coffee, more wandering through the woods looking for WITNESSES, and a bunch of certificates stating we'd fulfilled twenty hours of continuing ed. "Look, I'm not saying you're in the wrong for ditching your meds. We all pick our battles. For this one, though...I decided I'm just gonna keep my head down and go with the flow."

A prickle danced across the hairs at the nape of my neck, and I veered off the main trail onto a side path.

Jacob followed. We squeaked along the packed snow for a long while without a word, frittering away all the time we could have been speaking openly without fear of being tapped and recorded, both of us too lost in our own thoughts to fill the silence. We passed the stump where I'd found Allison earlier, and I thought about the impact a missing girl can have on her entire family. I multiplied that by the number of people who disappeared every year, considered how many of those were probably foul play, and wished again that Auracel's side effects were tasty enough to make me forget. "I met this witness. Her sister disappeared a couple years ago and I don't like the way it sounds. I need to look into it."

The snow-squeaks went thin as Jacob paused and fell behind a few steps. I stopped too, turned and shone my light at his crotch so it didn't catch him in the face and blind him. "What?" I demanded.

"Vic, that's just a story."

"I'm not an idiot."

"Don't put words in my mouth, I'm not saying you are. But everyone here has a canned story. It's part of the whole routine. All the witnesses are actors who do summer theatre. They have certain lines they feed you, and if you manage to steer the interview the right way, they give you a card. This whole thing is one big improv."

I thought about Allison. Her fried hair. Her tacky keychain. The furtive way she hunched over her cigarette. If she was really a character actor playing a downtrodden, minimum wage twenty-something, she deserved a freaking Oscar.

But what if it *was* all just a line? And there I was, playing the sucker. Gullible enough to trust Laura Kim to dictate when I should or shouldn't take meds. Gullible enough to think Sarah was a real person, and not just the scripted figment of some trainer's imagination. Gullible enough to think I was doing something that even mattered.

I aimed my beam between the trees and went deeper. Jacob wouldn't see my cheeks flushing, not out in the dark by the light of a couple of flashlights, but he knew me well enough that he could probably read my chagrin in the set of my shoulders. If anyone knew better than to trust someone without a damn good reason, it should be me.

It would be easier to say *screw it all*, head back into the cabin, and stare at the rafters until I fell asleep. But I thought of Allison's sadness—not just a haunted look about her eyes, but a weariness that pervaded her whole self— and I just couldn't let the issue drop. "Look, maybe it really is nothing. But we're what, an hour away from home? This agency doesn't have access to the type of resources we do, not for a missing person with no evidence of foul play. And think about it, we're feds now, our jurisdiction's gotta reach way outside city limits."

"Vic, wait."

Jacob hung back while I stepped into a moonlit clearing with long, ground-eating strides. "We'll check it out first, make sure her sister exists." I was sure she did. Positive. "And then come up here and look around. We don't find anything, no one's any the wiser."

"Stop."

"I get that you're the rock star investigator and I'm just some guy who sees dead people, but give me at least some credit—"

"Get back here," he said urgently. "That's not trail, it's ice."

It wasn't the words that registered, not initially. It was the tone. He wasn't mansplaining, he was scared. In the way thunder follows lighting half a heartbeat later, it took me a second to understand what the fear was all about. Not the sort of ice I chip off the driveway, but a frozen body of water. And then Jacob's fear leapt over to me. Normally, I'd only need to worry about falling on my ass, but with the freakish warm snap we were having, things could turn ugly.

My breath caught and I held it, terrified that the wrong step would send me plunging to an icy grave. My middle school hockey coach's single piece of advice sprang to mind, *Don't be stupid.* I'd always thought it meant I'd better not put a move on any of my team members, but in retrospect, I realized he was discouraging us from skating on the frozen pond out by the railroad tracks. More convenient than the rink, but so not worth the risk. And now, there I was, adult-sized and twice as heavy, wondering if I should turn and carefully follow my own footsteps back, or forget about the precision and slam myself into reverse.

And then the ice groaned.

"Holy fuck."

"Slow and easy," Jacob said, in a tone he'd use for talking a jumper off a ledge. "Just back up." Slow and easy. Right. I shuffled back one step, then another, scanning the ice for telltale fissures with my flashlight beam. "That's right, follow my voice. Not much farther. You got this, Vic. You got it."

I'm not sure whether he was giving me encouragement or trying to cover any more panic-inducing sounds, but with my vision limited to whatever I captured in my flashlight beam, my ears were working overtime trying to make sense of my surroundings. Since I'm a city mouse, every outdoorsy creak and rustle immediately conjured images of rotten ice in the throes of disintegration.

"Keep going," Jacob said. I wasn't sure when I'd frozen, but suddenly it was imperative to see, to hear, to thoroughly understand what was going on. I swept my light across the surface, back and forth, back and forth, searching for a telltale puddle or spreading crack. "Vic, come on."

There. Movement. I fixed my flashlight beam, and I strained. Clenching all over never seemed to help, but I did anyway, trying to make sense of things through sheer force of will.

"Vic," he repeated, even more urgently. "Come *on*."

A flicker on the surface of the ice pack resolved into a shape that made sense. A...hiking boot?

"Vic!"

"Just a sec."

I scanned up and down, and if I really, really strained, I could see the boot was connected to a leg, to a whole body, a woman in jeans, a puffy ski vest and a fleece hat. But it wasn't a hiker out on the lake with me, not anymore, and it wasn't a sentient ghost, either. It was a repeater. I could tell by the way she flickered out, then reappeared a few steps back, only to start walking toward the spot where she'd vanished.

I opened up my crown chakra and pulled white light down from the heavens. The impulse to charge my batteries came to me automatically, but the focus wasn't all there. It felt tenuous and strange, like dropping a call in an area with shitty cell coverage. I could kick myself for taking that dinner dose of Auracel.

I took a deep breath and did my best to calm down. The ice groaned again.

"Vic," Jacob implored.

I considered keeping the repeater to myself, for all of two seconds. I didn't think Jacob knew my talent was so strong that a normal dose of Auracel couldn't squelch it, but it probably wouldn't come as any big shock. "Repeater. Two o'clock."

Jacob digested that information, then said, "It'll keep."

Maybe. Or maybe this elusive moment was my only chance of seeing what I needed to see. Repeaters are ten times thicker at night, so in the morning she might be gone. And even if we came back next week with a jug of Florida water and a solid plan, the ice might be too weak for me to get a look at her from any useful angle.

Most people have checks and balances, but not me. I was the only one who could determine if I was just seeing what I wanted to see—namely, a definitive answer as to what had become of Sarah—or if the remnant belonged to some other long lost hiker.

"Since when do you have a sense of urgency about

repeaters?" Jacob said. "They're not suffering."

"No...but their families are." I eased forward a few more steps as I silently begged the surface to hold me, but I was beginning to doubt the wisdom in consuming that extra cookie. The ice didn't groan again, but it definitely creaked. And while it was a more subtle sound, it was also a hell of a lot closer. Meanwhile, the repeater took a few flickering steps forward, then disappeared. "I can't see her face."

"Vic, please."

"I need to see." I waited, breathing as shallowly as possible, for the spectral film loop to start again. And just when I thought that maybe the ghost show was over for the evening, I caught it again. The woman took a few steps, flickered, and disappeared. Right before she blinked out, though, what was that movement? A shrug, or...? She was so transparent, the light so poor—or my inner vision was so clouded by Auracel—I couldn't tell. "Damn it all, I can't make it out."

"What can I do to get you off the ice?" Jacob pleaded.

I wiggled my fingers back at him in a gimme-gesture. "Either pipe down and let me concentrate or pass me some mojo."

"I'm not coming out there too."

"You shouldn't have to. I don't need to touch anything to gather up the white light, and neither do you. Funnel it in my direction—use your will."

I suspected *will* was probably a trigger word for an overachiever like Jacob, a point of character he prided himself on. I had no idea if he could psychically email me the juice, but if he busied himself with the effort, at least he'd be occupied enough to stop distracting me. I took a deep breath and centered myself, ignoring all the ominous creaking and crackling that filled the night air, and I focused on the flickery white haze of the repeater.

She was still a pale jumble of frozen moments. One

foot forward, then the other, then...was that a smile? She was smiling. Maybe. For a split-second, maybe. And then she disappeared. "Are you sending it?"

"I'm trying."

And I wasn't receiving. Damn it.

"Do the details really matter?" he asked. "For all we know, this death might be old news around here and she's already been ID'd."

Maybe. I tried to will the repeater to brighten and solidify anyhow. I'd done it before...but that was without Auracel, in range of a GhosTV. And even then, it had cost me. Out here on thin ice with my psychic ability pharmaceutically stunted? I should be grateful I saw anything at all.

"Kill your flashlight," I told him. "Maybe I'll see better by moonlight."

"Vic," he said desperately. But when I flicked off my beam, he did the same.

While I know I'm not seeing ghosts with my physical eyes, my brain must be hardwired so my sense of vision is still involved. Ghosts don't glow in the dark, and I can't see them with my eyes closed. But whether it really was an effect of the moonlight, or the absence of the flashlights just made the background trees less confusing, the next time the repeater cycled through, she looked more like a person and less like a degraded loop of film.

I eased toward her another few shuffling steps to see her face at a better angle, and the ice sighed beneath my feet. Jacob didn't say anything, but I imagined I could feel him begging me to turn around as a tug in the pit of my gut. I did my best to tune it out—really, to tune out my whole physicality and focus on that part of me that was made of light—and to see her.

The woods were dark and still, and utterly quiet. And then the woman appeared, walking, looking down at her phone. She scrolled to something that made her laugh.

Innocuous. Normal. But then, for just a glimpse, laughter blurred into something more like surprise as the ice gave way, and she was gone.

I waited one more cycle, focusing this time on the face. I wasn't positive, but I strongly suspected I was looking at whatever was left of Sarah. My heart felt heavy enough to sink me as I flicked on my flashlight beam and backtracked off the groaning ice. The moment I was on solid ground, Jacob grabbed my arm hard enough to bruise it and dragged me back a few more yards as if to stop me from changing my mind and charging back out there.

Once we were out of danger, he grabbed me and kissed me so hard I suspected he did it in lieu of punching me in the face—or maybe I was feeling the crackle of psychic energy that leapt over to me when we touched skin to skin. Though I do think he wanted to slug me. "It's okay," I said, when he let me come up for air. "We're fine. I'm fine."

He grabbed me by the head, mashed his forehead into mine so hard it hurt, and said, "Don't do that ever again."

"I'm fine."

"But one of these days, you won't be. Not if you keep following your inner eye, and to hell with what's going on around you." He gave me a shake. "You might not care much about your physical shell, but *I do*."

I covered his hands with mine and eased them off before he popped my head like a fleshy balloon. "Okay, okay."

"I mean it."

"I know." I eased myself against him and brushed my lips across his, and marginally, his shoulders relaxed. I pictured the white light flowing back into him, not as an electric rush, but a soothing mist. Who knows if it happened or not, but I like to think it was possible. "I know."

6

No one's ever accused me of being an optimist, and I'm the last person who'd try to profit from anyone's death, but once I called in the repeater to Laura Kim, she went into FPMP Regional Director mode and had a search and recovery team trudging through the camp by morning. The ridiculous trading card exercises were preempted. I tried not to look too self-satisfied about it.

I had myself positioned in the trees with a clear line of sight to all the action, close enough to watch, but far enough away to keep from tripping up the folks who actually knew what they were doing. No cheesy emblazoned sweatsuits here. Lots and lots of hardcore weatherproof and waterproof gear covered in reflective strips, lots of equipment, and lots of radio buzz going back and forth as they did their thing.

The clearing looked very different by daylight, and while the ice still gave an occasional moan, the workers didn't seem overly concerned. They drilled down with augurs, made some calculations, and marked off the safe zones with bright orange spray paint. I hadn't been in imminent danger of drowning during my ghost sighting after all. The part I'd wandered onto was able to hold three guys at least as heavy as me and a bunch of gear besides.

Bly looked a lot more like his usual self when he came out to join me in his overcoat and suit, and Jacob looked like his work self. They took position on either side of me and gazed out at the proceedings with looks of vague professional interest. I asked no one in particular, "Where are all the other INVESTIGATORS?"

"Relocated to the local community college," Jacob said.

Bly added, "And they're going nuts trying to figure out what happened here. I guess simulated crime just doesn't put you in the zone like the real thing."

"Oh, there was a zone all right," I said, "a pissing-contest zone." I dug the crime scene trading cards out of my pocket and picked through them. A perp with depression stabbed a victim with a hunting knife, left a blood trail and a set of partial prints, but there was an alibi. Maybe the final reveal was that evidence was botched or one of the witnesses was lying. I guessed we'd never know. And I supposed it didn't matter.

"Wait a minute." Jacob pulled his cards out of his overcoat pocket, and it struck me as funny that he'd bothered to keep them even though there was no chance of winning the game anymore. "How many do you have?"

I thumbed through and counted. "Seven."

"Me too," Bly said. Hilarious, he'd kept his too. He pulled them out and fanned them wide. "Seven."

And then the three of us went quiet while the recovery team broke out the power tools and sawed a triangular opening into the frozen crust. I was glad the WITNESSES had been relocated along with everyone else. Not because it meant someone other than me would break the news to Allison about her sister—that would be the real investigators' duty once positive ID was made—but because the sight of the divers dragging a decomposed body out from under the ice would give any civilian nightmares, whether or not it did turn out to be a missing relative.

From the glimpses I got—of the heart-shaped keychain, and of the repeater—I was pretty sure Allison's family would find out soon enough what had become of Sarah. And while it would close the door on the hope that she might someday turn up on their doorstep apologizing for making a really bad decision and running off with an indie hipster vegan polygamous folk band, hopefully *knowing* what had happened was better than not-knowing, and eventually it would bring them some peace.

When the chug of the generators died down, Bly said, "It

was a smart thing to ditch the meds." I thought he'd aimed that at Jacob, wondered how he'd figured it out, and then realized he was talking to me. And also that none of us had been given our antipsyactives that morning. Crap. Hopefully he wasn't reading anything from me other than startlement. "Talking to the witnesses psychically blindfolded, it definitely taught me something...but I'm not really sure what." He shuddered. "It was unsettling. Yeah, they were actors. But without empathy, it felt more like they weren't even people."

Of course he thought I was the one who hadn't gone along with the program. I'd seen a ghost, after all, so surely that meant I wasn't on the mega-powerful antipsyactive, Auracel. Not to mention the fact that my permanent record was the one covered in black marks for bucking authority. I wondered if Laura would call me on it. I should probably have an excuse ready if she did, though hopefully she'd pick her battles too and let it slide. And if I did need to bend the truth, I'd just need to do it without any other psychs lingering around who could read my heart or mind. Laura had been pretty dismayed that I'd pegged her for a low-level medium, but that discovery actually worked to my advantage—it guaranteed she wasn't a goddamn telepath staring right into my very thoughts.

I'm sure there was a time and place to shut off my extrasensory abilities, like wading through the same old intersection repeaters that I didn't have the privacy to salt. In general, though, I had to admit that *knowing* truly was better than not-knowing...even if it was distracting, and even if it did put me at risk of wandering into something ugly because I was more focused on my third eye than my physical sight. But it was also a relief that I was such a practiced liar, and that the man I was most inclined to share my secrets with was impervious to psychic probing. No one should have a say in what I was seeing or not-seeing besides me.

Maybe I did learn something during this training

exercise after all. Bly had drunk the Kool-Aid, Jacob held out, both of them had put forth actual effort while I did the bare minimum, and in the end, our score was the same. It's not exactly that training, effort and talent don't matter—obviously psychic abilities give us a major advantage. But life has never been fair, and chance tends to play a much bigger role than it should.

Eventually Bly's unaccustomed lack of body fat drove him back indoors, leaving Jacob and me alone to see the diver surface with a waterlogged hiking boot. I sighed.

"I know this is important to you," Jacob said. "If anyone understands what it's like to put your life on the line for strangers, it's me."

*But...?* I heard the disapproval in his tone, and if he wasn't going to finish the thought, I might as well. "But I was risking my neck, and she was already dead. Yeah, I know. It wasn't the repeater I was worried about, it was the family. Her disappearance put all of them in a downward spiral."

Out on the ice, the guy manning the winch must've had some signal from a diver, because he set the gears in motion and started hauling up something a lot bigger than a shoe. Generators chugged, and voices grew animated—edgy and loud—as the team scrambled to deal with whatever would emerge from beneath the surface.

Jacob stepped up beside me and his arm brushed mine. In the pale morning light, the worry line between his brows was chiseled deep. "Your family matters too," he said, just below the hum of the winch.

Even I wasn't blockheaded enough to shoot back, *What family?* Because families run deeper than blood. Connections are forged with things like affection and trust. Tolerance, too, since everyone's insufferable once in a while. Understanding and intimacy. Love. Obviously, love.

In every way that mattered, we were a family. Jacob, and me.

# About the Author

Author and artist Jordan Castillo Price is originally from Buffalo, New York, though she's been a Midwesterner long enough that she can pass as a born and bred Wisconsinite. Over the years, she's tried her hand at all sorts of creative endeavors, from wildly impractical to surprisingly useful —including art, music and design—but has found fiction writing flows the most freely and connects her with the greatest number of people.

In her spare time she spoils her cat, leads water aerobics, stuffs people full of cake, and daydreams about interesting ways in which society might collapse.

**If you enjoyed the book, please leave a review. Even a brief review is beneficial to the author.
It DOES make a difference!**

www.psycop.com